ELENA

DUNCAN LLOYD

authorHOUSE®

AuthorHouse™
1663 Liberty Drive
Bloomington, IN 47403
www.authorhouse.com
Phone: 1 (800) 839-8640

Edited by TW Brown
Cover art by Laird Ogden

Published by AuthorHouse 01/26/2017

ISBN: 978-1-5246-6010-9 (sc)
ISBN: 978-1-5246-6009-3 (e)

Print information available on the last page.

This book is printed on acid-free paper.

This book is a work of fiction. Names, characters, businesses, organizations, places, events, and incidents either are the product of the author's imagination or are used fictitiously. Any resemblance to actual persons living, dead, or otherwise, events, or locales is entirely coincidental.

Acknowledgements

I wish to thank all the fine writing teachers in the Creative Writing department of San Francisco State University where I got my BA and MA in the 60's and 70's. I also want to thank my editor, Adam Marsh, who helped me cut the fat out of this novel while, hopefully, leaving the heart. I especially want to thank Denise and Todd Brown, the owners of May December Publications, who gave my book a chance even though it did not contain a single zombie. (I may try to sneak one or two into the sequel.)

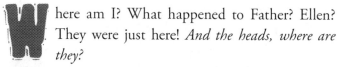here am I? What happened to Father? Ellen? They were just here! *And the heads, where are they?*

I sat in a chair, with darkness all around me except straight ahead, where there was a glaring whiteness with dark lines on it. The image before me quickly resolved itself into a newspaper projected on a white screen.

Then I understood. This was what I called the Time Machine, the microfilm viewer in the Weimar Public Library. Nothing had happened to my sister, Ellen, or to my father. I was still Theodore Edward "Teddy" Schoendienst; a boy genius according to my father, but not to the kids in Weimar Wisconsin. They called me "retard" (because of my stutter) or "the headshrinker's kid" or "the brain!" You might think that they couldn't call me retard and brain at the same time, but a bully doesn't have to be consistent. He just needs to know how to hurt. Some happy day I might wake up as someone else or in someplace else, but not today.

I must have dozed off. I had a strange nightmare

that left me shaky and bewildered. Details of the dream lingered in my mind, the way a lightning flash at night burns itself into the eye. I caught a glimpse of a knife blade flashing in a dark alley, then of a big dog being patted by a State Trooper—"good boy"—while he picked up what the dog had in his mouth, something horrible, then of a man in a dark robe leaning over a girl's body.

"No!" I shouted.

The scream echoed through the marble halls of the library. I felt ashamed. It was just a nightmare, after all. But this dream had seemed to go on and on, and I couldn't wake up no matter how awful it became. But how could it have seemed so long if I only dozed off? I hoped I hadn't slept too long. Mrs. Goethe, the librarian, would be mad at me for tying up the machine. She was one of my only friends and I didn't want to upset her.

I turned the crank and the pages sped by until I located the story I was looking for, dated July 27, 1925. Above the story, there was a drawing of an old farmhouse that looked strangely familiar, though I'd never been there. It had a long walkway leading up to the house, past a barn and silo, from a country road. A wooden gazebo stood in the front yard to the left of the path. It was night, and in the lighted front window stood a huge shadow of a man with an axe in his hand looming over several smaller shadows that looked like a woman and three children. The caption read: "The Killer and his Victims: Does this family still haunt the old Washburn farm?"

Probably not, I thought, with my usual skepticism. Anyway, it was getting late. I would come back to this story next time I was here now that I knew the date. Anyway, that strange dream had spooked me. I was scared enough; no point in frightening myself some more.

I looked up at the clock on the wall. It was after five. I had a couple of books on Wisconsin hauntings to check out. I'd better hurry or I'd be late for dinner, which our cook, Emma, always served exactly at six.

Outside, the globes of the street lamps around the town square glowed white against the darkening fall sky. Suddenly, I felt afraid to leave the bright space of the library. But I had to go now; it would only get darker if I stayed.

I called on Sam Spade, one of my imaginary friends, who grew up in dark streets and didn't fear them. He puffed on a cigarette and buttoned up his trench coat

"Well, kid," he said in his best Humphrey Bogart voice, "If you've got an appointment with something, there's no point in keeping it waiting."

I picked up my books and walked downstairs to the main desk. Mrs. Goethe looked up with a wide smile. To most people in town, she was a caricature of a librarian: prim and severe in her dark, almost mannish suits; but she always had a smile for me. I think it was because she knew I loved books as much as she did. Also, I was the only one who pronounced her name correctly; (Gurte, like the German author), everyone else called her Mrs. Gothy

"Was that you I heard yelling? Are you all right?" There was concern in her smile.

I flushed with embarrassment.

"I-I'm okay. I just dozed off and had a nightmare."

She glanced at my books and smiled conspiratorially. "Ghosts, eh? Maybe that's what gave you the nightmare! I wonder what your father will think about these books. He's always so scientific, you know. I wonder if there aren't a lot of things on Heaven and Earth that he doesn't dream of in his philosophy. You know what I mean?"

I smiled. I'd told her once that *Hamlet* was my favorite Shakespeare play and I enjoyed her play on Hamlet's words to Horatio.

"You, on the other hand, are curious about everything. That's what I like about you. I hope you never lose that... open-mindedness.

She looked around and lowered her voice "A lot of people around here aren't like that. Especially these days, with Senator McCarthy still in power. Just the other day, a man wanted me to take *Tom Sawyer* out of the Library. Can you imagine that? *Tom Sawyer*! Said it was subversive!"

She opened up my books, took the cards out, stamped the due date on them and reinserted them.

"Actually, this is a fascinating subject. Did you know, according to some experts, Wisconsin has more ghosts than any other state in the Union? That's strange when you think how few people *live* here! I sometimes think—if there are such things as ghosts—certain places must act as doors to their world. If so, then Wisconsin must have the biggest welcome mat in the country."

I stared at her in alarm. She flushed and lowered her eyes.

"Of course, it may all be nonsense. I guess no one knows for sure," she said as she handed me my books.

Poor woman, she must think that I think she's crazy. But that wasn't why I'd looked so alarmed. When she mentioned the doors to the other side, I'd seen a door from my dream, utterly dark but outlined in bright light, and I'd felt such horror that I thought I might faint like a girl.

I paused at the library door. It was mixed up in my mind with that dark door and I was afraid to push it open. But this was stupid! I couldn't stay here forever! I called again on the spirit of Sam Spade and went out into the night.

What was I afraid of? My enemies might be waiting for me, true, but once I got on my bike, I could outrun them all. I could even outrun my nightmares. I walked down the stairs to the bike rack where I'd locked it up.

It was gone!

Someone had sawed through the chain. They took a lot of trouble for a cheap Schwinn bike. Bastards! That bike was the only thing I owned.

My anger turned to panic. How was I going to get home? I could walk home, but the local bullies might be lying in wait for me. I was sure they were the ones who took the bike. Besides, I had no desire to walk into the growing darkness. Not after that dream.

"Hey, egghead!" someone yelled from the street in back of me

I turned around quickly and spotted Bobby Niebauer, my worst enemy, riding by me on my Schwinn! I should have known. Only Bobby or one of his gang would have the nerve to steal in broad daylight. He had often promised to make his gang as tough as the big city gangs. To prove it, he periodically staged "rumbles" with some of the kids from the Catholic high school, using sticks, chains, and knives. Everybody said that they'd kill somebody some day.

Bobby pedaled slowly, smiling insolently, hands clasped behind his neck

"You so-so-son of a bitch! Give me back my bike," I screamed.

His smile vanished and he sped up, heading towards the corner

"You'll never get your bike back if you keep talking like that!" He turned the corner and headed down past the movie theater.

I ran after him, shouting, "Bo-Bobby! C-Come on! I-I-I'm sorry I called you that. Gi-Give me back my bike."

"You forgot to say please!" He was halfway down the block now, headed towards the north side of the Square.

"P-P-Please give it to me. I ne-need my bike!" He was already down at the bottom of the square and turning towards the row of bars on the North Side. I was barely mid-block by the movie theater

"If I were you, I would call the authorities," said Sherlock Holmes, my other imaginary friend, in the clipped British tones of Basil Rathbone. "I quite sympathize with your dislike of the local police, but you can't take on this gang alone."

Sherlock was the one I called on when I needed to

solve a problem, just as Sam Spade was the example I needed when I wanted to act like a man. I looked around for someone who would let me use their phone. There was only a bored looking teenager sitting in the cashier's cage at the movie house and I doubted she'd help me. I could ask Mrs. Goethe, but then I would lose Bobby. Sorry, Sherlock. I can't use your plan this time. Anyway, I shouldn't have called Bobby that. My temper would get me killed some day! If I apologized enough, he might give the bike back. I started running again. My breath came in short gasps by the time I made it to the corner.

These bars were where the Town Square Boys hung out: a tough bunch, mostly Korean War vets. Some worked as deputies for Sheriff Carson, the son of the man who had arrested Old Man Washburn. These alleys were where they beat people up, like that labor organizer last summer. They beat him bloody before they dragged him down to the river and threw him off the old stone bridge. But I didn't think the Boys would bother a kid like me.

Bobby was nowhere to be seen. Either he'd gone into one of the bars, and I doubted even he had the nerve to do that, or he was waiting for me in one of the alleys. I crossed over to the North Side and walked towards the nearest one. The neon lights of the closest bars barely lit up the entrance of the alley.

"Bo-Bo-Bobby, please!" I said into the darkness. "I said I was sorry. Okay? I-I-I'll even tutor you like you asked me to do. I-I'll do anything you want!"

"Anything?" The voice from the nearest alley sounded soft and sinister

"Don't trust him," a voice in my head said. It sounded like my father. "It will only bring you humiliation, fear, and pain!"

I hesitated, startled by the voice, which had come uninvited, unlike my imaginary friends. Something else about it seemed...wrong. It was not like the déjà vu experience; just the opposite: "It didn't happen this way before." Was I having auditory hallucinations now? My father would call that a sign of serious mental illness! I decided to ignore the voice. It would be all right. Bobby had been at me for months to tutor him. I walked over to the entrance to the alley.

"Sure, Bobby," I said. Two pairs of hands pulled me into the darkness. Another hand covered my mouth as my books went skittering onto the pavement. I smelled the fetid breath of the boy who held me from behind. He seemed taller than me and much stronger. The hand on my mouth had a foul taste and felt slimy. I almost gagged. My heart pounded. I thought about what that voice had said. I should have listened.

The boy behind me removed his hand from my mouth. I swallowed and began to say something when a fist slammed into my cheek, snapping my head back and making a vivid row of stars dance in front of my eyes. The boy in back of me loosened his grip. I leapt forward, toward the entrance to the alley. Someone screamed "Hold him!" and a net of arms tightened around me, dragging me back into the alley.

"Hello, faggot!" Bobby said. "This fag says he'll do anything to get his bike back. Think he means it?"

A chorus of raucous laughter rose in reply. My eyes were growing accustomed to the light. I made out ten or twelve figures in the alley. They were all bigger than me. *Cowards!* I thought, but the thought brought me no comfort.

Another fist flew at me, hitting me in the stomach. I doubled over and fell to the pavement, fighting the urge to puke. I saw a dirty pair of sneakers, straddling a bike, my Schwinn. I looked up. Bobby was still grinning.

"Hey, egghead! You want your bike back?" I had no breath to reply, so I nodded. A heavy boot came out of the dark and buried itself in my side. The pain shot through me like an axe blade.

Bobby frowned and said, "Hey, knock it off!" I felt completely and absurdly grateful to him.

"Hold him up!" he ordered. Someone pulled me to my feet. Old slimy hands, foul breath had me from the rear again. I was beginning to regain my breath, though my side still ached

"W-w-what do you want?" I asked Bobby. Laughter echoed in the brick enclosure. Good, when they're laughing, they're not hitting.

"W-w-what do I want? You know what I want, Teddy. Don't you remember why you quit the Boy Scouts?"

As if I could forget! I'd joined the Scouts in one of my efforts to lose my shyness, but this attempt had turned out worse than I thought possible. The sheriff, who was also the Scout Master, was usually drunk at the meetings. This wasn't so bad, because he was nicer drunk than sober. But he couldn't keep order in the troop. Bobby and his gang joined the Scouts as a joke, but soon Bobby became the real Scoutmaster. He invented some badges not covered in the Scout manual, especially the Brown Badge. In order to advance beyond Tenderfoot in our troop, a Scout had to literally kiss Bobby's bare ass. I quit, as did most of the other kids who weren't already kissing his butt.

"You remember how you quit before you could get beyond Tenderfoot?" Bobby said. "Well, tonight you get your Brown Badge!" The other kids guffawed loudly. I couldn't understand how anyone in the bars just feet away couldn't hear it. Or maybe they heard it and didn't care. I couldn't count on any mercy from the men in those bars—any more than that union man they threw in the river.

The union made a big fuss over it afterwards, but the sheriff told the state patrol a deputy had seen the organizer climbing out of the river after the attack. So they never dragged the river like the union people wanted. But my father thought the labor man was still down there. I wondered if the river would be my last stop too. Well, so be it, I wasn't so in love with my life that it would be a tragedy to lose it. At least all the fear and the nightmares would be over! I wouldn't let them humiliate me, whatever happened.

"I-I-I'd rather be d-d-dead!" I told him.

Bobby smiled, nastily.

"It might just come to that, Tuh-Tuh-Teddy. But frankly, I don't think you're as tough as you think you are. I don't think you're tough at all! But we'll soon find out!"

As if on command, a fist came out of the darkness,

snapping my head back. This time the strong arms that held me didn't loosen their grip. I tasted blood and my tongue burned like fire. I must have bit it when I was hit. I was trembling and near tears.

Sissy! I said to myself. It's easy to play the martyr. But when they really start pounding in the nails, you start to cry like a little girl. Don't give them that satisfaction!

"Okay, Tuh-Tuh-Teddy, now is when you get your Brown badge!" Bobby said. "Bend his head down, Paul."

A strong hand pressed my head down. I stiffened my neck, but the hand easily forced me lower. I was like a toy to him. Out of the corner of my eye, I saw Bobby loosen his belt and pull down his pants. The boys snickered. Bobby paused as if he wondered if they were laughing at him. He pulled down his underpants. I thought of Father's voice telling me only pain and fear would come to me in here. I'd ignored him. Now, I was probably going to die in this dark, filthy place, because I would never do what Bobby wanted.

The hand forced me down towards the two globes of flaccid flesh sticking up towards me and the fetid stench which rose from between them. I fought down my nausea. The hand released its pressure a little.

"I-I-I think you should take a bath once in a while!" I said.

The boys laughed, but now they seemed to be laughing with me rather than at me. Could they be starting to respect my refusal to give in? I hated these thugs with their DAs and the hoods of their black jackets worn flipped up. In one way, though, I could relate to them better than I could to the good kids with their smiling, open faces and their closed little minds. Those kids seemed to live in Heaven already, but these hoods and I lived in the real world, and maybe we shared some knowledge of what that world was really like. Could they be coming over to my side?

"Shut up!" Bobby screamed at them, and they did. He turned to me. "Why, you little faggot! Work him over, Lonnie!"

The hand of the boy behind me pulled me back up, and another fist shot out of the darkness, hitting me in the chest. It hurt, but my nausea was gone, and I felt stronger. The grip on me relaxed and for a second, I was being held with only one arm.

I broke towards the alley entrance, past Bobby, who was pulling up his pants. I got past all but one huge boy, who spread his arms and blocked the light from the street. I darted to his left, but he grabbed me and slammed me to the concrete then the others were on me. Another boot buried itself in my ribs. A loud crack and I felt something give in my side. A wall of pain rose with every breath. They dragged me deeper into the alley.

"You stupid faggot!" Bobby screamed. "You want us to kill you?"

I hesitated, then nodded and his eyes grew wide.

"You are crazy! But you're not getting out of it that easy. As a matter of fact, I'm not going to have you kiss my ass at all. You're going to kiss something a lot better than that!"

"F-f-Fuck you!" I said.

The kids laughed again, but more softly this time. Bobby turned towards them and the laughter stopped as if a light had been turned off. *As if they and I could ever be friends!* I thought. They were all cowards or they wouldn't be here.

"You little faggot!" Bobby said softly. "But we'll see who fucks who! " He reached into his pants pocket and pulled out a small dark object. He flicked it with his thumb. There was a click and a blade flashed out in the dim light. I thought: I have seen this scene before, in the dream in the library!

He brought the blade up to my eyes, and then down by my throat. I heard gasps from the boys, but no one tried to stop him.

I had one chance. I felt the boy behind me shrink away from the knife when Bobby brought it close to me. I was pretty sure he was keeping a better eye on that knife than on me.

"Okay, faggot, now we have some fun!" Bobby said. His right hand still held the knife up to my throat while his left hand went down below the level of my sight. There were nervous laughs from the boys. I didn't think they liked this. In fact, they all seemed to be moving back from the scene. I could see a good-sized opening between them all the way to the entrance of the alley. I heard the sound of a zipper being pulled down.

I brought my foot down hard, scraping the shin of the boy in back of me. He yelled and loosened his grip. I darted towards the street. I felt a sharp pain in my throat as the blade dug in. I hit it with my arm and it fell to the concrete. Everyone was yelling. The big boy who had stopped me before reached for me. But then I saw his eyes get big and he backed away. In a minute I was out of the alley and I could not hear anyone running after me. I was free, and I had beaten them!

A nurse told me that I'd been seen by the ticket takers in the movie theatre bleeding copiously from the throat. Apparently Bobby had cut me worse than I thought. No wonder that last boy in the alley had backed away. I guess I had been too scared to feel how bad my wound was. I passed out while they were taking me to the hospital. The nurse told me it took five stitches to close the wound.

"That was a week ago," she had said. "You've been unconscious for a whole week."

I guess I must have needed the rest. So now, several weeks later, I lay awake in my hospital bed, listening to the wet hiss of the respirator and staring into the early morning darkness. The slow rhythm of the machine soothed me. As a child, I'd sometimes been afraid that I'd forget how to breathe during the night. Now, as this machine pumped oxygen into the plastic canopy over my bed, those old fears seemed silly. The first time the nurse buttoned me in to this tent, I had almost panicked at the thought of being trapped in this small space. Now, after several weeks, it felt like home.

The doctors told me I could come off the respirator today. They said my injuries could have been a lot worse. I had only one fractured rib; unfortunately, it had punctured my right lung and I wound up in intensive care. The worst part had been the fear I would suffocate. It was like being deep under water and not knowing if I would make it to the top. But now I had recovered enough to be put in a regular room, with this machine to help me breathe. Otherwise, my only pain was a throb in my throat where Bobby had cut it.

I still had nightmares. My father told me these were natural after such a traumatic experience. Some of the dreams I could trace to the assault: being dragged into the alley, feet and fists coming out of the blackness. But the three images from the nightmare in the library still haunted my dreams: the knife in the alley, the dog with the horror in its paws, and the man covering a woman's body with his cloak. One of them, the knife in the alley, had already become real. Had I projected the knife back into the dream? But no, I remembered clearly that there had been three images and that I had recognized the knife as one of them when I saw it in the alley. Were the others waiting for me in the future?

I'd had a recurrent nightmare like this when I was a kid, of a hooded figure with eyes as big as car headlights coming into the room and covering me with his cloak, and pressing me down until I could not breathe. The strange thing was that Ellen was having the very same nightmare about the hooded man. We called him the Man in the Moon, because of his huge moon eyes. He had looked much like the hooded man in my present dreams. I remembered how I had told my father about the hooded man and how he had told me how I could get rid of him. I had tried his suggestion and it had worked. But I still wondered how he could have appeared in both our dreams and how what I said to him could have caused him to disappear for Ellen as well as myself.

Most of the time, I'd been happy in the hospital, safe in my little plastic shell. No one bothered me, except to give me a pill, or meals, or a bath. I didn't have to talk to anyone so I didn't worry about my stutter. It was like a vacation in a way.

Ellen and Father came to see me every night. I was glad to see them together and not fighting for a change. Father brought me books from his library and Ellen talked about her classes or her many friends. For once, I was not jealous when she mentioned her friends. Once word got around about how I had stood up to those thugs, maybe kids would want to be pals with me, too. Sometimes, when my father went out to talk to the nurses, she and I played the old role playing games we used to love so much; the ones I had taught her: Sherlock Holmes and Sam Spade and some characters we made up. We each had our own play names; I was Edward and she was Elena.

Not all my visitors were so friendly. Sheriff Carson had come several times. His face and voice were always hard, and made me feel like I was the criminal. Especially, last night, when he had said, "Listen, boy, you have to tell me who beat you up! This is the last time I'm going to ask you. The boys who did this committed a crime, and if you don't tell me who they were, you're an accessory!"

I tried to picture going to jail for my own beating, but could not. So, I said nothing. My father finally turned on him.

"Don't you threaten my son!" he had shouted. "Just because you can't find the thugs who did this, you think you can blame the victim. Well, you're not going to do it this time!"

The Sheriff's jaw tightened and his hands clenched. "How am I supposed to find them? Your son won't tell me and there are no other witnesses."

"Don't make excuses! You know damn well who the thugs are in this town! Half of them are your deputies and your son is in with the other half," my father said. His hands were also clenched. I was afraid they were going to fight right there.

"You leave my son out of this!"

"I will when you leave my son alone and let him heal! It's your job to catch these hoods, not his!"

"Don't tell me how to do my job!"

"Someone had better. You certainly didn't catch the thugs who lynched that labor organizer. I wonder if you tried!"

The sheriff flushed red and put his hand on the club on his belt. My father stood facing him, hands on his hips. Finally, Carson turned and walked away. On his way out, he gave my sister a little smile that I didn't like. It was not the first time I had seen him give her the eye, but this time, he looked particularly menacing. I saw her shrink back from him, fear in her eyes.

I felt proud of Father. Not many men in this county dared to talk to the sheriff like that. But I also felt a twinge of fear in my gut. Carson was a bad man to have as an enemy. I was afraid my whole family would pay for this defiance, but later, my father came to me and asked if I was really unable to identify the boys who had attacked me

"I'm sorry, Father. It was just too dark."

He caught my eye and I was afraid that he would force me to tell the truth. I could never hide a lie when he turned that all-knowing stare on me. But this time he just shook his head and said nothing more about it.

I was proud of myself. I had stood up to both Carson and my father and not told them about Bobby and his gang. I didn't want those punks to say I was a snitch or a coward. I wanted them to know I was a better man than they were. After all, they were the ones with brown badges, not me!

I reached under the flexible plastic hood over to the table by my bed and turned on the light. It was very early, but I wasn't sleepy. I'd been sleeping twelve hours a day for weeks, and was sick of it. I picked up my Social Studies textbook from the table and began to read. Most of my teachers had given me no homework, so I could rest in the hospital, but Mrs. Freitag, my Social Studies teacher, insisted on giving Father homework for me. This was ironic, because it was my easiest class. She wanted everybody to work at the same pace, unlike my other teachers, who gave me extra credit assignments and more advanced books. As a result, I was almost through with my reading for that class for the whole year. I had no idea what I would do after I finished the book. I'd complained about this to my father just yesterday, and he'd replied cryptically that there would be a lot of changes in my schooling from now on, and I was not to worry about it.

I was excited about going back to school. The kids must have heard about my beating, and they'd know I hadn't named my assailants. Would they respect me for not being a snitch; or would they think I remained silent out of fear? I had to show them I wasn't afraid. If I did, maybe they'd think more of me. Maybe I'd think more of myself and not be so nervous around them. Maybe, even, I could stop stuttering!

Daylight started coming through the windows. A cart rumbled down the hallway outside. A bell rang; the hospital had begun to waken. I'd become familiar with the routines here, and I felt some connection with the other patients and the staff, even though I had only caught glimpses of them through my little plastic womb. I'd listened to the World Series broadcast with them and shared a little of their joy when the Braves upset the mighty Yankees. I was very grateful to this place. It had saved my life and given me a necessary rest. I would miss it.

It was full daylight when Father walked through the door. He had a grim look, like the one he'd worn when he'd shouted at Carson. Ellen was not with him; she would be in school. I caught his eye and he forced a smile

"Good morning, Teddy! Ready to go home?"

"I...I guess so. Did the doctors say it was okay?"

"I am a doctor, remember? You'll be fine." He reached over and disconnected the respirator. I took a deep breath and was pleased to find I could do so without pain.

"Your breathing is almost normal now. Staying in bed will only keep you sick! You need fresh air and exercise."

He unhooked the plastic hood. Then, he laid a suitcase out on the end of the bed and brought out a change of clothes for me.

"Let's get going. You don't need a shower. I've already checked you out!"

I rose uneasily and looked around the room that had been my home for the weeks since I got out of intensive care. Yes, I'd miss it.

Driving home, my father stayed silent, his face set. I wondered if he and Ellen had had another fight, but I didn't dare to ask any questions. My father's silences were always intimidating, but this day...even more so.

When we arrived home, I was surprised to see a blue sedan in our driveway. My father grunted and pulled in beside it. That car's door opened on the driver's side and a short fat man in a light blue suit got out. It was Mr. Thompson, the school principal. Father got out, slammed his door and walked right past Mr. Thompson, who had extended his hand. My father opened up the trunk and extracted my suitcase. My principal looked startled by his rudeness but he followed my father to the rear of the car. They both seemed to ignore my existence.

"I...I'm sorry to bother you, Doctor Schoendienst, but I have to see you," Mr. Thompson said.

"I told you before there was no point in further discussion. The decision has been made!"

"But what about your son?"

"He is my boy, not yours!"

"But he is also my responsibility!"

"Not any more!" Father said with a tight smile. I began to worry. What decision had been made?

"Listen to me, please!" said Mr. Thompson. "The boy needs to be around children his own age."

"So they can cut his throat and puncture his lung? I doubt that very much!"

"That is a very small minority of the children!"

"Then it shouldn't be too difficult to get rid of them, should it?"

"If Teddy could help us identify them..."

"Please. I have work to do. I believe this conversation is ended!"

"If you're afraid to have him attend our school, at least consider other alternatives! There is a good Catholic school—"

My father snorted. "My son will never attend a Catholic school or any other religious school while I'm alive!"

"There are some quite good private schools in Lacrosse—"

"I'm sure my son wouldn't wish to travel so far or to be away from his family. The issue is closed!"

"Look, doctor, you're a psychiatrist! Surely you

know that this boy, any boy, needs to be connected to his community..." My father snorted again. "To other human beings outside his family! If you cut him off from any outside contact, you will be making a tragic mistake! Please reconsider!"

My father turned and stared at the man. He'd put down my suitcase. His hands were knotted into fists.

"How dare you tell me my business as a doctor or as a father! No one knows my son like I do! He is a genius. His IQ scores are off the chart! Your school has done nothing to develop his intellect, even before the attack. Now get off my property!"

Principal Thompson flushed and his own hands knotted. Then he looked over at me with an expression that was too much like pity. He sighed and walked over to his car. I watched his car drive onto Seminary road and turn towards town. I felt lost, empty. I wished he'd come back, and force my father to change his mind. I wished I'd said something to support the principal. But I knew my father would have taken that as disloyalty, and I didn't think he would allow that today.

"I'm sorry you had to find out this way," Father said. "I was going to tell you this morning."

"I'm not going to school any more?"

"No, I'm going to be your teacher now. From now on, you won't have to let those kids or those teachers drag you down to their level. You'll be free to live up to your own potential. Won't that be a lot of fun?"

His smile faded a little as he waited for an answer.

I wanted to say to him: Now they'll never respect me!

They'll be sure I asked to be taken out of school out of fear! They'll think I'm a coward! I'm not a coward! I beat Bobby and his gang! I beat them!

But what I said was, "Sure, Father. It's going to be a lot of fun."

On my first day of 'freedom' I stood in my bathrobe looking out the front window at my sister going off to school. She had her blue book bag over her shoulder and was waving at some friends on the big yellow bus. Then she turned and looked at me. She waved, and I waved back. She had a soft liquid look in her beautiful gray eyes that I didn't like: more pity

She doesn't understand, I thought. *I'm free!* All the other kids have to pile on the bus, answer to the bells and mill in the crowded hallways with the rest of the herd. Only I can go where I like and do what I like without answering to anyone! So why do I feel so empty, so ashamed?

My father stood at my side, watching Ellen leave. He didn't answer Ellen's wave, perhaps knowing it wasn't for him. After the bus had pulled away, he brought me into the dining room and sat down beside me. He smiled broadly. Clearly he enjoyed having bested the principal and the whole town. They couldn't even provide his son with a decent, safe education. He had to do the job himself! This just proved what ignorant rubes they were.

Even though I agreed that the townspeople were mostly rubes, I didn't believe all of them were. Some of my teachers were really nice; especially Mr. Hall, my English teacher, and I would miss them. Mrs. Goethe and our cook Emma were also nice, even if Emma seemed a little slow. But I knew that he would fly into a rage if I defended anyone in this town. Why did he hate them all so much? And why did he stay here, in a town he despised?

He laid on the kitchen table a typewritten outline of my new course work and went over it with me. The subjects and the basic texts were the same I'd had. However, I had to read several additional books each semester either from the library or my father's bookshelves. Furthermore, I had to write one essay each week on one or more of the subjects. Father would approve the topic of the essay during our Saturday session. I also had midterm and final essays due on all subjects, plus one final, interdisciplinary essay covering two or more subjects. He'd make reading assignments each Saturday. Otherwise, my time was my own, as long as I completed all the assignments. Did I have any questions?

Yes I did, but I kept it to myself. How was I supposed to do twice the workload I'd had in school, and still meet my father's high expectations? I wanted very much to justify Father's faith in me and make him proud.

My father gave me a list of my first week's assignments and then walked out the door. I watched him go through the gate and up the long driveway to the big red brick asylum towering above our house. The sudden silence of the house spooked me and I realized, as if for the first time, how dark it was in this huge old house, even in the daytime. The walls were paneled with dark wood everywhere, and there was only one big window in the big old dining room with its long mahogany table. Even the family photographs lined up in the front hallway were poorly lit and murky. I'd seen these pictures thousands of times, but now I paused to study them. Perhaps the history they held could tell me how I'd arrived at this dead end in my life and provide a clue on how to break free.

The first picture, as you came in the front door, showed Pastor Schoendienst, my father's father, standing at the head of our huge refectory table. (Our house had been both his rectory and the dining hall for his small Lutheran seminary, which was now the asylum just up the hill.) His hands were raised in supplication while perhaps two dozen young seminarians bowed their heads.

The next photograph showed the pastor with his arms around the shoulders of his teenage son, my father, his bony fingers grasping his boy's arm like talons. How proud my grandfather looked and how insecure and resentful my father seemed! I had never seen him like that.

I'd often wondered why he'd left this unflattering picture up. Maybe because he'd got his revenge against the man who had so dominated him. After the pastor died, my dad had come back to Weimar from the University at Madison, with a doctorate in Psychiatry and his father's inheritance. He converted the seminary, which the Lutheran church had leased from his father, into the private insane asylum it was now. He hadn't even permitted the church authorities to deconsecrate the chapel.

"There was nothing sacred there, Teddy!" he told me later. "If I could have converted it into a public toilet, I would have!"

The townspeople hated him for his sacrilege and started calling Seminary Road, which led past our house, "Nuthouse Road." My father didn't care. He hated them back; as much he did his father, and God.

I shuddered. I hoped that my father's large capacity for hatred would never be directed at me. But I was his favorite. Ellen bore the brunt of his anger and I always tried to protect her from him as much as I could.

The next picture showed my father and mother on their wedding day. He looked so young and handsome in his tuxedo, and she appeared so lovely in an old fashioned wedding dress whose train swirled around her feet. He had brought her back from Madison where he had treated her in the University clinic. His arm circled her shoulder and he wore the same expression of proud possession that his father displayed in the previous photograph. She looked radiantly happy, but also insecure, as if fearing that such happiness couldn't last. It hadn't lasted; she'd died giving birth to Ellen. I'd always suspected that Father had blamed Ellen for her death. Strange, for a man who prided himself so much on his rationality! But I had no right to judge him. He was my father, and in his own way, a great man.

He had published several books on psychiatry and had been presented with honorary degrees from a host of universities which hung above the family portraits. But as I looked at the unease in my mother's eyes, I wondered if it was the beginning of madness and if she had bequeathed it to me.

The next picture, my favorite, showed Grandpa Varner, my mother's father, with me at three years old, clinging around his neck. I remembered that piggyback ride: it was like being on top of a moving mountain. A huge, jolly man, he always smiled, always brought goodies for my sister and me.

He'd say to me, "I love you, Teddy, and God loves you too."

Whenever I thought of God, I would always give Him my grandpa's face. But my father would frown when he said these things; either because he resented any mention of God in his house, or because he was jealous of any expressions of love towards me. And I'd always felt guilty for loving this interloper in our home. For the last several years, Father had made sure that Grandpa Varner and God stayed away from our home. I suddenly wanted to talk to Grandpa. I didn't know his phone number, but surely I could get that from Information. But I'd better not; it was a long distance call to his home in Milwaukee and my father would find out.

The last photograph showed my father, his strong arms around my puny shoulders. I was a scrawny thirteen-year-old—begoggled and wimpish. Weak, too weak! The same possessive pride shone in his face as his father had shown. As for me, I showed the same insecurity, but not the resentment. He had done too much for me for me to feel any resentment. I had to be properly grateful.

I sighed, deeply. Studying these old images only increased my feeling of being in a trap, one that was built before I was born.

I had to get out of there! I took a quick shower and dressed. Then, I threw my book bag over my shoulder and walked into the back yard where I'd parked the new bike Father had bought me. It was just a Monkey Ward bike, but it gave me back the feeling of independence I'd had with my Schwinn.

I wheeled the bike through the narrow passageway between Old Man Koenig's fence and our house. Once I hit the gravel of our driveway, I jumped on the bike and started pedaling. At first, I panted and my chest hurt a little, but as I got into the rhythm of pedaling, exhilaration replaced pain. The wind blew through my hair, taking with it my fears and doubts. Yes, I was free!

As I picked up speed, the red autumn leaves crunched beneath my tires. I thought of wounded men lying on a battlefield, screaming as a tank rolled over them. This horrible image jolted me so that I almost fell off my bike. Where had that picture come from?

"From you!" My father's voice again, the same one I had heard outside the alley. I had the same feeling of wrongness I had had then. This didn't happen this way. But I had to admit that the voice had been right, then and now. Where else could the image have come but from myself? Some of my nightmares were like this, bloody and sadistic, and they came from me too. I seemed to see a black chasm opening under me. Was I really a sadist or did I like tormenting myself, just like Bobby and his friends did? Neither alternative seemed very cheerful.

I suddenly realized I was passing the school, which towered above me on the hill to my left. I lowered my head, glancing at the three-story red brick building as I went by. Fortunately, all of the kids were still in their first period classes. But Mr. Schroeder, the janitor, was out front raking leaves. He gave me a startled look as I went by and I looked away.

I imagined him saying to himself, "That little truant is as bold as brass, riding right by here like he doesn't have a care in the world!" It seemed to take a year until the school was behind me.

Finally, I was rolling over the stone bridge and into town. The streets were empty. Thank God! Huffing and puffing, I made the long climb to the top of the square. I put my bike in the library's rack, carefully threading my new bike chain through the spokes. As I walked up the steps, a smile broke out on my face. From now on, I'd be spending five days a week here in my favorite place in the world. Oh, I'd take out my assigned books, all right, but nothing could prevent me from spending an hour or two a day reading anything I liked. I could even read the detective novels I loved so much, but which my father loathed.

"These books have no relation to reality!" he'd say. "What are the odds that any one will ever ask you to solve a murder?"

But what was wrong with a little fantasy? Here I

could meet my friend, Sherlock Holmes, pursuing master criminals across the foggy moors of England, shouting: "Come, Watson, the hunt is up!" Or I could meet my other friend, Sam Spade, turning up his collar against the equally foggy San Francisco night. I loved being with them, even though I knew they were only imaginary.

"I value your companionship too, young man," said Sherlock.

"Yeah, kid, you're all right," said Sam.

I bounded up the stairs to the library and went inside. I was expecting to see Mrs. Goethe. Instead, a youngish blonde woman was seated behind the counter. She looked at me suspiciously as I walked towards her. I asked her where Mrs. Goethe was. She gave me a thin smile and told me my friend only worked on the weekends. Then her eyes locked on mine. She had cold gray eyes, the color of Ellen's, but without the love.

"Shouldn't you be in school right now, son?"

I blushed and began stammering, "I-I-I'm in a sp-sp-special home study program with my father."

She stared at me dubiously then went back to stamping her books as if I was not there. Suddenly the library wasn't so much fun anymore. I read in her eyes what I had read in Mr. Schroeder's: *You aren't supposed to be here.*

My steps echoed as I walked across the tile floor to the card catalog. I looked up one of the books on Father's list, but in that instant I decided to cheer myself up by looking at something I would enjoy. I walked up the marble stairs to the second floor. The stacks, always so warm and welcoming before, now looked like dark hiding places where anything might be waiting for me. I imagined Bobby and his friends jumping out at me, shouting insults.

"Hello, faggot! Bookworm! Queer! Hermit!"

Hermit! That one fit. I felt cut off from everyone and everything even here in my favorite place. I decided to go where no one ever bothered me: The Time Machine. I took out the microfilm roll for 1925 and soon reached the story about Old Man Washburn's farm.

"Just a few miles outside Weimar, at the end of a beautiful coulee, stands the old Washburn house. There, just over eight years ago, occurred one of the most sensational crimes in Wisconsin history. And there, according to reliable witnesses, a brutal murderer and his helpless victims still appear, silhouetted against the farmhouse's plate glass window

On a quiet Monday morning on June 21ˢᵗ, 1917, Samuel Washburn walked into the office of our Sheriff Carson, and announced that he had killed his wife and three daughters on the day before. When asked by the Sheriff why he had done it, he said that they had refused his demand that they read the Bible for several hours after they had attended church. It seemed it was the youngest girl's birthday and the mother and her girls insisted on celebrating it in a local ice cream parlor

"They were willful and disobedient!" Washburn stated. "But they will mind me now!

"The sheriff immediately jailed Washburn and went out to the farmhouse with three deputies. Upon entering, they were greeted with a hellish sight, which shook even these experienced lawmen. The walls were drenched with blood, which somehow continued to flow more than twenty-four

hours after the massacre, defying all the laws of physics. The savagely butchered bodies of Mrs. Washburn and the three small girls, the oldest nine years old, lay in the living room. The murder weapon, a blood-boltered axe, lay beside them. The bodies were cut up in so many pieces, that they had to be gathered into large bags to be transported to the morgue."

I skimmed over the details of the short but sensational trial. The jury was only out for an hour before returning with a guilty verdict. Washburn was duly hanged three weeks later. Then came the part of the story that had interested me.

"Shortly after Samuel Washburn was hanged, residents of the little coulee began to tell stories of hearing earsplitting screams from the Washburn house late in the evening. Some bolder spirits went onto the property and reported seeing silhouettes of a large man, standing over a woman and three small children, wielding an axe. An unearthly blue light shone behind the eerie figures casting their shadows on the drawn shades. Sometimes, the larger figure brought the shadow axe down on the smaller figures and then the eerie screams began again. Some people who went into the house in the daytime saw large quantities of blood flowing down the walls."

I had thought that reading the gory details of the murders might excite and entertain me. I usually enjoyed scaring myself that way; it took me out of my sad, drab life, and, of course, I was never really in danger. But something about this story seemed too familiar, as if I had seen something like it in my dream in the library. I decided to go to one of my other favorite spots: the art section

I opened up one of the big books, Blake's illustrations of *Dante's Inferno*. The first picture I saw showed a drowning sinner reaching a hand up in supplication to Dante, who stood in a boat. But, Dante was driving the sinner away with a paddle.

How cruel! I thought

"No!" said a voice inside my head, which sounded like my father's. "No man can save another from Hell! Each man must save himself! Remember!"

That voice again, But my real father would never talk about Heaven or Hell, except as a joke. What was wrong with me?

I opened up another big book: *Goya's works*. The first thing I saw was a huge, maddened face, eyes glittering, shoving into its huge maw a red and pink mass of human flesh. Below the place where the flesh merged, I made out smaller human forms up to the neck. I was shocked, sickened. Something about the thing's glittering eyes seemed horribly familiar. It reminded me of the nightmares I had about the Man in the Moon. I looked down to the title: "Saturn Devouring His Sons."

This was turning out all wrong! I slammed the book shut and looked up at the clock. It was only half past ten AM on the first day of my new life!

I looked over the marble railing at the librarian. She was on the phone and looking up in my direction. Her eyes met mine and she looked down. It was time to leave. I hurriedly got the book I'd been looking for and went down to check it out. I was almost running by the time I reached the door. It was just after eleven and I wanted to be past the school before noon, when the kids would be coming out for lunch. I put the book in my bag, unlocked the bike and took off as if hellhounds were following me.

The cool rush of the wind against my face made me feel good again. I crossed the bridge at a good clip. I'd be home soon and all this anxiety would be gone.

Suddenly, I felt rather than saw something very large coming up fast behind me. I glanced back and saw the Sheriff's black and white cruiser almost on my rear wheel, looking as big as a tank. Then, the flashing lights came on and the siren screamed.

I stood up on my bike, spinning the pedals as hard as I could. I heard a deep engine roar and suddenly the cruiser was beside me and then cutting in front, and I saw my distorted image reflected in the rear bumper's chrome. I jammed on the brakes but the bike hit the car. I flew over the roof and smashed down on the hood. Things went black for a second, and then I found myself in the mud and the leaves just beyond the cruiser's grille. My chest hurt and my breath came in pain. I thought: there goes the lung again. But in a moment, I could breathe more easily.

"Jesus Christ, boy! Are you all right?"

It was the Sheriff, his blue eyes wide and his face redder than ever.

"I-I-I think so!"

"Why didn't you stop when I put on the siren?"

"I p-p-panicked."

"Well, you're supposed to stop. You're lucky you're not dead! Can you get up?"

I nodded. He leaned down and pulled me up by the shoulder, not too gently. I could tell he was angry but his words were solicitous. He was probably thinking about a potential lawsuit.

"What are you doing out of school at this hour anyway?" he said.

"I-I-I'm in a special home study program. D-d-didn't my father tell you?"

"Nobody told me nothing!" he said. "But listen, I'm sorry about your accident! Are you sure you're okay?"

I took a deep breath and took stock of myself. My heart still beat fast but then it had a good reason. I had a skinned palm from my landing, and gravel and mud had been driven up into my hands, mixing blood and dirt. I held them out to him.

"You better get those cleaned and bandaged before you get an infection! You get in the car now and I'll take you to the school. The nurse can look you over while I sort this home study thing out with the principal."

He opened up the back door to the cruiser. I thought of what the kids would say if they saw me coming to school in the back of a police car.

"P-p-please don't take me to school. All you need to do is c-c-call my father at the Asylum. H-h-he'll tell you all about it!"

The Sheriff got a mean smile on his face. I knew that he was thinking how I'd crossed him by not telling him who attacked me, and how my father had humiliated him at their last meeting.

"Get in!" he said.

There was no arguing with that tone. I got in the back seat, ducking my head to avoid the roof. I felt like a criminal.

"P-p-please, sir, just c-c-call him!" I said again. "Or call the principal!"

He said nothing, just picked up my bike, threw it in the trunk and got in the driver's seat. But when he started the car, he turned towards town, not towards the school. Soon, he pulled up in front of the police station that was just off the square, by the old city hall. For a moment, I thought he was going to arrest me. Then he said, "I'll be back as soon as I make a phone call!"

While I waited, I sat as far down in the back seat as I could, with my head down and my eyes closed. I hoped that no one would come by and see me like this. Suddenly, the door next to me opened and I heard the Sheriff's gruff voice

"All right, boy, you can go home!" I looked up. His face looked as angry as his voice. "The principal backs up your story. He doesn't seem happy about it, though, and neither am I. But I guess I got to let you go! Now get out of my sight. You know, I'm not very happy about what you did to my hood!"

I kept my mouth shut, just happy not to be in school or in jail. He took my bike out of the cruiser's trunk and threw it on the sidewalk. He sped away with his dented hood but my bike was in much worse shape. The front tire and the rim were warped and the handlebars of my Monkey Ward rocked like a horse in stride as I rolled along the pavement

Once I got home, I went up to the upstairs bathroom, washed my hands, and put disinfectant on them. The sting of the iodine distracted me a little from my dark feelings. I went up to my room, which, as always, felt secure and private. Gradually, my feelings of isolation and vulnerability were replaced by a feeling of power. They hated my freedom, but there is nothing they could do about it. I had beaten the town just like I did Bobby and his gang!

4

The next day, as I watched Ellen's yellow bus drive away, I realized that I needed one more thing from my dad before my new life could be complete. And safe

"Father, can I ask you a favor?"

He put down his coffee cup on the kitchen table.

"What is it, Teddy?"

"I wonder if you can give me a ride to the library on Saturdays. I don't think I want to go there on weekdays any more."

"Why, did something happen yesterday?"

"Oh no, nothing happened."

"But I thought you loved it there."

"I do, when Mrs. Goethe is there. It turns out she's only there on the weekends."

"Well, can't you take your bike in on Saturdays? I'm pretty busy."

"I know, but I'd really rather go with you. You wouldn't have to stay. You could come back and pick me up in a couple of hours."

Father sighed, heavily. Then, he put his hand in his pocket and brought out a key.

"Here, Teddy, this is the key to my room. You can go into my study, which is on the other side of my bedroom. It has hundreds of books and a desk where you can do your writing. If after you look at what I have in there, you still feel you need to go to the Library then we'll work out something. One thing though, I do not want you rummaging around in my bed room and I especially do not want you to look in the bookshelf at the head of my bed. Do I make myself clear?"

"Yes, Father."

My dad could always make himself clear. But I was smiling as I watched him climb the hill to the Asylum. I had handled that well. He appeared to suspect nothing. I just had to keep my banged up bike out of his sight and hope that the sheriff didn't tell on me. I didn't believe he would: he disliked my father even more than he did me

Meanwhile, Father had given me the keys to his inner sanctum, the place I had been forbidden to go even as a small child. It would be fun to look at all the books in his study and when I was done with that, well, I might just see what I could see in his bedroom.

"Better not," my father's voice said. I jumped as if he were in the same room with me. No, it was that strange voice that sounded like my father...but said things he would never say.

"The secrets you'll find there are better left unfound. You will wish you had never seen them!"

I said nothing. What was there to say? This voice

could read my every thought and knew what I was going to do. It was pretty much like God, if I believed in God. Fortunately, my real dad was not so omniscient.

I took the key and went over to my father's room. I put the key in the lock, but my hands began to shake so much that I dropped it. I leaned down and picked it up. My hands were still trembling, but I was able to open the door.

The room was dark and I fumbled for the light switch. I found it at last and turned on the light. The room was still extremely dark; the only lights were one over the bedstead and one in the study. The walls in here were also paneled in dark wood and the two windows in my father's bedroom were covered with dark drapes. There were no windows in the study. The walls were covered with books, on bookshelves set into the walls. I took in the rich odor of old, well kept books. This should be fun! A desk and chair sat under the light. *This must be where the pastor wrote his sermons*, I thought. The furniture had that heavy, 19th century look which showed up in some of the photos on the wall.

Well, let's see what we've got, I thought. It would be fun to find out what my father was really interested in. But after a search of the book titles, I felt that I was no closer to finding that out than when I started. Tons of books on psychology, of course, mostly Freudian, old and new, though I did find some Jung and Adler. Case studies by the thousands, many of them taken from the files of the Waupun Asylum for the Criminally Insane. I wondered how he had obtained all these files, since he had never worked there. There were also hundreds of fine reference books, encyclopedias, thesauruses, dictionaries, and yearbooks. A smattering of books on chemistry, pharmacology, and the use and misuse of illegal drugs. Quite a few history books, especially on the Second World War, in which my dad had served in as an intelligence officer. No books on art and only one on music. The only works of fiction were large editions of the classics: Shakespeare, Dante, Homer, etc. No books on philosophy, and of course, none on religion. I thought of what Mrs. Goethe had said about him: More things on heaven and earth than are dreamt of in his philosophy. But was that all there was to him? Did he never wonder about anything that wouldn't fit in a textbook or a reference book? Did he have no desires, no dreams, no secrets?

Once again, I heard his voice.

"Oh, yes, I have secrets that you would not believe. And, yes, when you find them out, you will wish that I *was* only what shows up in these books!"

Damn his threats and warnings! I have a good mind to call his bluff. I don't believe this voice is really my father's. He says too many things my father would never say. I looked over at his bedroom. If he has any secrets, there's the place I'll find them. And why not? If I hear him coming in, I'll have plenty of time to put away what I'm looking at and go back to the study. I would find out what I needed to know no matter what.

I went over to his bedroom. I saw nothing remotely personal on the dark walls, just some diplomas that apparently wouldn't fit in the hall. But I did see a splash of color on his nightstand. I moved closer; it looked like a small portrait of a young man. At closer range, I saw that it was my dad at about the same age as he was in the photo in the hall. But what a difference! The teenager I saw in the portrait was staring directly at the artist, and he was smiling. There was a hint of uncertainty in the smile, as if what he was looking at was too good to be true. But he looked happy. He looked as if he were in love. I had certainly never seen a look like that on my dad's face. Here was a secret for sure. But it made me feel better about him, not worse.

I examined the picture for clues. The initials ESB appeared in the lower right hand corner, in a fine feminine hand. The young man was seated at an old-fashioned roll top desk. Behind the desk, I made out an old style poster bed festooned in blue and white. The same blue and white motif appeared in window curtains at the far end of the room. The room seemed very large and I was sure I had never seen it before. The hand that created the painting was also fine and feminine, or I missed my guess, and possessed of real talent.

I wondered how I would go about tracking down this ESB. It could be that I might find more clues in the books at the head of Father's bed. Of course, he had forbidden me to look into those books, but I had gone too far to turn back now.

All the books were large and seemed to have a lot of pictures in them. I grabbed one from the middle of the row and flipped it open to a random page. At first, I could not make out what I was looking at. A young officer in a black uniform smiled as he stood in front of a huge pile of rags. Then I saw that there were human beings inside the rags. It was hard to recognize them as human because their skin was as gray as the rags they had worn, and their bodies were shrunken and distorted.

No! Not my father. He can't enjoy this stuff!

I ruffled through the pages, hoping to find anything sane and normal, but every picture revealed a new horror, another way to torture and dehumanize. A young boy with his genitals torn off, a pitifully thin woman, her blood cascading through smashed teeth. And always, the ovens, stuffed full of bodies, some with their eyes still gleaming with life. I felt like vomiting. My God, he must be insane!

There had to be an innocent explanation for why he kept these things by his bed. He had been in Germany during and after the war. That was it. He must have been responsible for keeping a record of these atrocities. Maybe he could better fathom the minds of these sadists by looking at what they had done. But why keep this stuff right by his pillow? What sweet dreams they must give him!

I closed the last book carefully, making sure to put it back in its proper place. If he had any inkling that I had looked at these books…what? What would he do to me? I had always been afraid of his rages, of course, but I had been sure that he was a rational man and would always be under control. Now, I wasn't so sure.

I decided to go back to my own room. His room seemed suddenly full of darkness, the kind that all the lights in the world would not dispel. I began to feel it creeping into my own mind.

It was only about two but once I was in my room, I felt very tired. I took my glasses off and lay back on the bed. I soon drifted into an uneasy sleep. I was lying on the poster bed in the picture. Someone was painting me, nude. I wanted to see who the artist was, but when I tried to look up, a girl's voice said, "Don't move!" I quickly looked down. It was then I realized that I was the boy with his genitals torn off.

I woke up, my heart beating fast. I listened to it for a while until it calmed down. I reached gingerly down to where my genitals should be. Still there, thank God.

Just then, I heard the front door slam. Ellen, probably. I was glad not to be alone with these kinds of thoughts. I heard her coming up the staircase. She opened the door and looked in on me. Her eyes looked sad, and a little scared. For a moment, I thought that she had seen into my dream.

"What's the matter, Ellen?"

"Nothing. Why do you ask?"

"I don't know. You just looked…so, how was school?"

"We heard that the sheriff took Bobby in for questioning."

"Really? I didn't think Carson was going to do anything about my case. Did he say why he was questioning him?"

"Nobody knows. The kids are mad about it."

"I don't blame them. I couldn't identify anybody, and I was the victim. I can't imagine what kind of evidence he could have against him."

"I don't know. Well, I'll see you later."

"See you."

She went into her room and closed the door. I wondered what was with her. Maybe something had happened to her at school. It didn't seem likely: almost everybody there liked her. Well, maybe she would talk about it later. Meanwhile, I had to start on one of my writing assignments. Father would be both angry and suspicious if he found that I hadn't done any real work that day. He might wonder if I had been violating the privacy of his bed room, which of course I had.

About five-thirty, I heard him coming in the front door. He called up to me to come down. I obeyed instantly. He smiled up at me as I came down the stairs.

"How was your day?" he asked.

"Fine, Father, how was yours?"

"As well as could be expected, if you have to play nursemaid to a hundred female psychotics all day. What did you do today?"

"I went into your bed…into your study and checked out your books."

"And what did you think?"

"Well, you have a lot of great reference books. But if I need specific information on one topic, I may need to go to the library."

"Really? Well, that's all right. I can take you in to the library for as long as you want on Saturdays. I might even stay with you. Who knows? I might find something of interest!"

"Really? That would be great, Dad. Thanks a lot!"

He really seemed to be in a good mood. He didn't even seem to mind my calling him "Dad". I felt really bad about snooping into his books, and thinking he was some kind of pervert and sadist. How could I? He had given me more than I had asked, and he had given me another victory over the town. No longer would I have to worry about the kids or the cops. There was no way they could hurt me now!

We had dinner at six, as usual. Emma served us silently, as she always did. She never talked when my father was around. I guess she was afraid of him. She was friendlier with us kids. She even prepared special treats for us when my dad wasn't looking.

After dinner, I told him that I wanted to go to my room to work on my report. He nodded. As I went upstairs, I was feeling really good. I had almost everything I needed right here at home.

Just then, I heard something heavy hit the house. Then came the raucous sounds of contemptuous voices. Lots of them. I ran up to my room and looked out the window. I saw twenty or thirty kids in our front yard. Some of them were in Bobby's gang, but there were some of the good kids. I even saw Doug Hobart, the closest thing I had to a friend in the school. He always smiled at me and said "hi" and we helped each other in class. The sight of him out there cut me worse than Bobby's knife had.

They were calling me "Snitch, coward, faggot!" I knew I was none of these things, but now they would never know. Some of them threw stones or garbage, but the older kids were passing around bottles of beer that they would smash against the house when they were finished.

Then my father rushed out and began screaming at them. They yelled "Shrink!" and "Egghead!" at him, but they backed off. In a few minutes, the sheriff arrived. The kids were gone. But they'd done their damage. I now knew I'd won nothing. Bobby and his gang had won. They had made me the enemy, the outsider, even to the good kids.

I remembered a similar mob of kids standing outside another house down by the river. They too had been yelling and throwing things at the house. Only I'd been one of them. I had been out biking and joined the mob out of curiosity. I had no idea who the people were in the house or what they'd done. I only heard the hatred in the kid's voices and the whining scream of the woman inside. Something in her tone seemed to invite violence. I picked up a stone and threw it at the house. I felt the exhilaration of being part of the mob.

I later learned the boy who lived in the house had just returned from Waupun State Hospital where he'd been held for molesting a little girl. I felt at the time that we had done right in attacking that home and that boy.

But now the tables were turned, and I *was* that boy.

I ndian Summer in Northern Wisconsin is like a rebirth. One day, fall leaves are drifting down and the smell of their burning is everywhere. The cold air gives a hint of the long months of snow to come. Winter waits just over the next line of bluffs and summer is as dead as the leaves. The next day, the air is still and hot while wispy summer clouds float high in the sky. You can put away your rubbers and your winter coat. You can begin to feel again.

The day after I became an exile in my own home was just like that. The night before, after my father had driven the kids away, I'd lain awake thinking about how I would end my life. It wasn't the first time I'd considered it. But this time, the pain of existence burned like a hot coal in the center of my chest: I couldn't stand this agony for another day, much less for fifty or sixty years! I told myself that the other kids were all punks and that I didn't care what they thought. I couldn't look away from the mirror of myself they showed me, or the weak, disgusting image it held. The kids were right! I was something queer, strange—a monstrous birth. I felt the pain of my wrongness as deep as my soul.

Raised in a bad house by one, maybe *two* insane parents. I should never have been born! But it wasn't too late to remedy that unfortunate mistake. I went downstairs and opened the hall closet, where my father kept his old medical bag. As I rummaged through the bag, I heard his deep regular snoring from his bedroom. So far, so good! I took out his scalpel, which gleamed in the dim light. Since he wasn't a surgeon, he had never used it except for dissections in medical school. Well, I had a use for it.

I took it up to my room and held it against my wrists. I drew it lightly across the veins. It stung a little. A bright line of blood appeared, and I flinched at the sight. *Oh, no!* I thought. *Father will see it!* I began to wonder if I was really serious about this thing. If I were, I'd be dead and I shouldn't care what he saw. This seemed so…sloppy. A gun would be quicker and surer, but my father never kept a firearm in the house. If only I could just fall asleep and never wake up! I sighed heavily. Maybe I *was* a coward! I put the scalpel under the mattress. I could always finish the job if the pain of living got too bad. Thinking this, I became calmer and finally fell asleep.

But when I woke up, the sun shone bright and clear and the birds were singing. For a moment, I forgot all about the night before, and the trap my life had become. When the memory did come, it seemed like a nightmare, which quickly dissolved in the sunshine. Only this bird-song morning was real. I felt my spirit climb out of its black hole and look around, blinking and rubbing its eyes.

After all, I was still free to come and go as I pleased, at least while my enemies were in school. But where in all this wide world could I go? I had no friends and Grandpa, the only relative I cared about, lived in Milwaukee, over a hundred miles away.

"I know a place you can go!"

The voice, low but seductively feminine, came out of the morning stillness. I started and looked around. I saw no one. That only frightened me more. Had I really heard that? Or was I having auditory hallucinations again? Next, I'd start seeing monsters or feel bugs crawling on me, like the people in Father's medical journals! But this voice didn't give me the same feeling of wrongness my father's voice did just before the attack in the alley. It fascinated me; a woman's voice, husky and rich. As if an unseen person was whispering in my ear: someone really interesting. So lonely was I, so cut off from any other person, that I longed for human contact. Especially a woman's contact.

"Come on, Teddy, let's go!" the voice said. "Or are you too afraid?"

This was getting too strange. *Don't answer it*, I thought. But I heard myself saying: "Sure. Why not?"

I found myself walking into the back yard. I felt the warm weight of the sunshine on my shoulders. What did I have to fear on a day like this? I walked my bike out to the road. *Okay*, I thought, *which way?*

"Through Lepke's Woods!" the voice said.

I stopped and put my hands over my ears. My father would definitely consider this a pathological symptom. But then, he would never have to know.

Why not let my imaginary friend be my guide, I thought. If she's part of me, then she's a very interesting part. I'm going to be spending a lot of time with myself in the next few years, so I might as well get to know all the sides of me.

But what if she wasn't a part of me? The thought stirred me. If she wasn't, then I had a real mystery to solve: Who was she and what did she want? I began to feel intensely alive. My favorite line from Sherlock Holmes came into my mind.

"Come, Watson, the hunt is up!"

I walked the bike across the road and into the woods. It was slow going through the high-piled leaves. I was also afraid that Old Man Lepke's groundskeeper, a big scary man with a shaved head and a shotgun, might show up, But the woods were deserted. The sunshine was warm and I was sweating by the time I broke through to the other side. I got on my bike and bumped down a dirt road until I reached a paved county road. I felt excited to be riding down a road, only a block or so from my house, which I'd never been on before. Perhaps my life was not over after all. New doors to adventure seemed to be opening for me.

When I reached the county road, I paused to wait for instructions.

"To the left!" the voice said very distinctly.

I looked to my left. That way, the road wound its way

up a high hill, while to the right; the way was flat and level. I shook my head.

"To the left!" the voice said more insistently and with a hint of menace. I didn't feel like arguing with myself so I went to the left.

It was hard going, climbing the hill. I had to stand up and pump hard in order to make any headway. The hill got steeper and steeper and my breath came in short painful gasps. I was worried about my injured lung. I weaved from one side of the road to the other, to avoid a head-on assault on the hill. Finally, the front wheel began slipping when I pumped it and I got no purchase on the road. I was actually going backwards.

I dismounted and began to walk the bike up the hill. I was pleasantly surprised to find I'd made it almost to the top. I had no idea I'd climbed so far so fast. When I reached the summit, I stopped to rest. Looking back the way I'd come, I was astonished at how much I could see. In the near distance, I saw the roof of Lepke's old house. Ellen and I used to call it the House of the Seven Gables, though we could only count three sticking out of its roof. It had the same air of gloom and mystery which had surrounded the place in Hawthorne's novel. Old Man Lepke lived alone there and never let anyone inside. Beyond it, I saw the spires of the Asylum, which blocked off the view of my house. Further back and to the right, I picked out the river, gleaming silver through the trees. The morning mist rose above it, making it look hazy and indistinct like an Impressionist painting. Closer, I saw the school, towering above the road. I even saw the kids on the playground. I hoped they couldn't see me.

Even the town looked beautiful from here, especially the town square, which resembled something out of a Norman Rockwell painting. You couldn't see the bars and the alleys, or the run down old bandstand, or the boarded up shops along the square, just the library, its marble facade gleaming, then the tall trees in the square below it, and then the river, winding its way through swampland to the west. I saw the dark figure of a hawk, soaring like a blessing over this quiet, beautiful town that had caused me so much pain.

I turned away and looked over the other side of the hill. I was looking down into a beautiful little coulee, one of the many glacial valleys of the upper-Midwest. The glacier had come in on the far side of the valley and hollowed it out like an ice cream scoop. The leaves of the trees glowed in such vivid reds and yellows I could hardly believe they hadn't been painted. The stubbled fields of the farms below me looked like a checkerboard of dark brown earth against the yellow of the hays and grasses. The fields were spotted with hundreds of cows, brown or black and white, leaning their heads down to feed. The roofs of the silos shone silver beside the red barns. So perfect, so peaceful; it might almost have made me believe there was a God. I thought of how scornful my father would be of such a thought, and quickly dismissed it.

But I felt good and strong. I'd won a right to this beauty and this peace by the effort I'd made to get up here.

"You still have a long way to go!" the voice said. "But it is downhill from here."

Damn you! I thought. *I don't care if you're a part of me. I'm getting tired of you. I'll rest here as long as I need to rest, then, if I feel like it, I'll go home!*

But within a few minutes, I was on my bike again, obediently coasting down the hill towards the coulee. Something about this voice didn't invite contradiction. In that way, it resembled my father's voice. The rush of the wind sucked the air out of me. The hill was even steeper on this side, so I was soon going so fast the fence posts looked like dots. *Too fast!* I thought and kicked backward on the pedals, but that only made me wobble back and forth. I had hardly slowed myself down. Soon, I was going even faster than before. The wheels were whining like miniature jet engines and I thought: I'm out of control. Involuntarily, I closed my eyes.

"Look out!" the voice shouted.

I opened my eyes and saw a metal sign right in front of me. I jerked the handlebars to the right and the sign grazed my shoulder. I spun around and pinwheeled off the bike and onto the cement. The road burned my arm and face and then I was off on the other side, skidding through gravel and grass. Finally, I stopped. I staggered to my feet, once again checking myself for broken bones. I found none. I was just scared, bruised and angry.

"You see how I take care of you, Teddy?" said the voice

"Damn you! You almost got me killed!" I shouted.

I looked quickly around, hoping no one had seen me yelling at myself. She laughed a deep husky laugh that was somehow very seductive. I took stock of my situation. I had no idea where I was. The sun was high in the sky. Time to go home! If I retraced my steps now, I could find my way back before Father got home.

"No!" said the voice. "There is something you need to see!"

How long would I follow this will-of-the-wisp and where would it take me? I wanted to go home! But I was also fascinated by this voice. I didn't want it to leave me. She had said there was something I needed to see. I felt she had something to teach me: something I needed to learn. This felt like one of those extraordinarily vivid dreams that comes out of the depths of your subconscious and that you must see through to the end or lose some valuable part of yourself. Every detail of the dream seems to have significance to you or to your fate. The kind of dream that Jung would have loved. The nightmare I'd had in the library, though I didn't remember it clearly, had been like that. It was horrible but it had a wonderful air of mystery; a deep personal meaning. Like a sign or a warning that I needed to heed, or else. I told myself I would learn everything this waking dream had to teach me, or die trying.

So I got back on my bike, which was dented and dirty but still in good working order. I weaved back and forth to slow myself down and was soon down to the bottom of the hill and pedaling towards the end of the coulee. This was a lot further away than it had looked from the top of the hill. I passed dozens of cornfields, which looked desolate and deserted after the harvest. I passed dairy farms, heavy with a sickening mixture of odors, sweet milk and sour manure. I wondered how anyone could live with that smell. I guess you get used to it, I thought. You get used to anything after a while.

The little valley didn't look as beautiful from up close as it had from the hilltop. In fact there was something desolate about it. I passed several ruined barns: the few slats that remained upright, bleached white by the sun, were like the ribs of a skeleton. The roofs had all fallen in. I saw no living being, except the cows, in that entire valley. This was not that surprising since the harvest was over, but it left me feeling uneasy and lonely.

I passed, very slowly, some Burma Shave signs, those little white signs that form a poem as you pass them one by one.

"Spring is sprung
the grass is riz
over where last year's
careless drivers is.
Burma Shave."

Very droll, I thought. I wondered if people really got paid for making up stuff like that. I was sure I could do better if given a chance.

I was getting close to the glacier-carved hills at the end of the coulee. They seemed steeper and taller than they'd looked from the hilltop. They were barren granite, unusual for Wisconsin, and gleamed an unnatural white in the sun. It almost felt like the ancient glacier itself loomed over me. The day seemed darker and chillier somehow, but when I looked up, no clouds blocked the sun, which still stood almost overhead. This eerie cold felt as if a chunk of that old glacier had broken off and been caught in this valley, ten thousand years after the Ice Age. I shivered. The Indian Summer magic drained out of the day, replaced by something dark and strange.

"Yea, though I walk through the valley..."

Where had that thought come from? Then I remembered. I'd been staying overnight at Grandpa's and woke up screaming from one of my nightmares. Grandpa had come into the room to comfort me. He'd spoken these words, which now unrolled in my head like one of those Burma Shave signs.

"Yea, though I walk
through the Valley
of the Shadow of Death..."

I began shivering. I felt as if I was in that Valley and that that Shadow hung over me. But what were the rest of the verses? After he recited the Psalm, I'd felt comforted and gone back to sleep. Why couldn't I remember the rest, the part that took away the fear?

"Stop! There it is!" the voice cried.

I kicked the bike to a stop and stared at the building, which had apparently been my goal all along. I'd run out of road, and there in front of me was an old farm. It looked eerily familiar though I knew I'd never been here before. Then I remembered where I'd seen it: in the Time Machine!

It was not exactly the way it had looked in the old newspaper. The silver roof of the silo had caved in and it loomed above the house like a round tower; the barn had collapsed into a mass of rotted lumber; and the stone walkway was covered with weeds, but the farmhouse itself looked exactly the same as it had in the newspaper drawing from thirty years before!

The old Washburn House!

I felt a rising panic mixed with a sense of unreality. How could this abandoned house be so intact, as if it had been frozen in time, when everything around it was in ruins? And how could I be here? I'd had little idea where this place was. How could a part of me lead me here? And if she was not part of me, why would she lead me to this horrible place, where a whole family had been butchered? What did the voice want me to see here? I thought: I don't want this! I don't want any of this!

"Don't be afraid, Teddy. Nothing in this house can hurt you. Now go up the walkway!"

I won't! I thought, and prepared to run. But somehow, I found myself getting off the bike and walking up the path towards the house. My breath came in short gasps as if I were riding my bike up hill again. It's really true, I thought. Right in that house, Old Man Washburn slaughtered his wife and daughters. And right there, in that window, they have been seen with his shadow looming over them as the glacier once loomed over this valley. And as I walked, the illusion of terrible cold grew so real that by the time I reached the front door, I was shivering and I even imagined I could see my breath! And I dreaded the mere thought that that huge shadow would appear in the window. But I saw nothing, only dark glass and...something moving in there!

Then I was running back down the path and somehow was on my bike, pedaling hard, towards light and warmth and sanity. And all the time, I felt the shadow of that old glacier looming over me, gaining on me! And the entire long road home, I thought about what I'd seen in the window.

After all, I told myself, *it could have been my own reflection*. Or it might have been a reflection of the clouds. Or, it could have been what I thought it was.

A man's hand, beckoning

6

The day after my strange experience at the Washburn place, Indian summer vanished as completely as if it had never been. The skies were once more a lifeless gray and the air smelled of the snows to come. I stayed in my room most of the day, trying to read my textbooks. But all the while, I was listening for that low seductive voice, half wanting to hear it, half frightened of where it might lead me this time. But the voice didn't come and I felt my spirit sink, almost to the dead level where it had been before the voice led me on that adventure.

But not quite. I didn't think about suicide any more. Another way out of my trap had been shown to me; a way through the Valley of the Shadow of Death! That valley was horrible, but I'd never felt more alive than when I'd been pedaling down that road towards the Unknown. Part of me wished I'd followed that road to its conclusion, no matter how terrible it might be. That waking dream had lifted me out of ordinary realms of consciousness, and it was horrible to return to them. Why had I chickened out? Why had I not followed that beckoning hand? It was my fault the voice wouldn't come now! But when I thought of Old Man Washburn and the monstrous things he'd done, I wondered how I could even think of going into that house!

But that day had marked me permanently, like the light scar I now bore on my wrist. (I used my father's styptic pencil to hide it from him.) I'd awakened myself out of an important, intense dream, more vivid than life itself. I wanted another such dream to come, granting me a special destiny, which would raise me above the common herd. If I refused such a dream, I'd have to accept the herd's image of me as lesser than they were. No, the dream had made me feel unique and powerful. The next time it came, even if it were the Devil's hand that beckoned me, I would not wake until the dream had come to its end.

For safety's sake, I altered my routine, as I'd suggested to my father. I only left the house once a week, on Saturdays, when Father would drive me to the Library. I didn't regret coming there so seldom. The place had been spoiled by my enemies, like every other place, including my home. It was nice to see Mrs. Goethe, but I felt too timid to speak to her. She must have heard about my leaving school, and I was afraid that she disapproved. Occasionally, I'd see one of the good kids there. I'd turn my head away and they never tried to talk to me. Usually, I just went in, found my books, checked them out and left. My father would hang around, browsing, while I did this and I didn't want to keep him waiting too long.

The first time my father drove me home from the

library, I heard someone scream, "Hey, faggot!" It sounded like Bobby but I didn't look to make sure. I ducked down in my seat though it was too late to keep him from seeing me. I didn't want to see or to hear him. I felt like dying. I heard Bobby beginning to say something else. Then, suddenly, I heard that seductive voice again.

"Come inside, Teddy! They can't reach you there!"

Come inside? I thought. How? But the next minute, I found myself following her voice inside myself. It was easy; just like falling into a dream. I saw only darkness, and heard a low roaring, like Lake Michigan on a stormy day. Amazingly, Bobby's voice had vanished. But where was I? And where did that voice come from? Had my father heard it? Was he watching me? At this thought, I instantly rose out of the darkness. Bobby's ugly distorted face was only inches from mine, outside the window. I sank back into the comforting darkness. I thought, *Is this what's at the end of the Valley?* If so, it didn't seem so bad! Bobby had vanished again, leaving only the dark mist and that peaceful sea noise. Only one thing worried me: a strange sense of déjà vu, as if I had been in this place before. Where exactly had she led me this time... and why? This vague unease brought me partly out of my trance. I could dimly see my father beside me. He appeared to be talking to me, so I came up out of myself, and instantly the darkness and the roaring disappeared.

"What did you say, Father?"

"I said, I hope you're not letting these punks bother you."

"Oh, no. I don't even hear them any more!" He looked at me strangely but said nothing.

I had told the truth. I'd found a hiding place much safer and more private than the Library or my room: my own mind. From that time forward, the minute I heard anyone yelling at me, I summoned the darkness and the roaring and my enemies vanished. They couldn't touch me in the cave I carried around with me everywhere. At first, I felt a deep gratitude to the voice for giving me such power. I felt also, by going inside myself, I was growing closer to the one who had drawn me there. It was a wonderfully intimate feeling, even though she never joined me in my cave.

But I soon began to worry that I might go so deeply into the Valley that I could not come back out. I had read a lot of psychiatric literature, and I knew what this kind of withdrawal could be: the beginning of a psychotic break! The symptoms were all there: auditory hallucinations, inner darkness, a ringing in the ears (though this wasn't a ringing, so much as a soft sea sound.) But as long as I knew that I could be going into psychosis, it meant that I wasn't there yet. I resolved to watch these episodes carefully, and, if necessary, to get Father's help

For whatever reason, the voice did not return for a long time. Perhaps, it had achieved its objective in drawing me into myself, and was temporarily satisfied. Meanwhile, as I'd feared, the darkness and the roaring seemed to be growing out of my control. Soon, any loud noise brought them on without my will. And it was harder and harder to come back up out of my cave. At first, these episodes lasted only a couple of minutes, but as time went on, they grew longer until I would spend up to an hour in this state. I felt too ashamed to confide my worries to Father. How disappointed he would be if he found out that his "genius" son had become a garden variety schizophrenic! One Saturday, I fell into this trance as we were driving home from the library. The next thing I knew, Father was shaking me violently. I couldn't hear him but I saw him moving his lips. Somehow, I brought myself out of it.

"You are losing control of your defenses!" he shouted. "You must keep control at all times!"

"Yes, Father," I said.

I felt deeply ashamed. He had seen through me, like he always did. But, because of my shame, I still could not confide my fears to him. Thereafter, when I was with him, I carefully avoided falling too deeply into these states. But when I was alone, they came more and more frequently.

My studies suffered. I'd sometimes stare at the same page for an hour at a time. Even when I wasn't in the trance, I didn't want to do anything except lie in my bed and listen for the voice to give me more instructions. I had almost no ability to think or plan anything on my own. One day, my father came in while I was staring at the ceiling. I had to make an effort to follow him with my eyes. I worried that he'd shout at me again, or even strike me. But his voice was gentle and his eyes were kind.

"Teddy, I understand how you feel. It is hard for a boy your age to be so alone. But don't cut yourself off from me. Above all, don't cut yourself off from yourself! You have always loved the things of the mind: your books, your researches. Don't throw them away now! They can still be your best friends. Better friends than those thugs you left behind."

And then, in a different tone, he said, "Above all, don't lose yourself fantasizing about someone else. Remember, too much love can be a trap! No one is worth losing your soul for!"

This last thing he'd said was so different from what had gone before that I had that same intense feeling of wrongness, that he had not said those words before, but something else. It felt like that time I heard his warning just before I was attacked in the alley. I looked up at him, startled. He never talked about the soul; he didn't believe there was such a thing. And how did he know I was fantasizing about the girl with the low seductive voice? But his warning echoed a question I had about this voice. If she were real, what did she want of me? Was it my soul, as my father seemed to be implying? So far, she had led me to the lair of a mass murderer and into a state of near catatonia. Based on her track record, it didn't *seem* like she had my best interests at heart! On the other hand, this voice of Father's had warned me about a real danger: the trap in the alley. Maybe this time, I should heed his warning.

So I tried to pay attention to things outside myself, if only to my books and our sad little family. Soon, I was able to live again in the novels and histories I read. I guess this was to live in fantasy too, but one which connected me to some degree with the outside world. I also began to enjoy the weekly tutorial sessions with my father. He seemed more friendly and encouraging than ever before, as if he sensed I needed that now.

One night, he took a bottle of cognac out of the fancy glass liquor cabinet in the dining room, and poured two glasses, one for me and one for him. I looked at him curiously, and he said, "Let's drink a toast!"

"What are we toasting?" I asked.

"Joe McCarthy died today. Here's to his death! Let's hope there are loyalty oaths in Hell!"

We both took a drink. I felt awkward drinking to another man's death, but I knew how much my father hated McCarthy for forcing him to sign an oath to keep his medical license. Besides, the cognac left such a warm, smooth feeling in my throat and my chest that I wished we could drink one or two more.

Another cold, clear October night, he gave me a special treat. He set up a long black telescope in the back yard, and invited me to look through the eyepiece. I drew in my breath: a thousand burning suns bloomed where only a few dim stars had been before. He told me that the light from some of these stars had been traveling for thousands of years and that some of them might have died already after flaring into a huge supernova. As he spoke, I felt small and insignificant, yet also enormous, as if my mind had grown to include this vast field of stars.

A few nights later, he invited me into the back yard again to watch the Northern lights. They were like cold fire, flaring and shimmering in delicate colors: red, blue, a ghostly green. So evanescent that you might think you had imagined them. Father called them the *Aurora Borealis*, and explained their origin in the Earth's electromagnetic field. This actually increased my sense of wonder. How could a gigantic magnet paint such lovely watercolors?

"Nature is the greatest artist, Teddy," he said, as if he'd been reading my mind. "She not only creates all this beauty, but she creates us to enjoy it. In fact, without us, the beauty wouldn't exist. So, in a way, the universe exists only for you and me!"

Looking into his blue eyes, I saw a reflection of the Lights, a cold crystalline fire. I knew then that I was loved, and I loved my father for showing me these things, Once again, I felt intensely alive.

I also began opening up to my sister again. She didn't have so much pity in her eyes now, and seemed to enjoy the time we spent together. As for me, I'd always loved being her big brother; teaching her, protecting her, loving her, and I felt that I could be that to her again. She talked to me about her friends, or her schoolwork, which I often helped her with. She talked about what she wanted to do with her life. She told me she wanted to become a nurse. I told her that career would be perfect for her; she'd always loved to take care of people and animals, and she was good at it. I had to conceal my jealousy though: I really wondered if I had a future now. When I thought of my future at all, I thought of the State Asylum at Waupun, where that child molester had gone, and where I might wind up someday if my mind continued to deteriorate. I'd heard terrible stories about this place, not only about the bizarre and dangerous inmates, but about the brutality of the guards.

It was also hard for me to hear about all of her friends, particularly when they asked about me. I couldn't bear to think of those people talking about me, judging me.

Finally, one day when she told me someone had asked about me, I snapped, "Just tell them I'm dead, okay?"

Her gray eyes opened wide and filled with tears. I regretted what I'd said, but she never again said anything about the kids asking about me and I was glad.

Sometimes, we tried to play our pretend games again, but I found they had undergone a peculiar change. I'd started these games years before, in an effort to bring her into the world of books where I spent most of my time. I told myself that I wanted to help her become interested in reading but I think it was because my world was so lonely. At first, I would just read from my favorite mysteries but she soon became bored with this and so we made up our own mystery stories, based on the books. We had even expanded our play world into other roles: like Knight and Lady, or Greek goddess and Hero. But now the games seemed to have changed in a disturbing way.

We were playing Sam Spade one day and suddenly my female client spoke in a husky, seductive tone which Ellen had never used before but which was strangely familiar, "Well, Teddy, are you ready to play the Game?"

"What do you mean, Ellen? We're already playing a game!"

"You know what I mean," she said, in that same strange voice.

"No, I don't know what you mean!" I said. I was

beginning to be frightened now. "And why are you talking in that funny voice?"

"I didn't say anything!" Ellen said, in her normal voice. "You know, you're really getting weird these days!"

Another time, when we were playing Knight and Lady, she reached into her dresser and brought out one of her nylon stockings.

"Take this as a token of my favor!" she said in that same strange voice.

I felt awkward accepting it, as if the gift had a dangerous meaning. She and I seemed to be changing into different persons, and the game had gone beyond our control.

I also had changed in my feelings about school. I'd always hated it and everyone in it. But now I found myself remembering the few good moments: the smell of chalk and new books in the fall; looking out at the town and the river from the top floor when I stayed after school, walking up the hill in the Spring when a warm wind was blowing and the last of the ice and snow was beginning to melt. On these days, I'd crush the dirty ice ledges with my feet and free the little rivulets of ice water to flow down to the street. I even missed the warm press and bustle of kids in the hall as they came in from a cold winter's day; the smell of wet fur and rubber. It was stupid to miss things like that, but I did.

One late fall afternoon; I heard the sound of drums and trumpets from the direction of the school. I also heard the high-pitched sounds of kids cheering. They sounded like they were having a good time. I got a lump in my throat, which disturbed and embarrassed me. To make it worse, my father came up in back of me as I stared out the hall window in the direction of the sound.

"Sounds like a damned pagan ritual, doesn't it? Perhaps they're sacrificing a virgin!"

"It's Homecoming!" I shouted, and ran up to my room. I felt his eyes on me as I ran.

I began to notice the bodies of the girls when they walked by our house, or when I rode with Father. Before, I might have noticed a pretty face or an attractive skirt. But now, their bodies seemed to explode into my consciousness, their breasts jutting out savagely against their fall sweaters, their hips and buttocks swelling obscenely against their skirts. All these changes in their bodies must have happened long before, but only now did I begin to see them. I was obsessed with how they looked—and I wondered how anyone could not be, how a boy could actually talk to a girl like that and not just stare at her body. I knew I never could. But then, I'd never get the chance.

I also noticed the ways the boys my age were changing into men. They'd developed muscles, their thighs and buttocks had swelled; they'd even sprouted hair on their faces. Only my body remained the same, a boy's body, thin and undeveloped. Of course, it didn't matter. I could take a Charles Atlas course and grow muscles like Superman's and the girls would never know, because no girl would ever look at me. Ever!

Except for one girl. One girl knew me very well; saw me every day, and knew all my deepest secrets. Well, almost all. She didn't know (I hoped) how I felt when I saw her budding breasts pushing out her blouse, or her nightgown, farther out than any girl I'd ever seen. At least I hoped she didn't realize what I was thinking. How I went over in my mind the large curves of her thighs, the light down on her legs. How I couldn't stop thinking about these things. One day, when she was coming out of the bathroom, her bathrobe flew open and I caught a glimpse of a line of dark hair between her legs. I'd had a throbbing in my penis before when I looked at girls, but now I looked down and saw it was growing wildly, pushing out the front of my pants. I rushed up to my room, hoping she hadn't seen.

I had read about erections in my father's medical books, and had a few, like when I'd had wet dreams, but I had never touched myself. I was somehow shy of my changing, strange body. But I touched myself now. The resulting physical sensation shocked me, so sweet, so painful, and so intense! I unzipped my pants and the thing sprang out, like a tiger freed from a cage. It was reddish-blue, swollen, and immense. Surely this was a man's penis, not a boy's. I wished I could show it to some of my tormentors. This was not the organ of a faggot! They were wrong about me!

I stroked it like a cat, and like a cat's back it rose to my touch. *Nice penis!* I stroked it again, down all its length, and it rose and swelled even more. Again I touched it. I moaned softly, surprising myself with the sound. The sensation was so lovely! I imagined a girl's soft white hand stroking it, again and again.

Hey! A goopy white liquid exploded out of it, spurting out over the covers, the pillow, even the wall! *Yecch!* I thought. *This is disgusting!* It looked even worse than the mess I found in my pajamas after a wet dream. But it felt so good. This is my semen, the essence of my manhood. Yeah!

Afterwards, I looked down and saw my familiar little nub again. But I felt an afterglow in my body, like someone had run an electric charge through it. I lay back on the bed to enjoy the glorious new sensations flowing through me. Then I felt a wet spot under my back. *Yecch!* I thought again. *I'm going to have to clean this up before Father or Ellen sees it.* I suddenly felt exhausted, sick, and ashamed. Ellen! I'd been thinking of Ellen when this happened! No! That couldn't be true! I'd been thinking of someone else, some unknown girl that looked a little like Ellen. It had been her hand around my penis, not Ellen's! Yes, I could almost see the girl; hear her low, familiar seductive voice. Yes, it had been Her. I thought of Her that way, like a goddess. And suddenly her name came to me: Elena. Yes, perfect! Ellen's old play name. Someone who did not exist and never could exist.

I masturbated several times a day after that, usually during the day when no one else was home. I usually thought of the fantasy girl, who was like Ellen but not Ellen. Yet, somehow I couldn't give her a definite shape and so the experience was unsatisfying. I wished I could get hold of one of those girlie magazines that Bauer, the grocer, was supposed to keep under his counter. But I never would have the nerve to ask him even if I had the money. I drew pictures of girls, but I was a mediocre artist and the pathetic stick figures I produced could excite no one. Finally, my father called me into his room.

"Teddy," he'd said after clearing his throat, "You are a growing boy, an adolescent. There are certain things you need to know about your development. Here are some books on the subject."

Then he had given me some medical books, which I felt grateful for because I hoped some of the illustrations would be useful for masturbation. But I was also a little ashamed because I assumed he knew I was playing with myself. But the women shown were clinical studies, not hot babes. It was hard to get excited by a woman whose internal organs were in plain view.

Then I came across a copy of *Psychopathia Sexualis*, by Kraft-Ebbing, in the books he'd given me. This seemed a little better; at least the case studies had something to do with sex. But I soon became disturbed by the nature of the case studies I masturbated to: incest, pedophilia, and coprophagia, even necrophilia. Afterwards, I felt sicker and more disgusted than I had when I first masturbated

Besides, masturbation only slaked my great hunger for a little while. The fantasy women I attacked with such ferocity were not what I needed. I needed the real thing, a real woman in my hands, and I knew I could never have it! Never.

The world was so brutally unfair! If I had believed in God, I'd have cursed Him. How could God give me such a powerful hunger and not give me any way to satisfy it?

I was like a man who could smell and see food but could never eat it!

In my despair, I began to practice strange rituals. I lay awake in my room late at night, my hand wrapped around my swollen organ, and began to chant Elena's name, softly so that no one could hear me. (Or did I hope the girl lying in the bed in the next room would hear me? The thought disturbed me.)

I went on like this for hours, waiting for my prayer to be answered. And at times, the image of the fantasy girl I longed for became a little clearer. I could almost see her, she looked like Ellen but more voluptuous, more wanton. I could even see something like a red bandana around her neck. At other times, I sensed something in the house itself moving a little closer to listen. It terrified me: it felt like the times when I was a kid, listening in the night for the Monster upstairs to make some sound. But in the end, nothing happened, and I masturbated quickly and went to sleep. Yet I couldn't shake the feeling that some one or something in this house was listening; that it had something it wanted from me before it would answer my prayer.

The thought fascinated but frightened me. What if my fantasy girl with the low lustful voice and impossible figure did appear in my bedroom one night? What would she ask in return for the one thing I so longed for? Would it be my sanity? Or perhaps my soul?

7

The man's face leaped out at me from the newspaper. Ed Gein! Even the name sounded inhuman, like the man's crimes. Gein was grinning shyly, but his eyes were blank, devoid of any human feeling. I turned my head away, disoriented and sickened. Gein's face gave me the same feeling that the painting of Saturn devouring his children did. But this man was real.

I read on, fascinated in spite of myself. There was his farm house and there the barn where they found the remains of his last victim. I was reminded of the old Washburn place. Could just living in these isolated places cause someone to go crazy and begin chopping people up? If so, I had reason to worry, because no one in the world was as isolated as I was.

Gein had pictures of Nazi atrocities all over his house. The stacks of emaciated corpses. The ovens with incinerated bones still in them. Ilse Koch's lampshades and the sofa coverings made of human skin. My stomach jumped as I read, but I couldn't stop reading. My father had many of the same pictures in his secret books. I knew now that he was fascinated with this type of extreme sadism. But at least he would never imitate the Nazis. Ed Gein had gone that one step farther, into actual murder. Gein apparently had German blood judging from his name. So did my father and I, and the Nazis. Could that have anything to do with what he'd done? But surely there were millions and millions of people with German blood who didn't do such horrible things! Think of my father, or of Mrs. Goethe, or of the great writer who was her namesake. But these thoughts didn't seem to help. I looked at my hands. Could they carve a human being up to make furniture?

There were many similarities between Gein and myself besides our racial heritage. He was much older than I, about my father's age, but he also lived in a small Wisconsin town; Plainsfield, only about fifty miles from Weimar. Plainsfield was a poor ragged town like mine. There, like in Weimar, hunters killed thousands of deer, making the woods around the town sound like a war zone. But not Ed Gein. Maybe, like me, he could never kill a deer. More likely, he had other game in mind.

Like me, he was a loner, an outcast from the town. He was a poor farmer and a worse field hand and hardly made enough to keep him alive. He lived alone in the house where his mother had died and rarely spoke to anyone. No one liked him, anymore than anyone liked me, outside of my family. But, like me, he apparently had ambition and imagination and dreamed of the day when he would make his mark on the world.

That time came on a cold November night a few

days ago. While I was lying in bed, praying incessantly to my goddess Elena, Ed Gein was hanging up a butchered carcass in his barn. Meanwhile, the sheriff of the county had obtained a warrant to search Ed Gein's property. It seemed a woman storeowner in Plainsfield had disappeared under suspicious circumstances and Ed Gein was the last person known to have seen her alive. Gein had a reputation as an oddball and, in that kind of place, to be different is to be suspect (as I well knew). So the sheriff had no trouble getting his warrant.

The first place he and a deputy searched was the barn. The sheriff told reporters that he thought at first that the carcass hanging there was a deer, possibly illegally poached. But no, it was too small. Then he realized that the thing hanging there was a woman's body with the head and the legs cut off. He didn't say whether he'd screamed or thrown up as I would probably have done. But he looked too stolid and unimaginative to have done any such thing. He looked a lot like Sheriff Carson, in fact.

However, he was spooked enough to call for reinforcements before going into the main house. When the others arrived, they searched the Gein house. They found the woman's head on the post of Gein's bed. They weren't able to positively identify it at first because Gein had cut off the face. He had made a mask of it which they found in the bedroom along with several similar masks. The police were able to solve one other disappearance when they matched one of the masks with a missing woman's photo.

They found a lot of other human remains in the house, all from women as far as they could tell. There were lampshades and sofa covers made of human skin just like Ilse Koch's. They found tables whose legs were human bones, and ashtrays made of human skulls. The police took it all away and, of course, took Ed Gein away, too, never to return.

Wisconsin may have its problems, but a high murder rate isn't one of them. So papers throughout the state, and later the country, put the discovery of this human slaughterhouse on page one. Later editions noted, apparently with disappointment, that most of the human remains had been dug up from graveyards. Police had direct evidence of only two murders. Apparently Gein did not even rank with Jack the Ripper among serial killers.

I got up from the periodical section of the library feeling that blend of excitement and nausea I always got from reading about Nazi atrocities. My father, who had been reading a magazine, asked me what I'd been reading. After a moment's pause, I told him.

"Very interesting," he said. "Do you intend to write an essay about it?"

"No!" I said, sickened.

"Why not?" he asked. "The subject is inherently interesting."

I paused for a moment. I didn't want to tell him I was ashamed to be interested in such things. He shared that fascination and might be insulted.

Finally, I said, "You always tell me to write on subjects

I can tie in with some universal theme. I don't see any such theme here. These are just random, irrational crimes."

"Teddy, the irrational is never random. Hell, as it were, has its laws, just as Heaven does, which is to say that the sick mind has its laws. And if you can find those organizing principles, you will find the universal theme you're looking for.

"As it happens, I have some inside information on these crimes, which never made the newspapers. I'd like you to take a look at it. It may help you to write a very interesting essay."

I promised to take a look at his material when we got home. Later that night, my father called me into his room. He had a medical case folder spread out on his desk.

"Take a look at this, Teddy, and let me know what you think," he said.

I sat down at the desk and began to read. I was astonished at what my father had shown me. He had somehow obtained a transcript of an interview with Ed Gein, at Waupun State Hospital, which was only three days old! What the newspapers wouldn't give for a peek at that! The file also contained a short monograph by one of the doctors who had been present at the interview. My amazement must have shown on my face because I heard my father laugh. I looked up and saw him smiling.

"I always told you I have my sources! The doctor who wrote that monograph is Bill Kunsler, an old friend from the University of Wisconsin. I asked him to send me a copy as soon as I found out he was involved in the case."

I read on. It appeared that Ed Gein had loved his

mother and, after her death, kept her room spotless and inviolate—like a shrine. The rest of the house had been so filthy and cluttered with decayed food, human body parts, and other junk, that the police had hardly been able to move around, or even to breathe. Searchers described the stench as worse than anything they'd ever experienced.

Ed Gein vehemently denied having had sex with any of the dead women, saying they smelled too bad. Dr. Kunsler accepted this as probably true, saying that Gein was probably incapable of sex with women, alive or dead. He went on to say that Gein had an overbearing mother and a weak father. Citing Freud, the doctor claimed these parents had produced strong homosexual tendencies in Gein. He theorized that Gein so loved his mother that, after her death, he tried to become like her, in order to keep her alive. So he had put on the faces of women, had cut off their breasts and strapped them on himself, made a skin skirt, and had even cut out vaginas, which he fitted over his penis. He didn't want to make love to women; he wanted to become one.

On clear nights, he would put on his woman suit, go out into the deserted farmyard and dance and chant. As I read, I could feel the rotting skin over my skin, feel myself growing excited, hear myself screaming incantations to Elena.

I suddenly realized I was getting an erection. I felt sick to be excited by these horrible fantasies. No! My father was looking at me sternly as if he knew. He must not know! I leaped to my feet and ran out of the room. I heard my father calling my name, but I couldn't stop. I had to get up to my room!

Once inside, I closed and locked the door. Then I lay down on the bed, my mind spinning wildly. I refused to masturbate, or even acknowledge the monstrous growth, which pressed against the inside of my pants. Soon, it began to recede and then was gone. But I still felt horror at myself. How could such things excite me? How could I have any fellow feeling for such a monster? I remembered the beckoning hand I'd seen at the Washburn farm. Was the old man inviting me in to see his bloody handiwork? Did he sense a kindred spirit? Was that my destiny: to become like Ed Gein or Old Man Washburn? I would rather die first!

I lay on the bed for hours, fighting the darkness and the soft sea roaring, which had risen soon after my excitement left me, and threatened to engulf me. I kept repeating two things "I'm losing control." and "I must not lose control!" If the darkness and the sea sound overcame me now, I might be capable of doing any horrible thing without even knowing it. But, I was not a monster! I would maintain control!

After a long while, I fell into a stupor, unable to sleep, but utterly exhausted by my internal struggle. Then I heard what sounded like sobbing coming from Ellen's room. I tried to ignore it at first, but then I heard her call my name.

I said nothing, and after a while the sobbing on the other side of the wall stopped. *I failed you again, Ellen*, I thought. *I love you more than my life, but I can't even open my mouth to help you in your pain.*

The feeling of being out of control of my body and my mind grew more intense after the Ed Gein incident. I was overwhelmed with sexual fantasies, often disturbingly violent. The worst involved Ellen. They were always the same. I'd sneak into her bedroom and wake her with a kiss. She'd smile at me at first, but as the kiss became deeper and more passionate, her eyes would grow wide. She'd try to push me off, but I would force her back onto the bed. Her moans and struggles just excited me more and then I...would force myself to think about something else. But all the time, the dark fantasy ran on in my mind like an unwatched movie until finally I had an orgasm. Then I would lie there, exhausted with my struggle not to see what was happening in my own mind, and filled with shame.

One night, I lay awake staring at the ceiling and trying not to hear the creaks from my sister's bed in the next room which might bring on the dark fantasy again. But a movement in the corner of the room interrupted my struggle with myself. There! By the closet, a flash of white.

I sat upright, my heart racing. Had I really seen something? I looked over at the closet but saw nothing but darkness. But when I turned my head away, I saw the white thing coming out of the closet! I did see it! I put my trembling feet on the cold floor and pushed myself off the bed. I walked slowly towards the white object. But when I looked directly at it, it vanished. I turned my head again, and the pale thing reappeared in the corner of my eye.

Of course, I thought. *I'm dreaming!* And this dream, like all dreams, had its own rules. The first one was, don't look at the white thing directly. I walked towards the figure again, but this time kept my head turned so it was always in the corner of my eye. I stopped, drawing in a deep breath. The figure had resolved itself into a girl, or rather a young woman. She was full-figured with large breasts outlined clearly by a flimsy nightgown! A bright red scarf covered her neck. This was she! The girl I'd fantasized about so long, with a figure like Ellen's, but without her shyness or the inconvenient ties of blood. And now she stood in front of me! She seemed to be smiling, but I couldn't see her clearly enough to be sure. If only I could look at her directly!

"Someday, Teddy! Someday, you will see me just the way I am! But not yet."

I staggered and almost fell. I didn't know what astonished me most; the fact she had read my mind, or the familiarity of her voice: a deep rich contralto that seemed to well up from those marvelous breasts. But where had I heard it before?

"What's the matter, Teddy? Don't you know me?"

"You're Elena!" I said in wonder.

And then she laughed, a deep sexy chuckle, and I recognized the voice. It was the one that led me to the old Washburn place and then inside myself, to the darkness and the roaring. It was then that I felt the appalling cold, which came off her like a wave. I shrank back, suddenly afraid.

"Teddy, you disappoint me! I've come a long way just

to answer your prayers. Don't you want me any more?" There was harshness in her voice which somehow excited me even more. She chuckled again, looking down at my body.

"No, I can see you still want me!"

I did want her. Even though hers was the voice that had led me into all those dangers, she was also the one whose name I'd invoked so often, who I'd prayed to on so many long, lonely nights. And now she stood right here in front of me! She was the answer to my prayers and I didn't care what else she might be

She moved closer to me and the waves of cold became more intense. Goose bumps rose on my bare arms. In spite of my desire for her, I moved back. She took another step forward and sat down on my bed. Astonishingly, the springs creaked under her weight. But then I thought, *If this were a dream, of course the bed would creak.* The sound only added to my desire as I imagined her soft flesh sinking into the mattress. This beautiful young woman, clad in almost nothing, was sitting on my bed! And I did not repel her. In fact, she seemed to want something from me. But what?

"W-why are you here?" I stammered.

"You know why, Teddy... I have heard you all these nights, calling my name I have seen you in the darkness forming my body around yourself with your hands! And I want to help you!" She paused. "Of course, I will want something in return."

My shivering grew so violent I had to put my hand on the dresser to keep from falling down.

"W-w-what do you want from me?" And I was thinking again: *My soul?*

She laughed. "Don't worry, little Teddy. I won't hurt you! In good time, I'll tell you what I want. But just now, all I want is you!"

Her hand touched my thigh. I jumped. Her skin was soft and smooth and yet cold as ice. I was trembling with fear and desire.

"Sit down by me, Teddy. I want you to be comfortable."

I obeyed, although comfortable was not exactly how I'd describe my feelings at that moment. I felt her thigh brush mine. I felt her hand move up to my hip and then down, pushing down my pajama bottoms. Her hand paused, just above my genitals. My organ moved up towards her hand like a flower towards the sun.

"Of course, I'll ask for other things after we've come to know each other better. But first you must learn to trust me and not be afraid of me. Can you do that, little Teddy?"

I just moaned in reply. I was beyond words. Her voice was so hard and yet so sensuous. She was like fire and ice together, and I could feel myself swelling to an incredible size. *Touch it!* I thought. *Just touch it!*

She laughed again.

"Not just yet, Teddy. I don't want it to be over quite so soon. I'm going to teach you to last for a long long time. Wouldn't you like to learn that?"

"Oh, yes!" I said, and realized I hadn't stuttered. She was the only person, or whatever, who I hadn't stuttered with outside my own family.

"That's right, Teddy. Just think of me as one of the family."

Her hand moved down a little more, lightly brushing the head of my penis, which jumped as if hit by an electric charge. I moaned again. She leaned over towards me and I felt her soft, heavy breast brush my arm.

"I can tell you're ready to play the Game. And I want to play it, too. But first I have to tell you the rules! All right?"

I just nodded. She seemed to know my thoughts and feelings even before I did, I didn't need to speak

"Some of the rules you know already. Never look at me directly, not until I tell you to. And always let me make the first move. Never try to grab me. I hate that! Just let me lead, like we were dancing. If I want your hand to go someplace nice, I'll put it there. Okay?"

"Sure!" I said. It all sounded wonderful to me. I wondered what kind of nice places she might put my hand. She can do anything she wants with me! I thought. Anything!

"That's a good boy, Teddy. We're going to have such good fun, you and I!"

I was just about to say something stupid in agreement, when I felt her cold smooth hand slide over the head of my penis and down, down, while a thrill of the most delicious sweetness coursed through the whole length of it. I moaned again.

So began my instruction, and I was an avid pupil. Her hands roamed all over my genitals, bringing me time and again to where I thought I couldn't stand it, that I must explode. Just at that point, she'd squeeze my penis very hard and the explosion wouldn't come. The resulting mixture of pleasure and pain was almost more than I could bear.

I felt as if I were being buoyed up by a violent sea of desire, which would lift me higher and higher until I was torn almost out of myself, let me down into the gulf between the waves, then raise me even higher. Finally I felt my blood and semen shoot towards the ceiling, carrying me with it. I'm dead, I thought. I looked down and saw myself, lying on my bed, curled up like a baby. There was something large and white, with a splash of red at the top, looming over me, and I dimly heard myself screaming.

"Shush, shush, Teddy!" the white thing said to me, laughing. "You must learn to be more quiet."

I heard a knocking at the door and then I was back inside myself.

"Teddy!" It was Ellen's voice. "Are you all right?"

"Yeah," I said, "I just had a bad dream. I'm fine now."

And I was. I felt wonderful in fact. Lying back in my bed, I felt a marvelous lassitude, a deep satisfaction. The hungry man had eaten at last!

"Oh, no, Teddy!" the voice said. "Don't be satisfied so easily! We've just begun, you and me."

Her deep sensual voice and the promises she was making were getting me excited again. This was not the end, just the beginning.

"Yes, Teddy, just the beginning. I'll teach you to play the Game the way it should be played. And when you have learned that, I'll teach you other games that will be even more fun!"

A touch of mockery in her tone made me uneasy. I remembered the vision of her I had from the ceiling: an indistinct, menacing white and red mass. Was that what she really was? My whole body was shivering, as if suffused with a deep icy cold. How much of this wonderful relaxation was from the cold? I'd read that people who had nearly frozen to death all described a feeling of deep peace and contentment, much like what I was feeling now. Was this what death felt like then? If so, it was not so bad!

She laughed again, as if she'd been reading my thoughts. I heard the springs creak as she got off the bed. I saw her walk towards the closet. My heart felt like someone was squeezing it. *Don't go*, I thought.

"I have to go, Teddy. It is time."

"But when will I see you again?"

"Soon, darling, soon. Remember, all things come to those who wait." She paused, as if considering something. "But there is one more rule you must remember. You must never tell anyone about me until the time comes for me to reveal myself. Do you promise?"

"But why?"

"Promise or you will never see me again!"

I gasped. Never see her? Never have this feeling again?

"I promise.

And then she was gone.

8

The next morning as I came down to breakfast, Father and Ellen were staring at me as if they'd seen a ghost. I wondered for a moment what could have shocked them so much. Then I realized I was smiling, probably for the first time in weeks. The realization made my grin even broader. *I know something you don't!* I thought. I sat down to breakfast and ate more heartily than I had for a long time: eggs, bacon and cereal. When I got up, I walked out into the back yard. The sun was shining brightly and the day was full of promise, but the night! I couldn't wait! I felt their eyes on me through the kitchen window. *Yes, I've got a secret you can't even imagine!*

All that day, I thought only of Elena. I roamed around my room hoping to catch a glimpse of her, or a hint of her smell, although when I thought of it, she didn't seem to have a smell. Here was the closet she'd come out of. I looked all through it and felt the back wall but of course there was no sign of her and no back door she could have come and gone through. As if someone like her needed a door. There was the place on the bed where she had sat down. I looked and felt of the place but there was no sign of the impress she must have made. And, this was the most peculiar thing, there was no sign of my semen; although I knew I'd come and come. What had become of it?

It didn't matter! She had been there and she'd been real! I was sure of it. I felt my whole body glow again when I thought of what she'd done to me. There was no way it could have been a wet dream. No dream had ever made me feel so alive! I had a moment of unease when I thought of the death-like state I'd been in and the waves of cold which had come off her body. But this made her all the more real, because she was not perfect, because she was a mystery, because she had taken me to places where I could never have gone on my own. I remembered looking down on my own body, contorted in ecstasy, and fear. How could I have fantasized that? Or how about the way she'd led me to the Washburn place? That was certainly no fantasy. I had not known exactly where that place was before she showed it to me.

No, she was real, and she was mine. And the fact that she was mysterious and maybe even dangerous made her all the more fascinating. I had embarked on an adventure no one else on Earth had ever gone on, and she was on it with me!

This must be love, I thought. She was mine, or would be soon. I thought of those heavy breasts, half seen, half felt. Of those long, full legs brushing against mine. Of those wonderful hands! Elena! Elena! I found myself repeating her name over and over under my breath, and then wondering if I'd done so aloud. In a daze, I copied down what I thought was my math assignment. When I read it, I found I'd written her name a dozen times.

The house was full of her presence. When I felt her near me, I would glance around out of the corner of my eye but could see nothing. I almost thought I heard her whisper: Be patient, dear Teddy, this is only the beginning. But I couldn't be patient. I longed for her to lay her hands on me once more, if only for a moment. I wished I could talk about her to the boys who held me in such contempt. I would tell them: I have something better than anything you will ever have. But they'd only laugh at me. And besides, I'd promised Elena not to tell anyone about her.

I spent most of the day in my room. I couldn't even look at my books, and I had no desire to talk to Father or Ellen, because I couldn't tell them about the one thing in life that interested me. The soft fall breeze was too like her touch, gentle but with a chill that went down to the bone. The sun seemed to take an eternity to slide down the sky.

At last, however, Father called me down for dinner. As usual, we ate in virtual silence. I was not hungry this time and barely touched my food. I could feel Ellen's eyes on me. Usually, I'd have eaten something just to please her but this night I was obsessed with my own longings. I kept repeating "Elena! Elena! Elena!" under my breath. I heard a sharp intake of breath and looked up quickly. Had I said it too loud? My sister was staring at me with an expression which I took at first to be disapproval. Only later did I realize that it was horror.

I went up to my room almost immediately after dinner. As I was getting up, Father asked me if I felt sick.

"No," I said, "Just a little tired." But all I really wanted to do was to lie in bed and think about what she and I had done last night and how we would play the Game again tonight. I lay there waiting, barely breathing. At long last, full darkness came, and I heard Ellen settling down for bed. In a few minutes, the creaking of her bed stopped and I heard her high soft snore.

I began chanting. "Come, Elena!" I said I had my hand wrapped around my organ as if she could hear me better that way. But she didn't come. There was no flash of white, no husky, seductive voice, no icy silken touch. Hours passed and still no Elena! I fell asleep, still repeating her name.

When I woke next morning, I ached with emptiness. She had not kept our appointment! I went down to breakfast and ate nothing. After breakfast, my father called me into his room for our weekly conference. It went badly; I couldn't keep my mind on what he was saying, nor could I say anything myself. I began to hear the roaring in my ears and see the darkness gathering around my eyes. Father again asked me if I was sick and this time I nodded.

He stuck a thermometer in my mouth. When he pulled it out, he told me that I did have a temperature. I was not surprised, I felt weak and utterly exhausted. He sent me up to bed, after pouring me a big glass of orange juice. I couldn't even touch the juice, although I felt hot and thirsty. As I lay in bed, I kept saying to myself: *She could not be so cruel! How could she leave me alone, when she must have known she was the only good thing in my life?* Finally, just before dark, I fell into a deep sleep.

When I awoke, the sun was shining. I'd slept the whole night, almost thirteen hours, and still she hadn't come. I don't know how I got through that next day. I stayed in bed the whole day, except when I came down for meals. All day, I fought the darkness and the roaring that threatened to pull me under. By nightfall, I felt more exhausted than I had the day before. When Father called me to dinner, I called down that I was too sick and tired to eat. In a few minutes, I heard a knock on my door. I said: "Come in" and Ellen entered, carrying my dinner on a tray. She stood there in the doorway, staring at me with that same strange expression on her face.

"Are you all right, Teddy?"

"Of course I'm not all right. I'm sick and I have a fever! Now, what do you want!?"

As soon as I said this, I regretted it. She just stood there with this hurt, confused look on her face. Then she laid the tray on my dresser and walked out the door. I felt guilty but also angry. If she had something to say, why didn't she just say it? And if she was offering pity, I didn't want any. As long as I had Elena, I had everything I wanted. I didn't care if she was a dream. She was more real to me than Ellen or my father!

I lay awake for hours that night, hopelessly calling her name. But I couldn't even feel her presence: only blank emptiness. Then it occurred to me that my frantic calling might have driven her away, just as looking directly at her caused her to vanish. So I began to feign indifference, thinking: if she wants to come, fine; if not, that's fine, too! Just as I was about to fall asleep, I was rewarded with a flash of white, just at the edge of my vision.

"Elena!" I breathed, just a little too loudly. She said nothing at first and I was afraid I'd frightened her away again. But then I heard that low throaty chuckle and I knew it would be all right.

"Teddy," she said, "you've been a very naughty boy!" From the corner of my eye, I saw her shaking her finger at me.

"I'm sorry!" I said. "What did I do?"

"You know very well what you did. You've been saying my name out loud! And writing it down where other people could find it. You must never do these things again! Do you understand?" I nodded. "If you do it again, I'll go away and never come back. Do you want that?"

I shook my head violently. The thought of losing her for good terrified me. What would I do? How would I live?

"Someday soon the time will come for me to reveal myself. But until then, our relationship must be our little secret. Okay?"

I nodded again. I was wondering why she would reveal herself and to whom. But I didn't want her to reveal herself to anyone else. I wanted her all to myself!

She laughed again.

"That's good, Teddy. I want you all to myself too. But I don't want you playing with yourself. That's my job!"

She placed one of her icicle hands on my thigh.

"Remember this. I'm not your plaything. You're mine!"

I was quite content to be her toy that night. Once again she seemed to read my mind, using her hands to drive me to the heights of excitement, only to squeeze me hard and bring me down again just when it seemed I couldn't stand any more. She kept prolonging it, bringing me closer and closer, until I was almost frantic with excitement. And then she actually climbed on top of me! I felt myself slipping into a silky smooth tunnel of ice. I was inside her! I came almost immediately, and again it was like a death. But this time, she seemed to draw my soul out of myself and catch me in that cold dark tunnel. I saw only a terrible darkness and felt as if I couldn't breathe. And then, when I had returned to myself prostrate and shivering, she began again, for I was somehow still erect. At the end of the night, I felt as if she'd almost drained me of life, yet I was aglow like an ember in an almost extinguished fire, and utterly happy.

Just before she left me, she leaned down and placed her icy lips on mine. I felt her cold breath but, strangely, though her ample breasts were pressed against me, I could feel no heartbeat! Shouldn't I be able to feel it, if there was one?

"Just remember, darling!" she breathed, "no one else is to know until I say so!"

"All right!" I said. I was thinking that I never wanted anyone to know. She was totally mine now, and I was hers!

The next morning, when I came down to breakfast, I was smiling again. Ellen and Father looked startled, and were even more surprised when I again ate a hearty breakfast.

"You seem to be feeling better!" Father observed.

I smiled and nodded, and he smiled in reply. And indeed, I felt as if I'd never been sick. But Ellen seemed agitated and unhappy. Didn't she care about my happiness? What could be bothering her? She kept seeking out my eyes for the first time in days, but I avoided hers. I didn't want her problems to bring me down out of my cloud. Later, I felt guilty about this. *She needs me*, I thought, *and I'm nowhere to be found*. I promised myself I would find out what was upsetting her when she got back from school.

But when I opened up my notebook later that day to look up my assignments, I found a note. It was on the blue notepaper she had gotten for her birthday and was in her handwriting.

"Teddy: I need to talk to you alone today!" the note said. "I'm afraid! Please meet me in our special spot in Lepke's woods after school."

The note worried me. *I'm afraid*, it said. Afraid of what? And why meet in Lepke's woods at this time of the year? Summers were wonderful there, with the sun filtering through the green leaves, making us feels as if we were underwater. But now it was bitter cold and the trees were bare. Something must really be eating at her! And it all started when Ellen heard me say Elena's name. Could her secret have anything to do with Elena? The thought disturbed but also intrigued me.

The day went very slowly; I was impatient to solve

these mysteries. I felt well enough to do my homework. But in my mind I was putting on my deerstalker cap and my cape, and saying:

"Come, Watson, the hunt is up!"

It was difficult for me to wait for her to get back. I decided to get there a little early. The dead leaves were almost knee high in the wood which made for slow going. Our secret spot was a small hollow where the roots of several trees grew together around it. The floor of the hollow was two or three feet below the level of the roots so no one could see us when we were in there. It was kind of a magical place where Ellen and I had played and fantasized for years; all the more magical because of the hint of danger: we never knew if and when Lepke's guard with the shotgun might show up! But he never had, and it was a good place for the sharing of secrets.

I watched as the sun dipped lower through the bare branches and wondered if Ellen had played a trick on me. But in a few minutes, I heard someone coming through the wood, crushing the leaves under their feet. Ellen's face appeared above the root edge of the clearing and I was shocked to see terror in her eyes.

She walked down into the clearing and sat down on the ground. Neither one of us said anything for a while. Then, she stared at me hard, almost accusingly.

"Why did you say 'Elena' the other night?" she asked.

I stared at her. I was trying to think. What lie could I tell her? If I told her the truth, I'd lose Elena for good.

"Why do you want to know?" I asked, stalling for time.

She looked at me for a moment and then apparently decided she'd answer my question even if I wouldn't answer hers

"Because I have been having dreams about her!" she cried. "Terrible dreams! Oh, Teddy, I'm so afraid of her!"

I stood there staring at my sister, trying to make sense of what she had just said. All the while, the hairs on the back of my neck were standing up like porcupine quills.

"You've seen my Elena?" I finally managed to get out.

"You've been dreaming about her, too! Haven't you? It's just like that time when we both dreamed about that monster with the big white eyes! The one we called the Man in the Moon? Only these dreams are worse!"

"How could they be worse?"

"They just are! Horrible, disgusting dreams. I can't talk about them?"

My mind was racing. How could the same girl who was giving me such delicious dreams be haunting Ellen's dreams, and frightening her to death? And why, if she was revealing herself to Ellen, did she want me to keep quiet about her? Unless...she wanted to prevent us from comparing notes, as we were doing now. Elena was playing some kind of double game with us, and I didn't like it. But I couldn't tell that to Ellen.

"Ellen," I said. "I remember the Man in the Moon too! And how he scared us both for so long. Do you remember his big white eyes, like headlights? I was heck of scared! But do you remember how I got rid of him?"

She shook her head

"Father gave me the secret when I told him about my

nightmares. He said all the characters in our dreams are really us! And when the Man in the Moon came that last night, I told him "Get out of here! You're not even real. You are just of part of me!" And he just walked out the door and never came back!"

"So?"

"So Elena is really you!"

She shook her head violently. "No, no! You don't understand. She isn't me in the dreams. I'm her! Someone totally unlike me. Someone I don't like! And she makes me do things I don't want to do, that disgust me! And when I try to wake up, she won't let me!"

I tried to gather my thoughts for a reply. but something she'd said put a horrible suspicion in my mind. What if Ellen's dreams and my dreams were the same! What if the person Elena forced her to do horrible, disgusting things to was me? Then, while believing I was making love to Elena, I had actually been making love to...the thought was too terrible to bring to consciousness.

It can't be true! I thought. I wouldn't do such things; Ellen wouldn't do such things! Besides, remember that first time, when I screamed and Ellen knocked on the door to ask what was the matter? That proves Ellen and Elena aren't the same!

Unless that little detail was just part of the dream.

I had to avoid sharing my terrible suspicion with Ellen. Also, I had to convince Ellen that Elena was not real, or risk losing Elena. I couldn't bear that: liar or not, real or not, she was the most important person in my life.

"I know it feels like this person is real, but that is

impossible. Father told me no one can get into your dreams and that only makes sense! How could they? Elena is just a side of you that you have never seen before. You're a teenager now and your body is changing and developing, just like mine is. It's just natural that new parts of you should come out in your dreams. I know I have seen sides of myself lately I wouldn't have believed possible!"

"But how could we be dreaming about the same person if she wasn't real?"

That was a very good question and I didn't have a good answer. I decided to deflect the question.

"Ellen, the Man in the Moon wasn't real, and we both dreamed about him. You and I are very close and so naturally we think and dream about the same things. Besides, don't you remember: Elena is part of the games we used to play. She is you...your play name. She isn't a stranger. Besides, how do you know we're dreaming about the same person? Have you ever seen her in these dreams?"

"No. I'm always behind her eyes when I'm doing these terrible things!"

I definitely did not want to know what these things were or who she was doing them to. In my authoritative, big brother voice, I said, "Maybe these things are not so terrible after all. You're becoming a woman now and it's natural you should have, shall we say, grown up thoughts and dreams. You shouldn't be ashamed of your desires. You can't help them! They're perfectly all right for some one your age. Believe me, I have the same kinds of feelings. Everybody does!"

Ellen was looking deep into my eyes. I hoped she didn't see the fear and doubt behind the big brother voice.

"Then…you think it's all right?" she said, her voice quavering.

"Of course it is!" I said, with a smile. "I'm your big brother, remember? Have I ever lied to you?" But I was thinking, *I've never told you a bigger one.*

She smiled though, and seemed to relax. We walked back to the house without speaking about the matter any further and I congratulated myself on a fine piece of dissembling.

That night, I lay awake for a long time, trembling. I had an idea what the "it" was I had so confidently told Ellen was all right, but no idea what the consequences of my advice might be. How could I play games with her life like that? That night, for the first time, I was afraid that Elena might show up. What kind of double game was she playing with Ellen and me? I wasn't sure I wanted to know. I don't know what I would have asked her if she'd showed up that night or what she would have replied. But thankfully she didn't appear, and eventually I fell asleep.

The next morning when I came down to breakfast, I was quiet and a little sullen. But Ellen was glowing. I hadn't seen her that animated and happy in months. It was as if my words had resolved some internal struggle for her, just as Elena had resolved mine. Were our struggles about the same thing? I was startled to hear her ask my father if she could buy some lipstick.

"Of course not!" he said. "Whatever gave you an idea like that?"

Ellen flushed and looked down. But that afternoon, when she came home from school, she had on what appeared to be lipstick. My father blew up when he saw her.

"Didn't I just tell you not to use lipstick?"

"No, Father," she said. "You just said I couldn't *buy* any. Barbara Schmidt let me borrow hers. Besides, this is lip-gloss!"

"Don't mince words with me, young lady! You know very well what I meant. Now, go wipe that lipstick or lip-gloss or whatever it is off your face! I won't be disobeyed and I won't have my daughter parading around like a whore!"

At this last word, Ellen colored and ran up to her room. I ran up the stairs after her. But when I heard her sobbing through the door, I paused and then went into my room instead

That night, Elena came again. She said nothing, only laughed that deep laugh of hers when I asked her where she'd been. I asked her nothing about what she'd been doing in Ellen's dreams, or about anything else. I was too happy to see her and to feel her hands on me. I could no more resist her advances than I could stop breathing. When I felt her frigid hands on my thigh, I thought: Ellen could never have such cold hands!

Or could she?

One thing was certain: Ellen was a different girl, or should I say, woman after our discussion in Lepke's woods. She didn't wear lipstick, but she did pull her skirts up a little higher to show her legs, and her sweaters down a little lower to show her woman's breasts. She walked differently, too, with a swing to her hips. I wondered who had showed her how to do these things. Could it have been our mutual friend, Elena? Whoever taught her these arts, I could see the way the boys on her school bus watched her all the way from the bus to our house. Something about their stares angered me. Could I be jealous?

But it was my fault! I'd been glib and dishonest, when I talked to her in our sacred spot and told her "It" was all right. I now knew what "It" was and how she had interpreted my words. I was angry with myself for taking a parental role by discussing sex with her, and even angrier at Father because he'd obviously never assumed that role with her.

Father had noticed the changes in her and I saw in his eyes that he was upset. But though he had succeeded in banning her lipstick, he said nothing about the swing in her hips or the sideways glances she gave the boys. For the first time in our lives, he seemed too angry to speak.

The blowup finally came over Elvis Presley. Father had given her a small record player for her fourteenth birthday and she had taken to playing Presley's records at night in her room. I hated rock and roll. I associated it with Bobby and the other bad kids—the only ones I knew who played it. But one night, I heard her playing "Love Me Tender" through the door. It sounded so sweet and sad and romantic that it almost made me cry, thinking of her listening alone there in the dark.

Then one day, she came home with a big rolled up

piece of paper under her arm. My father asked her what it was, and she just muttered something and went up to her room. My father followed her and I followed him. The set of his jaw made me afraid of what he might do. We heard a rustle of paper. My father knocked on the door and demanded to know what was going on.

"Go away!" Ellen screamed, "Let me alone!"

Instantly, my father yanked open the door. We both saw a black and white poster showing Elvis in black leather thrusting his guitar and his pelvis towards the camera.

My father just stared at it for a moment then shouted, "How dare you!"

He ran towards the offending poster and grabbed it at the top. Ellen grabbed his hand and he pushed her away violently. She landed on the bed. Then he tore the poster right down the middle and ran out.

Ellen shouted, "You stay out of here! This is my room!" Then she collapsed on the bed again, crying.

I slunk out and went into my room. A little while later, I heard more rustling from her room. I went out into the hall and stared through the still open door. She had neatly taped the poster together and rehung it on her wall. She looked up at me and smiled. I smiled too. It was as if she and I were in some kind of conspiracy against my father. But then came the guilt and the fear. I had no right to go up against him

That night, I replayed the fight in my head. The violence of it and my father's anger upset me. But I had to admire the way she stood up to him. Maybe I'd worried too much about Elena's influence on her...and mine. So far, it all seemed to have done her some good. She was becoming more independent, more herself. Maybe things would turn out all right after all.

The next morning, at breakfast, she still had that proud, defiant look. My father just stared at her and said nothing. The intensity of his stare worried me but Ellen didn't seem to be concerned. She walked out of the door without a word to him, but when she met her friends on the bus, she smiled and laughed. I felt happy, and a little envious. I wondered if the day would ever come when I could stand up to Father like that. But why, when I was his favorite?

That afternoon, she didn't get off the bus as usual. This worried me, as she always caught the bus. Then I saw her coming down the street riding on the back of a boy's bicycle. Her skirt was hitched up and you could see almost all of her shapely thigh. She smiled at the boy as she dismounted and he smiled back. Then he smiled up at me as I looked on from my window. It was a cruel, sardonic leer.

The boy was Bobby Niebauer.

9

My English teacher Mr. Winslow taught us once that in every tragedy a time comes when the Wheel of Fortune, having lifted the hero to the top, turns over, and drags him down to Hell. I'd never been on top of anything, but that moment, when I saw my sister with my deadliest enemy was when I realized how far I still had to fall. And the descent to Hell was faster than I could ever have believed.

My father blew up when he saw Ellen getting off Bobby's bike. "How dare you associate with a thug like that!" he screamed.

The irony was that neither of them knew that he'd almost killed me. I began to regret playing the strong, silent type and refusing to rat on Bobby. My silence had won me nothing but contempt from my enemies. Now, listening to the argument downstairs, I realized I might lose Ellen because of it.

"He's not a thug!" said Ellen. "He's a very nice boy. He just gave me a ride because I was late for the bus!"

"Oh, certainly he's a nice boy!" said my father. "That's

why he's the leader of a gang that beats up other nice boys. And fights other gangs with chains and even knives. That's your nice boy!"

"That's all gossip!"

"I have this on very good authority!"

"From who? The sheriff? So why doesn't he ever arrest him? And why is the sheriff's son one of his friends? Huh?"

"He is a hoodlum!" my father roared. "I forbid you to have anything to do with him!"

"You can't do that!" Ellen said. "We go to the same school!"

"Well, then I forbid you to ride home with him or talk to him outside school!"

"You can't tell me who my friends should be!"

My father said very slowly and distinctly, "Ellen, I am your father, and as long as you live in my house, you will do as I say. Do you understand? I can tell you who you will associate with!"

I knew my father well enough to know it was at these moments of seeming calm that he was closest to the ultimate explosion. But Ellen replied, "Well, I just won't listen!"

"Then go to your room, young lady! And don't come down until you're ready to apologize!"

"That will be never!"

I heard her run up the stairs and into her room. Then I heard things being slammed around in there. I was afraid to approach her while she was in this mood. But I also feared what might happen if I did nothing. I saw again the light glinting off Bobby's knife. He was crazy and he hated me. There was no telling what he might do to Ellen just to get back at me.

I knocked at her door, at first gently, then a little louder.

"Ellen?" I said.

"What do you want?"

Her tone was so hostile I almost decided to let it go. But then I thought of her and Bobby, and I said, "Can I come in?"

"Oh, all right!"

I pushed the door open. She was standing in the middle of the room, looking up at the picture of Elvis as if she were asking him for guidance. I wondered if she saw Bobby as the kind of romantic rebel Elvis played in his pictures

"What do you want?" she asked again.

"I...I saw you come home with Bobby Niebauer."

"So what! Are you going to harp on me, too!"

She faced me, her hands on her hips. This was not going well.

"No, but there is something you need to know."

"What?"

"You remember the time I got jumped in that alley?"

"Of course I remember. What about it?"

"Well, it was dark, and I couldn't see much, but I thought the leader of the group might have been Bobby!"

"You're lying!"

"No, Ellen. I'm not. Of course, I can't be sure—"

"You're lying! You told the sheriff and Father you couldn't recognize anyone. And now you think the leader might have been Bobby! I thought you were on my side! But you're just like Father! You don't want me to have any fun. You want me to have no friends and hang around this freaky old house all the time just like you!"

"That's not fair! I just want you to be safe—"

"Get out!" she screamed. She ran at me, her fist upraised, and I really thought she might hit me. I ran quickly through the open door and closed it quickly behind me. I heard her hit the other side with her fist.

That was a catastrophe! I'd alienated her and maybe made her believe that Bobby was her only real friend. I felt my life spinning out of control. It always did whenever I began to care too much about another person.

I suddenly heard my father's voice, just like I heard it before I went into the alley, "Remember, Teddy, only when you care for yourself first are you in control."

The feeling of wrongness came again. *That voice was not there last time!* I thought. But when was last time?

The next day was a Friday, and again, she didn't come home on the bus. Just when I was becoming frantic with worry, I saw her and Bobby walking hand in hand out of Lepke's woods. They had been in our sacred spot! I couldn't bear the way he grinned up at me, or the way he was combing his DA back like "Kookie" on that stupid TV program, *77 Sunset Strip.* I went to my room and lay down, pulling the covers over my head. The darkness and the roaring came, and this time I welcomed them, like old friends.

I made no attempt to talk to Ellen that night and she

pointedly ignored me. The next morning, I ate early in order to avoid seeing her.

I went up to my room to read. I was reading *Doctor Faustus*, by Thomas Mann. I could always get into a book so completely that I entered its world and lived there. And then I wanted to stay; particularly when my own world was falling apart. This novel especially interested me. I'd always been fascinated by the Faust legend, and had already read Marlowe's play and Goethe's novel on the subject. The question always was: could you deal with the Devil and come out on top?

I had never believed in God, but when I read history, or the newspapers, or just looked into my own heart, it was hard not to believe in evil. The power that drove Ed Gein to develop his unique interior-decorating scheme could not be just some amoral psychosis. Something in my own heart preferred death, destruction, and pain; in a word: Evil. It seemed so powerful, and Good so bland and weak in comparison. That was why the idea of dealing with the Devil was so fascinating and so scary. What was worse, to be a perennial victim like me, or to become the victimizer—to inflict pain rather than always suffer it? The Bobby Niebauers of the world might be hated, but they were never the objects of pity or contempt like me.

These were the thoughts that *Doctor Faustus* brought into my mind. I'd got to the part of the novel when the hero, Leverkuhn, first meets the Devil. I pored over the passage avidly, eager to fully inhabit this dangerous world, which was so much more interesting and full of possibility than mine. But something about the scene made me back out of that world and reread the passage, carefully. It was the description of how waves of cold came off the Devil towards Leverkuhn. Waves of cold! That was exactly the sensation I had whenever Elena came to me in the night

I felt as if someone had hit me with a baseball bat. The darkness and the roaring rose up around me with terrible speed. Elena was a demon! I had suspected and feared as much but this was proof. She was after my soul

Just at that moment, Sherlock Holmes' voice sounded in my head. "Teddy! Think about it. Do you have any evidence she is a demon? Has she ever asked you to sell your soul, or to sign anything? Has she ever asked you to do anything besides to conceal her existence? She wants something from you, but not your soul. Panicking now won't help you. You must try to figure out what she does want! Now I want you to take a few deep breaths and calm down!"

Obediently, I began to breathe deeply. I was astonished to find the darkness and the roaring vanished almost immediately. *How wonderful*, I thought! *I can control these things—they don't have to control me!* Following the second part of Holmes' instructions was more difficult: to think carefully. What did Elena want? I could make a good case that she was a demon. She had me so under her spell that I'd do almost anything to keep her around. And certainly she'd played a double game with Ellen and I, and she had caused Ellen to undergo a frightening change. She also had also opened up a huge rift in our family. But, as my father had said, there was no evidence she wanted my soul. What else could a demon want?

A sudden suspicion struck me. I went to the dictionary and looked under "S". There it was. "Succubus: a female demon who lies with men at night for her own sexual pleasure. Taken from the Latin, meaning to lie under." For her own sexual pleasure! Perhaps that was what she wanted. But what pleasure could she have in making love to me? I was hardly the world's greatest lover; mostly I just lay back and let her do things to me. And what pleasure could she get from inflicting nightmares on Ellen, or changing her personality? And why was she always saying she'd soon reveal herself? Reveal herself to whom and as what?

No, I couldn't, wouldn't believe that my Elena was a demon. Maybe she had done some suspicious things but there was always certain tenderness in the way she touched me, and the changes she had made in Ellen were not all bad. Ellen was certainly stronger and more independent than ever, even if she'd made a terrible choice in boyfriends. And I was happier than I'd ever been. Could all this come from pure Evil?

The fact was I was in love with her! I couldn't bear to lose her. Yet I had to find out who she was, and what she wanted with my family and me. If she intended us harm, I had to know, before it was too late.

Suddenly, I heard a high-pitched scream from downstairs and then a low roar of anger. While I had been musing about my "demon" lover, I had half-heard the shower running downstairs. Now it had stopped, and I heard the shocking 'thunk' of flesh on flesh. *My God*, I thought, *he hit her!*

In a moment, I was at the top of the stairs and headed down. I could hear her sobbing uncontrollably. I heard him too, screaming with a rage I wouldn't have believed possible.

"You slut! You dirty little whore! You left that door open on purpose! You wanted me to walk in! Is there nothing you won't do to torment me? But I won't let you tempt me again. Not this time! Now get up to your room!"

Once again, I heard him hit her. She ran past me, naked, soaking wet, and sobbing. I didn't have time to avert my eyes. I couldn't help but see her large bobbing breasts or the brown tuft of hair between her legs. I also saw the red mark of his hand across her face. She ran into her room and closed the door. I was glad, because I felt myself getting excited.

My father was standing at the foot of the stairs staring up at me. His eyes were bulging and his face was so red I was afraid he might be having an attack. One of the earpieces of his glasses had slipped off and he looked as if someone had hit *him*. I'd never seen him so out of control. It frightened me, because I felt like one of the foundations of my universe was cracking. If he couldn't control himself, how could I?

I walked down towards him but he gave no indication he saw me. He seemed to be looking through me to some other place, some other time. His eyes were full of anger, even hatred. I turned away, shocked and uneasy, and walked back up the stairs. I stopped outside my sister's door. I heard her crying, the choked breathless sobbing of an injured child. I knocked once, and then again. She made no reply but her sobs began to come a little more slowly.

Nervously, I opened the door. She was lying face down on the bed. Fortunately, she'd put a bathrobe on. She turned her head a little and I saw her frightened eyes. She sat up, clutching her diary. She hurriedly put it in her desk drawer, where she always kept it.

"Are you all right?" I asked, stupidly.

She shook her head, violently. "I thought I'd locked the bathroom door. I always lock it when I take a shower! But then he opened it and came right in. Oh, Teddy, you should have seen his eyes!"

"I did."

"I'm so scared, Teddy. He hit me twice, hard! What will happen now! What will happen to me?"

I put my arms around her, being careful not to touch her breasts. Clearly she was even more frightened than I was by Father's loss of control. I had to reassure her that our world was not collapsing.

"Don't worry. He'll come around. I'll talk to him. And remember, I'll always be here to protect you. I won't let anyone hurt you!"

I felt her body relax. She looked up at me and smiled that trusting little-sister smile. I congratulated myself on having calmed her and handling the situation well. But, although I didn't know it, I had just told her the biggest lie of my life.

The next few days were difficult ones for our little family. My father wouldn't look at Ellen and when he did talk to her, it was to tell her something she'd done wrong, like leaving a drawer open. He got that terrible look in his eye when he spoke to her, like the one he had just after he hit her: His pupils were dilated as if he were on drugs and his tone was the one you would use on a disobedient dog.

Also, he would go into the attic every afternoon when he came home from work and spend hours in there. He hadn't gone up there in years, and it got me thinking about the Monster that Ellen and I had invented as children to explain Father's strange actions. The Monster was something out of a Gothic novel: a female relative, maybe an aunt, whose body was so distorted that our family had locked her away in the attic out of shame. My father would go up there in the afternoons to give her food and water and to be with her. Only, he never had anything in his hands when he went up there, and we never heard a sound from the attic. It seemed impossible that anything living could be so silent, which made me wonder if the Monster might be dead. Now, my father's behavior was even stranger than in those days. He didn't come down for dinner most nights. When he finally came out of the attic, he had a faraway look in his eyes that was even scarier than his anger. But I made up my mind I'd keep my promise to Ellen and talk to him about her. I was terribly afraid to do it but even more scared to lose Ellen's trust. I was so upset, I almost forgot about Elena, which was perhaps fortunate, because she hadn't come in almost two weeks

I chose a moment one early weekend morning when

Father and I were eating breakfast and Ellen was still asleep.

"Ellen sure is snoring away!" I said, with a little laugh. He grimaced in reply.

"She gets lazier and lazier as she gets older!" he said.

I took a deep breath and plunged in.

"Oh, come on, Father! She's not that bad!"

He gave me a startled look and said, "Oh? You really think so?"

I swallowed hard, but pressed on. "Yes, I do. She's really a good kid and I don't believe she meant any harm. Don't you...don't you think you might have been a little hard on her?"

"No," he said quickly. But he averted his eyes. *That might be a good sign*, I thought.

"You know, Father, things have been a little tense around here."

"That isn't my fault!"

"Well, maybe, but I don't think it is all her fault either. She really didn't mean to upset you. She just made a dumb mistake."

"And how do you know that? Did she tell you?"

"Yes, she did."

"Well, I don't believe it! She isn't so stupid that she can't lock the bathroom door! I think she did it on purpose to...to provoke me!"

"You wouldn't say that if you knew how unhappy she was. She's really sorry she upset you!"

"Then why isn't she apologizing to me directly instead of getting you to do it?"

"Oh, no, Father. She had no idea I was going to talk to you. This is my own idea!" He grunted, as if in disbelief. "The fact is, Father, she is afraid of you!"

"Why should she be afraid of me!"

"Because you hit her. Hard."

"Oh, it wasn't all that hard." he said, but he averted his eyes again.

"Hard enough to frighten her! But she really is sorry, and if you would talk with her, you'd find out I'm telling the truth."

He met my eyes this time, with that hard stare which made it difficult to look away.

"You really think so?" he said.

"Yes, I do."

"Very well," he said. "We will see. But she must apologize and she must agree to do what I say if she wants to live in this house. I won't be made a fool!"

He got up from the table and started walking towards the stairs.

"Are you going to wake her up?" I asked.

"It is high time she got up! She and I need to have this little conversation!"

He knocked on her door. After a moment, it opened and he went inside.

I sat down and nervously scanned the morning paper. *Well*, I thought, *I got the ball rolling*. It's up to them now. I could only hear the tones of the conversation but that was enough to tell me how it was going. He started out low and harsh and her voice was high and breathless like a little girl's. After a while, some of the harshness had gone from his tone; and her voice, while still querulous, seemed lower and more deferential.

Then I heard a totally unexpected sound: Laughter! That was a sound I'd never heard between them, and never expected to hear! A moment later, I heard her door open. I was astonished to see her reach up and kiss him affectionately on the cheek. He leaned down and kissed her on the forehead. After I'd got over my astonishment, I laughed a little myself. I had certainly done my job well in bringing them together! I was getting this big brother thing down pat.

During the next week, their relationship got even closer. They were always laughing when they were together, as if at some private joke. I was even beginning to get a little jealous at their closeness. Then, that Friday, my father made a little announcement to me as my sister looked on, smiling.

"Teddy, I have something I should tell you. As you know, your sister is becoming a young woman and she needs some new clothes. So, tomorrow, I'm taking her to Milwaukee to let her pick out a new wardrobe. I know shopping is boring for you so I'm not going to make you go with us. You don't mind, do you? We'll be back on Sunday afternoon."

I was dumbstruck. There was an embarrassed silence for a moment until I managed to say what he expected to hear. "Of course, Father. No problem.

They smiled at me and then at each other. But there was a problem. The fact was that I was jealous: He never took me on any long trips! He never took me anywhere. It was like he was ashamed of me, although I was supposed to be his favorite! For another thing, the excited look on Ellen's face reminded me a little too much of the expression my mother had in the wedding picture in the hall. Perhaps I was afraid that this joy wouldn't last any longer for my sister than it had for my mother.

But my worst fear was that I'd be home alone with Elena. Ordinarily this would have made me very happy, but that passage I'd read in *Doctor Faustus* still haunted me. What if she *was* a demon? I had no one to protect me from her; only that phantom voice of my father which must be part of me. What if she did offer to buy my soul? Suppose she offered, in exchange, the power to take vengeance on my enemies, or a cure for my stuttering, or complete fulfillment of all of my sexual needs, whenever I wanted it? Would I have the strength to bear that!

The next morning, my father and Ellen were busy packing and looking at store catalogs together. I stayed alone in my room and rehearsed what I'd say to Elena if she offered to buy my soul. No! I said to her a hundred times. Get out! But the fact was I couldn't lose her. I couldn't stand to have that tremendous sexual hunger again, hunger that could never be satisfied. So I didn't know what I would say if she made that offer.

Just before my father and Ellen were due to leave, I heard a knock on my door. I opened it, and there was Ellen with a sad look on her face.

"I'm sorry you can't go on this trip, Teddy! But maybe you and Father can go on a trip another time."

"Yeah right!" I snapped. "Maybe he'll take me to a Braves game!"

Her eyes opened in shock and sadness and I saw a tear forming. I felt terrible about what I'd said.

"Don't worry about it, Ellen. I'll be fine. I'm sure he'll take me on a trip someday soon." I kissed her on the cheek and drew a rueful smile. "Hey, don't look so sad. It's not like you're going away forever!" I kissed her again and this time the smile was not so sad.

She left the room, and shortly after, I saw them piling into the car laughing like two kids going on vacation. Again, I felt a twinge of jealousy. My father never behaved like this with me! But then, I had been the one who brought them together and set up this trip, so I had no right to complain.

Still, when I saw them drive away, it left me with a cold, empty feeling. I was alone in the house, night was falling and soon Elena's time would come. I decided to go on one of my reading binges. I hoped this would tire me out and I'd fall asleep before Elena could show up. I'd finished *Doctor Faustus* and was starting on Shakespeare's tragedies. I read all the way through *Hamlet*. I had read it at first at age eleven to show Father what a prodigy I was, but, as I read it again and again, I began to actually enjoy it. Now, I could feel for the characters and put myself in their places. I felt sorry for Ophelia, because she reminded me a little of Ellen. The way her father manipulated her and refused to love her seemed very familiar. So did Ophelia's doomed little rebellions and her hopeless quest for love. But I identified with Hamlet more. I deeply felt his isolation and his feeling that something was rotten in his world that he was powerless to remedy. Also, like Hamlet, I was having problems with a spirit. But unlike Hamlet's ghost, mine wouldn't tell me what she wanted. If only it was something simple, like avenging her murder!

After *Hamlet*, I started on *Macbeth*. But this time I found the first scenes with the witches disturbing. They reminded me too much of Elena. Their prophecies to Macbeth were like her prophetic promise that "her time" would soon come. I'd read somewhere that witches also had waves of cold coming off of them, like Elena. Could she be a witch? But if so, the question remained, what did she want from me?

After reading for hours, I found myself going over the same passages again and again, like the description of how Macbeth's sword "smoked with execution." That seemed unrealistic: Why should blood smoke when it came out? Then the print began to blur before my eyes. *Good*, I thought, *now I'll be able to sleep*.

I lay down, and almost immediately, I felt myself begin to drift up over the bed. But then I looked down and saw that same white shape I'd seen before, coming out of the closet. The sight snapped me back to my unguarded body. I was trembling. Once again I felt the cold flowing from Elena

"What's the matter, little Teddy?" she said in that husky voice. "Are you afraid of me?"

"No!" I lied.

She laughed.

"I don't believe you! You think I'm a demon. You think I want your soul! Don't you, little Teddy?"

"No, I..."

"Why do you bother to lie? You're like a pane of glass to me! And now you're worried that I'm going to break you! But I'd never hurt my sweet little Teddy! Besides, yours isn't the soul I want!"

"What do you mean?"

"Don't worry about it; it will all be clear very soon. Meanwhile, think about this. I can't be a succubus! That word means "to lie under" and as you know, I like to be on top! Now, come over here, you silly boy! It's time to play the Game."

And so I went. Of course I went! I couldn't resist those silken, teasing hands or that luscious body—as smooth and cold as ice! Still, I cringed when her icy flesh first touched mine. She laughed again.

"I'm really not a witch or demon, Teddy. Very soon, you will find out what I am."

"When?"

"Tomorrow nigh, it will all begin."

I was still confused and apprehensive, but somehow the fear made the things she did to me all the more exciting. Once again, as if to prove her point, she got on top of me and rode me for hours. She left me without a word but I was not sad. I couldn't wait to see what tomorrow night might bring.

I was awakened by the sound of the car pulling into our driveway. I bolted upright in surprise. Could I have slept all the way into the afternoon? But when I looked at the clock, it was just past nine in the morning. Something must be wrong! I got up and went to the window. My father was unlocking the trunk and Ellen was running into the house. Her eyes were red and her lips were set in a tight line. I heard the door open and then slam shut. Something was wrong all right!

I heard my sister run upstairs and into her room. A moment later I heard my father opening the door. I was expecting him to call after my sister or to ask me to help with the luggage but he said nothing. I went over to the door between my room and Ellen's. I only heard a soft sighing. I opened the door. I saw her putting her diary in her desk drawer, and then looking up angrily at me.

"Get out of here!" she yelled.

I quickly closed the door. A few moments later, I heard her begin to snore. *Well, that's good anyway*, I thought. Maybe she didn't get much sleep last night. Maybe that's when the argument started. But I felt helpless and angry. I couldn't talk to her, and the look on Father's face told me there was no point in talking with him. All my best efforts to get them together had failed and I wondered which one of them had messed it up. Or maybe they both had!

As hard as I try, I can barely remember anything about the rest of that day. I remember reading Shakespeare in my room, coming down only for lunch and dinner. The other two walked around with their eyes down as if they were in their own world. This was all right with me; I was too angry with both of them to want to talk. After a while, my anger subsided a little and I told myself: Give them a little time. They'll come around like before. I have a vague recollection of eating some kind of cold leftovers for dinner (Emma was on her day off), and of Ellen, her eyes still red and downcast, drifting up to her room. My father stalked off to his room, and I went to mine.

The rest of that evening is vague, dreamlike. I remember reading *Richard III* in my room, trying again to tire myself to sleep. I remember rooting for that dwarfish, evil, grand little man to win, just because he'd been hurt so much, because they'd all insulted him and they deserved what he gave them! Suddenly, I heard a horrible, inhuman scream. I couldn't locate the source of the sound. At first, I thought it was coming from just above me, and for a moment, my heart stopped. I thought about the Monster in the attic and how that was just the sound it would make. But then I made out some of the words and they were so bizarre they might well have come from the asylum up on the hill. But the voice could also have come from Ellen's room. It was high pitched enough to have been her voice.

The first word was so distorted I couldn't make it out. It could have been a name. But the rest of it was clear enough and the fear and horror in the voice made the darkness and the roaring close around me. "Why did you come back?"

I don't remember when I came out of the darkness and the roaring. My next clear recollection is waking up to a strange but somehow familiar metallic whine, with a deeper whirring sound beneath it. It seemed to be coming from somewhere below.

Then came the dream. I had a vague sense of flying out of my bed, of going out my window, of soaring through the darkness, guided by someone or something. Then I was shown things; things so horrible that I woke up screaming!

10

I sat upright in the bed, heart pounding. The screaming continued, although my lips were pressed tight together in fear. It took me a moment to realize it was coming, not from me, but from downstairs.

"Get up, both of you. I'm tired of fixing breakfast and no one coming to eat it! Get up! Now!"

It was my father and he sounded very angry. This looked like another very difficult day, especially for Ellen. I looked over at my clock. It was just after nine. Usually he let us sleep in on a weekend. I swung my feet over onto the floor. My stomach was a knot of anger and foreboding.

"I'm coming, Father!" I yelled.

"All right," he said, after a moment. "But where is your sister? She'd better get down here."

The naked menace in his voice wound the knot in my stomach even tighter. I'll bet this argument was mostly your fault! I thought. What right have you got to get so angry! But what I said was:

"I'll get her up, Father! Don't worry!"

"Make sure you do!" he said.

I walked over to the door between our rooms and knocked, at first softly and then more firmly.

"Get up, Ellen!" I said in a stage whisper. "Father is really mad!"

I put my ear to the keyhole but heard nothing. Usually when a person is in a room, some sound will give them away: a faint breathing, a creak of the bed or something. But from Ellen's room, only dead silence. I couldn't even feel her presence in the room. The panic I'd felt in the dream was beginning to return. I hesitated for a moment, and then opened the door.

She was not there. Not there! Her bed was made, which was unusual enough, and the room was completely clean. I walked inside, my mouth open with astonishment. Ellen never cleaned her room; it was even messier than mine. This room looked as if no one had been there in weeks.

Where could she have gone? Ellen never went anywhere without me or Father, except to school. Could she have run away? And if so, where to?

The darkness began rising towards my eyes and the roaring towards my ears. Not now! I told them and they receded. I couldn't afford to pass out now! I had to find out where she'd gone. I looked up and realized my father was watching me from the door.

"She's not here!" I said. He looked at me gravely and nodded.

"So much the worse for her!" he snapped. "Let's go eat breakfast."

I stared at him in disbelief and then ran after him.

"Shouldn't we try to find her?"

"Why should we? You and I both know she has run off somewhere to sulk. When she's had her little tantrum, she'll be back."

"But she never runs away! Where would she go?"

"How would I know? Now, do you want breakfast, or don't you?"

"No, thank you, Father. I'm going to try to find out where she's gone!"

He looked at me, anger in his eyes. But he must have seen something of the same in mine because he just snorted contemptuously.

"Suit yourself!" he said, and walked down the stairs

I walked back into Ellen's room, slamming the door. *If you don't care about her, I do!* I thought. There must be some kind of clue to where she has gone in this room.

The unnatural cleanliness and order in her room again struck me. There was a certain finality in it as if she'd known she was going on a long trip and was uncertain when she'd return. I went over to the bed and lifted up the neatly tucked in covers. The bed was cold and held no imprint of her body. I was sure she hadn't slept here last night. But I knew she had gone into her bedroom. So where could she have gone in the middle of the night? The question again brought the darkness and the roaring. No! I said again, and again they retreated. *I have to be strong for her*, I thought. I have to figure this out!

Surely she hadn't run out in the middle of the night just to sulk. I was almost certain she was in some kind of danger. But how could I convince my father of this? There must be other clues here! I went to her desk. A pad of her blue writing paper was on it. I saw the impression of some kind of writing. The top page had been torn off jaggedly, as if in a hurry. I looked around for a pencil. I had read in some detective novel that if I ran the pencil over the top sheet, I could raise the impressions so that they'd show the original letters. But before I could find a pencil, I found the torn off sheet of paper itself, crumpled in her wastebasket. I fished it out and smoothed it on the desk.

"Dear Edward," it said. "I'm afraid." Nothing more.

Curiouser and curiouser! "Dear Edward." She never called me Edward unless we were playing our games. And this didn't sound like a game.

"I'm afraid." Afraid of whom or what? Suddenly I remembered: She'd used the same words in her note asking me to come to our secret spot. That letter was about Elena. Could it still be Elena she was frightened of? I remembered what Elena had told me: It all starts tomorrow night! That was last night. What had started last night? And why had it made Ellen so afraid?

But if she was afraid of Elena, what made her write the note, then discard it? Surely she'd have knocked on my door if she was worried about a bad dream. And surely she couldn't have had a bad dream between the time she started the letter and when she tore it out of her pad? No, she must have heard or seen something that startled her. Did Elena finally reveal herself to her face to face? If so, why would Ellen care whether she saw the note or not?

I had no answers to these questions. But now, at least, I had some evidence I could show my father. He couldn't deny that she'd been afraid of something; enough to tear the letter out of her pad and try to hide it. Surely, he'd call the Sheriff now! I started down the stairs, the letter in my hand. But halfway down, I reconsidered. Was it really a good idea to show this to him? Might it not enrage him further, particularly if he suspected he was what she was afraid of? I had to admit I suspected as much.

I went back up to Ellen's room and put the note in her desk drawer. As I did, I noticed that her diary was missing. That was strange. She always kept it in there unless she was writing in it. I'd even seen her put it in there the day before. Could she have taken it with her, wherever she was? And if so, why?

My father was just finishing his morning coffee when I got down to the kitchen.

"Would you like toast or cereal?" he said, getting up from his chair

"That's all right. I'm not hungry. Listen, Father, Ellen's bed doesn't look as if it's been slept in all night!"

He smiled

"And how did you deduce that, Holmes?"

"The bed is all made up and it's cold!"

"I grant you that the neatness of her bed and her room is a little unusual, but perhaps she was feeling guilty about her slovenly habits. God knows I've told her to clean up that room often enough. And as far as the temperature of the bed, how long does it take for a bed to cool down? Teddy, the fact is you're no detective. I think you should leave that kind of thing to the professionals!"

"Fine!" I said, picking the phone off the receiver and

handing it to him. "So call the professionals! I'll be more than happy to leave this to them!"

My father slammed the phone down. The receiver jangled with the impact.

"There is no need for this kind of melodramatics. It isn't time to call the sheriff yet!"

"When will it be time? If we wait too long, it may be too late!"

My father looked at me intently.

"You really are worried about this, aren't you?" he said. "Well, I'll tell you what. Why don't I come up there and have another look around?"

"Good!" I said.

I ran up the stairs two at a time and he followed close behind. When he entered the room, he went straight for the desk. I was hoping he wouldn't notice the torn off page on the note pad. Apparently, he didn't because he then walked over to the closet and looked carefully through my sister's clothes. Then he said, "Just as I thought!"

"What is it?"

"All of your sister's clothes are here. If some had been missing, I'd have been worried, too. It could have meant she'd run away."

I felt stupid. Of course. My father was right and I was being melodramatic. I had no business playing Sherlock Holmes.

But wait.

"Father, are you sure all her clothes are here?"

"Of course."

"Then she must be running around the neighborhood in her nightgown!"

"What? No, of course, not. She probably is wearing the clothes she had on yesterday."

I went over to her hamper and looked in.

"No, here are the clothes she had on last night!"

"Well...well...I can't vouch for all of her clothes being here. There might be a few missing!"

"Then you can't be sure she didn't take a few articles of clothing."

"Well, that makes sense. But do you really want me to call the sheriff just based on that?"

"Yes, he can at least start an investigation."

"He would laugh at me. The odds are she is simply sulking someplace and will be home by lunchtime. She seldom misses two meals in a row!"

"Well then at least let me look for her. I have an idea where she might be."

"All right. I won't do anything further until you get back. Although..."

He looked as if he had just remembered something. I was glad that he was at least thinking about the possibility that something might be wrong.

I ran into my room and hurriedly threw on some clothes. As I was going downstairs, I was startled to see my father on the phone. He had some sort of psychological case file spread in front of him, and I could see tension and anger on his face.

"Well, all right, I understand all about your procedures.

But if she isn't back by this evening, I'm going to call you again, and I want you over here!"

Father slammed down the phone. He glanced over the case file again and then went over to the hall window which looked out on Koenig's house. He was staring intently at the house and seemed preoccupied, so I didn't disturb him. I was glad he'd decided to call the sheriff, but I wondered why he'd changed his mind. Could it have anything to do with the case file on the table?

I felt better when I was on my bike and pedaling over towards Lepke's Woods. That was where she met me the last time she sent me a note saying "I'm afraid" and I was praying she'd be there this time. But if she wanted to meet me, why had she discarded the note before she finished it? Unless she hoped I'd find it. It was a long shot but the best hope I had.

But when I got to our sacred spot, she was not there and there was no sign anyone had been there. I was the only one who had left my tracks in the duff that day. Now, I really had no idea where she was.

"I'm afraid!" she'd said. Who would she go to as a protector? She'd thought of me first, and then thrown the thought in the trash can. It was a bitter knowledge—she hadn't trusted me to protect her. But who else could she see as a guardian? I could only think of one person and that thought was even more bitter.

I walked the bike back to the road and then jumped on it and headed towards town. Bobby Niebauer had once told me where he lived when he had had me do a paper for him. I hoped to God she hadn't gone to him, but it was possible she thought of him as some kind of romantic rebel who could save her from Father's anger. I was hoping Bobby wouldn't expect me to come looking for him in his lair. Anyway, I didn't care about the danger. I only wanted to find her and for her to be okay.

"The wrong side of the tracks" is a cliché, but I guess all clichés start out as truths. Once I crossed the tracks that ran on the other side of downtown, the houses became smaller and the lawns more unkempt. Old cars and trucks rusted on the scraggly lawns. As I went on, first the outbuildings and then the houses themselves seemed to be crumbling, with paint peeling and shingles missing on the roofs. There were even some rundown old barns where people lived as I got further out into the country. By the time I got out to Bobby's street, the houses were just underground concrete basements with tar paper on the roofs. It was as if they'd run out of money before finishing the houses. Only the windows were above ground: you had to climb down steps to get to the front door.

Bobby's "house" had no doorbell, so I had to knock on the door, the paint of which had almost peeled off. I wondered how cold it got in this house in the winter, when it was thirty degrees below zero outside. I heard someone moving around inside and then the door opened. Bobby was wearing only dirty underwear. His eyes opened wide when he saw me. Inside, I hear a raucous female voice screaming:

"If that's one of your hoodlum friends, tell them to fuck off, you little asshole!"

I stepped back, shock registering on my face. Could that be his mother?

"What the hell do you want?" Bobby snarled. "Get the hell out of here!"

I stood my ground.

"I j-j-just wanted to know if you had seen Ellen."

He rubbed his eyes and stared at me.

"Ellen? When would I have seen Ellen?"

"Today or last night."

"She's missing?" There was something like concern in his voice

"Yes."

Suddenly, he leered broadly.

"Oh, yeah. I forgot. I've got her here in bed with me. I'll send her back when I'm finished!

I ran up the stairs, his derisive laughter ringing in my ears. Coming here was a stupid idea. Had I really thought he had her in his house? And now he'd probably spread it all around town she was missing. But, at least I knew now where she wasn't. Unless Bobby was a natural actor, the confusion and surprise on his face when I asked him about Ellen had been real.

So if Ellen was not with Bobby, and wasn't waiting for me in our sacred spot, where could she be? Then I remembered the way my father had been staring over at Koenig's house. He had had that case file in his hand. It had looked a lot like Ed Gein's case file, and I bet it came from the same place: Waupun State Hospital for the Insane! And after he looked at that file, he'd changed his mind about calling the sheriff.

So my father suspected Koenig and seemed to have some evidence for his suspicion. I remembered how Koenig had grabbed me one time when we were picking berries off his bushes. He had let me go right away but the glazed look in his eyes had scared me. Kids also talked about the way he looked at girls when they walked by his house. If the sheriff wouldn't investigate Koenig and his house, then it was up to me. Tonight might be too late!

I got on my bike and rode towards home. As I rode, I tried to tell myself she would never allow herself to go to that filthy, decrepit house or to be touched by that equally filthy old man. But Ellen had always had a soft spot in her heart for strays, for the rejected and the outlaws of the world. She might think of that despised old man as a stray and his house as a refuge. My father had told us both not to go near that house but that might have made it all the more attractive in the mood she was in. The thought made me pedal faster.

I got off my bike by a deserted wooded area just west of Koenig's house, and dragged it into the trees. I left it there behind some bushes and went deeper into the woods. I climbed to the top of a little hill which gave an excellent view of the house. Ellen and I had spied on Koenig from there more than once. The fence on that side was closer to his house than the one on our side because the vegetable garden was between his house and ours. My vantage point was not more than twenty feet from Koenig's back porch.

I squatted down on my heels in the loose duff and waited. I was not quite sure what I was looking for:

perhaps just something out of the ordinary. The trouble was that Koenig had no fixed routines. On a nice day like this, he might work in his garden or just sit on his back porch and drink his whiskey. Or he might not come out of his house at all. He always kept his blinds drawn so no one could see inside. As far as I knew, no one besides him ever went in there. This day, he seemed to be staying inside.

As I squatted there waiting for some sign of him, the sun rose higher in the sky. I was sweating feverishly. I shifted my weight off my heels which were falling asleep. This was stupid! Ellen could be sitting at home eating lunch while I sat there being eaten alive by ants and chiggers. The chiggers were the worst; they burrowed deep beneath the skin and you couldn't get them out.

Wait! Something was moving onto the back porch. It was Koenig, with his usual dirty tee shirt, torn jeans and bottle. He had a dirty glass in his left hand, which was a little unusual. Usually, he drank it straight out of the bottle. I wondered what he might be celebrating. He walked over to his rocking chair and sat down. He looked out onto his back yard which was littered and overgrown with weeds, smiled, and poured himself a drink. I wondered what in that filthy landscape could cause him to smile. Or was the smile about someone he might have trapped in that horrible old house?

After a few drinks, his head began to tilt forward and the glass began to lean sideways. But just when it looked like he was bound to spill the drink, the head would jerk back up and he'd bring the glass up to his lips. Then he'd smile, and drift off back to sleep, until he seemed again to sense danger to his drink, and he'd rescue it once more. It was hard not to laugh aloud; at that moment he didn't seem like a threat to my sister or anyone else.

And then I heard the sound. At first, it sounded like a voice on the radio or a TV. But something was wrong with it. It sounded inhuman, or as if someone were under a terror no human could endure. It was high pitched and could have been a girl's voice. It kept screaming something over and over. And the more I heard it, the more it sounded like: "Let me out! Let me out!"

For a moment, I couldn't breathe or think. Ellen was calling for help! I was sure it was her voice. She was in there in that dark filthy house, and God only knew what he'd already done to her! Maybe she was injured or even dying. I had to help her!

But how? I could go to Father. He'd know what to do. Obviously, he had some kind of suspicion of Koenig. Of course, I was assuming the case folder I saw was Koenig's. But what if I was wrong? I could imagine him saying

"You think you hear your sister's voice because that is what you want to hear. But you can't really hear what the voice is saying and you have no proof it isn't coming from a radio or TV. You're getting yourself all excited over nothing."

And while I argued with him, she might be dying in there or waiting for Keonig to do... something terrible to her. Could I call the sheriff? I dismissed the idea as quickly as it arose. If he hadn't come for my father, he certainly wouldn't come for me.

So it was up to me to rescue her if she was in there.

But how could I get in, with him standing guard at the back? The front door was closed, and, for all I knew, locked. It was hopeless! And after all, I was just a kid. I couldn't be expected to do this kind of thing.

Suddenly the darkness swarmed around me again, along with the roaring. Only this time, in the middle of the darkness, I seemed to see Ellen's face shining in its own light. Her eyes were open, as if in horror. The mouth was open as if to shout: Let me out!

I found myself moving towards the fence. On this side, the downslope hit the fence so that it was only about four feet high. In a second, without thinking, I was up and over it. I had a moment's sensation of flight and then I hit the ground hard. The impact knocked the breath out of me. I rolled over and over until my right knee hit the side of the house.

I lay there for a moment looking up at the fence. It looked much higher on this side, perhaps six feet high. No wonder I hit so hard. I got up unsteadily, and checked myself for injuries. My right knee was throbbing a little but nothing seemed to be broken. Then I remembered where I was. I must have made a tremendous racket coming over the fence and hitting the house. I listened for the sounds of Koenig coming after me, but all I heard was a soft rhythmic sound. He was snoring! I couldn't believe my good luck.

I moved slowly in a half-crouch towards the back of the house until I reached the porch. I peeked my head cautiously over the stone railing. Koenig was still sitting in his rocking chair—his head back, and his mouth open.

Somehow he'd managed to put his bottle and glass down without spilling either. He obviously knew what was important in his life. I couldn't see any weapon near him.

The back door was wide open; another stroke of luck. But Koenig was right in the center of the porch, and I'd have to get by him to reach the door. If I moved slowly and quietly, I might be able to sneak by without waking him. But what if he did wake up? He would have a legal right to shoot me as an intruder... And what if Ellen wasn't in there? I would have died for nothing!

I stood there for a long time, frozen in fear. And then I heard that voice again. It was clearer from here, although I couldn't quite make out the words. One thing I was sure of, that was no radio or TV. It came from someone alive. I thought again of my vision of Ellen's despairing face. and had that feeling of déjà vu. I knew I'd seen that vision before. But where? Was it in the dream?

It didn't matter. In a moment I was over the railing and onto the porch. The board I landed on creaked, loudly. Koenig gave a loud snort, opening his mouth and lifting his head as if snapping at a fly. I stood absolutely still, waiting for him to open his eyes and see me. Instead, his head went back down and he began snoring again.

When I was sure he was asleep, I began tiptoeing towards the door. There were no more loose boards, and within a few minutes I was inside the house. The place seemed to exude darkness and I had to inch my way forward. The smell of filth and decay was so strong that moving against it was like moving underwater. I could vaguely make out that I was in the kitchen. It smelled as if the garbage of a dozen years was festering there. I could feel, and hear, rotten things being squashed beneath my feet

I moved out of the kitchen into what must have been the living room. The smell became even worse. Under the garbage smell, the odors of urine and feces rose up, my gorge rose with them. I fought down the urge to vomit. My eyes had become somewhat accustomed to the darkness. I saw piles of trash and garbage spread out all over, in between and even on the furniture. I couldn't believe anyone could live in such squalor. Several times, I almost tripped over the piles or on some foul, slippery thing. Once, I did fall and, putting my arm out, caught myself on a piece of furniture, perhaps a couch. The material was cold, smooth, and slimy, the way I imagined a snake's skin might feel.

I started away from the suddenly sinister fabric. I was thinking about Ed Gein's house with its piles of garbage and feces, and its slip covers made from human skin. Could there be two Ed Geins in Wisconsin? I fought down a wave of fear and nausea. There was no proof of that, I thought. And even if it were true, it made it all the more important that I get Ellen, and myself, out of there, before we both became part of his interior decorating scheme.

Moving forward, I slipped again and steadied myself by putting my hand on a pile of magazines. I picked one of the magazines up and rolled it into a cylinder. It wouldn't make much of a weapon if Koenig did come in, but it was better than nothing. Anyway, I didn't think even the Nazi's ever made a magazine out of human skin.

The sound was closer and clearer now, although I still couldn't make out the words. I moved towards it. Suddenly, I was caught in something yielding and soft. Spider web! I used the rolled up magazine to break the web. Something was crawling on my shoulder, something that felt like a small hand. I shuddered convulsively and brushed my shoulder again and again until I was sure the spider was off me. I made a sick noise in my throat: "Yennh!" I stopped and listened. I couldn't hear anything from the porch. Not even snoring! He was awake!

You must hurry! I told myself. Just a few more steps. Almost there. I dimly saw the door a few feet in front of me, and heard the voice from the other side. I could almost make out the words now. There *was* someone in there! I moved closer and put my hand on the cold glass knob. Now I could recognize the words being screamed over and over. And as I did, I felt the darkness closing over me again.

"Elena," the voice was saying, "why did you come back?"

As the darkness and the roaring closed around me, I thought, *I'm going to pass out*. But suddenly, Holmes's voice came out of the darkness.

"No, Teddy, you must not! Think! There is a logical explanation for this!"

Holmes was right. If I passed out now, it might be fatal, for Ellen and me. The darkness and the roaring receded and I could again see the door and hear the absurd, impossible words.

"Elena, why did you come back!"

Why would Ellen or anyone else call out my lover's name in this dark filthy house? Only Ellen and I knew her name, but why would she use it here, instead of something sensible, like, say, "Help!" But if it were anyone else, how could they know the name? Well, there was only one way to find out. I turned the glass knob. To my surprise, the door opened.

The sound was coming from something bright and red in the middle of the room. Like a flame. A living, talking flame! I felt the solid edges of the world begin to dissolve and flow. So this was madness!

No, wait! A shaft of sunlight was coming through a hole in the window shade lighting the red thing up like a flame. It was a bird! Thank God! I felt sanity return to my world, the way sunlight flows into a darkened room when you pull aside the curtains.

It was just a parrot or parakeet. She was beautiful, whatever she was. On closer examination, her feathers were more bright orange than red, and she had a tall beautiful comb and a yellow curved beak. She was strutting around on her perch in a metal cage, uttering the sounds which must be meaningless to her, but meant a lot to me. Still, she seemed to be agitated, as if something had disturbed her and she couldn't calm down.

And suddenly, I knew what had disturbed her and why she was saying these words. She had heard the same words I heard last night, only she heard them more clearly, and was repeating them exactly as she heard them. So that voice had been no dream, and I was willing to bet it hadn't come from the asylum, unless Elena was invading their dreams too.

Since only Ellen and I knew about Elena, it must have been Ellen who screamed out that bizarre phrase. But what did it mean, and what relation, if any, did it have with her disappearance?

I thought of what Elena told me the night before: Tomorrow it begins! Had Elena come back to Ellen last night in a dream, or maybe in the flesh? Ellen's voice had been terrified. Had Elena appeared to her as she really was, as she had promised to do to me? Was her real appearance so horrible that it could cause madness, or even death? But if so, we would have found Ellen's body in her bedroom. No, I was being unfair to the woman, or whatever, that I loved. *Sorry, Elena*, I said inwardly, as if she was watching my thoughts. I had a terrible feeling that she might be.

I moved closer to the bird. She hopped to the far side of the cage and turned to regard me with her unblinking yellow eyes. Her cage was large and had several perches and a plenty of food and water. Moreover, the cage and the room it was in were very clean, except for papers and magazines covering the bottom of the cage. There were bookcases filled with books all along the walls. The bird and the books were obviously well loved and cared for, although their owner lived in filth and excrement. I thought of Ed Gein. They had found one room in his house not covered with filth and decaying body parts: his mother's bedroom, preserved like a shrine. Koenig, too, had built a shrine in this room. Was it to this bird, or to his books, or perhaps just to sanity? Whatever it was, it made me feel better about him. He was capable of love; for this creature, for these books, and his lush garden. He just didn't seem to love himself. It made it hard to think of him as a murderer.

"You are really a beauty!" I told the bird.

"Elena!" she replied.

"I know about Elena!" I said. "But who told you?"

I went over to the cage and put my finger through the bars. She hopped over to the furthest perch from me.

"Don't be scared of me. I'd never hurt you. I wish I had a pet like you!"

She hopped up to the highest perch. Clearly, something about me was frightening her. Perhaps it was the magazine I still held tightly rolled up like a weapon. I let it fall to the floor. The pages fluttered open to reveal a little blond girl, about eight. She was naked and she had her legs spread wide open! *My God*, I thought, *Old Man Keonig is a pervert!*

"What are you doing here?"

The harsh, guttural voice came from directly behind me. I whirled around and saw Koenig in the doorway. He was wielding a large butcher knife in his upraised right hand.

"No," I said quietly, unable to gather enough breath for a shout. "P-p-please don't!" My hands were shaking as I raised them to shield my face, or perhaps just to avoid seeing the blow when it came.

"Answer my question!" he shouted, raising the knife higher above my head. I felt my bowels loosen and I thought, *I'm going to shit all over myself.* A sense of embarrassment replaced my terror for a moment and I blurted out:

"I-I-I heard the bird and I wanted to see him!"

Koenig stared at me. The hand holding the knife trembled a little. Then his expression softened and he lowered the knife to his side.

"You're the boy next door, aren't you?"

I nodded, unable to speak.

"He's a beauty, isn't he? But you should never have come in here!"

"I-I-I never saw a more beautiful bird

Then I happened to look down at the magazine, and his eyes followed mine. Our eyes met; he knew that I knew. He gave a low growl and charged at me, his knife once again raised. I screamed and fell backwards, knocking over the bird cage. The bird squawked and fluttered, hitting the bars of the cage with his wings. Koenig instantly knelt down and righted the cage. The knife hit the floor with a metallic clang.

"That's all right, my beauty!" he said. "I won't let anyone hurt you!"

Sensing his distraction, I scrambled to my feet and ran towards the door. As I did so, I grabbed the magazine to use as evidence. As I ran into the darkened room, I slipped on the cluttered floor and fell over a sofa. I heard him cursing and growling like an animal close behind. He had all the advantages here; he knew this house as I didn't, and he had the knife. I half crawled, half ran towards the sunlight coming in from what I hoped was the back door. I screamed again as his hand gripped my shoulder. But I pulled free, and I heard him slip and fall as he lurched after me.

I was in the kitchen now and could see the back door a few feet away I heard a swish in back of me, and felt something hard and sharp dig into my arm. It stung like Hell; he had drawn blood. Pain and fear propelled me out the door. But I heard him just one step behind me. I ran straight towards the side railing and vaulted over it. I hesitated for a moment, not sure which way to go then I heard him hit the ground right beside me. I knew I could never climb the fence before he got me, so I sprinted down the narrow passage between the house and the fence, hearing his curses and labored breathing right behind me. I kept waiting for the knife to dig into my back, but he was apparently too busy trying to keep up with me to strike the killing blow. I burst out into his front yard and broke for our house. I risked a backward glance and saw he was several feet behind me, doubled over and fighting for breath.

He waved his knife in the air and shouted, "You tell the cops I didn't do anything to that little girl! You tell them!"

I ran on without a further backward glance, saying to myself, "I'll tell them all right."

My father was sitting at the kitchen table still looking at that medical file when I burst in.

"Father! You have to help me! He's got her! I'm sure he has!" I said.

"Got her? Who's got her?"

"Koenig! I just left his house. I know he has her."

"What were you doing in his house? You know better than to go over there!"

"Please listen to me. He as much as admitted to me he did something to her! And he tried to kill me!"

I showed him the wound on the back of my arm. He blanched and rose to his feet.

"My God!" he said. "Here, let me look at that!"

He came over to me and pressed his hand over the

wound, very hard. It hurt at first but the blood soon stopped flowing. After he'd bandaged it, he asked me to tell him exactly what happened. I told him, leaving out the part about Bobby. I told him how I'd heard the sound from Keonig's house and thought it was Ellen. How I'd snuck in and found the bird. I also left out the part about Elena—something told me that would open a lot of doors better left closed. I looked in my hand and realized I still had the magazine all rolled up. I spread it out and showed it to him, explaining how and where I had got it, and how Keonig had tried to kill me because of it. He looked grim as he leafed through the pages.

"It was my fault!" he muttered. "I should have warned you both. But I did tell you long ago not to go near him."

He got up and went to the phone. As he began dialing, I said, "Father, one more thing. After I got away from him, he yelled after me, 'Tell those cops I didn't do anything to that little girl!' Those were his exact words. The thing is, I never said a word to him about Ellen being missing!"

"You did well, son," he said. "I'm proud of you! But you shouldn't have gone into that house. He could have killed you in there!"

I felt a glow of happiness at his praise. Then I heard the sheriff come on the line. I remembered that my sister was missing and that she could be injured or dead. I felt ashamed of myself for feeling anything but worried

"You bet I have something to tell you!" my father yelled into the phone. "My daughter is still missing and now that madman Koenig has attacked my son with a knife! Yes, you had better get over here. I have a lot to show you!"

About fifteen minutes later, the sheriff's car pulled into our driveway. I let Carson in. He gave me a perfunctory smile as he went by.

"So what's this all about, Doc?"

"Perhaps Teddy should tell you," Father said.

Once again, I felt that guilty glow of pride. They both sat down at the kitchen table and stared at me, while I told my story.

When I told them about going into Koenig's house, the sheriff said, "That's trespass!"

My father glared at him, but I ignored him and went on. When I got to the part about the magazine, my father spread it in front of Carson. He leafed through it as I finished my story. I don't think he even heard me when I told him what Koenig had said to me about the "little girl."

"Not in my county! We won't have this kind of pervert in my county!" he shouted after I'd finished.

"That's all very well, but you already knew he was a pervert!" my father snapped, pointing to the case file still lying open on the kitchen table. "I told you about it over the phone today."

"Well," Carson said slowly, "maybe I wasn't paying you the attention I should have. After all, you're not in law enforcement. Anyway, a convicted pervert is supposed to register with me!"

"Well apparently Koenig forgot that when they let him out of Waupun. The point is, he attacked a ten-year-old girl back in Milwaukee, and now I'm afraid he's done something to my daughter! What are you going to do about it?"

"Can't you just arrest him for having something like this in his house?" I said, pointing to the magazine.

"I'm afraid not, son. For one thing, you got the evidence illegally. But he did commit a crime by failing to register! That means I can get a warrant to search his house."

"I suggest you get right on that, Sheriff," my father said, "before you waste any more time!"

The sheriff nodded stiffly and left, his head down. My father said, "Teddy, can you keep an eye out from the front window? I have to do something down in the basement, and I don't want to miss the sheriff when he gets back.

I did as I was told, although I wondered what my father had to do in the basement at a time like this. But I knew that he liked to work in his workshop when he was tense. I devoted most of my attention to Keonig's house. I didn't want him to leave without us knowing about it. But nothing was happening over there. I soon grew bored and restless that my exhilaration at escaping from Koenig and bringing Carson in on the case had almost vanished, replaced by a growing fear. If Koenig had Ellen alive, it wasn't in that house. I had been all through it. But where else could he have her?

I returned to the kitchen and picked up the case file, hoping it might give me some clues. I noticed it was compiled by Doctor Kunsler, my father's friend in

Waupun. It gave biographical details for Keonig: age fifty, born and raised in Weimar. Mother died at an early age—like mine. Father died more recently. Had younger sister whom he lost at age ten due to a fatal accident. Fixated on younger sister, and unable to relate to older females. Poor social skills. Graduated from UW in English. Unable to keep a job. Lived on allowance from father. *And now he must live on the inheritance*, I thought. Got job at private elementary school in Milwaukee as a teacher, but was discharged for "improper contact" with a fourth grade girl. Finally was arrested for attack on a ten-year-old, whom he lured into his house with candy. Said to psychologists: "I never wanted to hurt her! I loved her." Girl was unharmed except for sexual assault, but kept asking: "Why did Uncle Willy hurt me down there? He was always nice to me!" History of alcohol dependence as well as pedophilia. Tentative diagnosis of inadequate personality, as well as the above problems. Possible schizoid tendencies. Poor prognosis for any kind of independent living in society.

I was not much wiser than I had been. Still, I was glad to read that he had no history of violence except for the sexual assault. Of course he had attacked me, but he might have been within his rights to do so. I was also relieved to hear he had no apparent interest in girls over ten. He could hardly have mistaken Ellen for a ten-year-old. Maybe he hadn't done anything to Ellen. But if not, why had he told me to tell the police he hadn't harmed her, even though I hadn't told him she was missing?

After a while, my father came into the hall. I quickly closed the case file, but he didn't seem to be concerned about it. He asked me if I had seen anything and I said no. We both went into the living room to wait.

After what seemed like hours, we heard several cars pull up outside. I ran to the hall door and looked. Several carloads of men had gotten out of their vehicles and were walking towards Koenig's house. A few, including the sheriff, were in uniform, but most were in hunting outfits and carried rifles. I recognized some of them as Town Square Boys. Some of them had excited grins on their faces and were pointing their weapons at Koenig's house.

Just then, a state patrol car drove up and a patrolman in a broad hat got out. He was carrying an official looking piece of paper. He brought it to Sheriff Carson who looked at it and nodded. He motioned some of the deputies to go around the back of the house. They did so, trampling Koenig's precious garden as they went. The rest he called to himself. They huddled around him and he showed them the magazine I'd brought out of the house. The looks of disgust and hatred on their faces were as eloquent as words. Then Carson rolled up the magazine tightly and put a rubber band around it. *That's an odd thing to do with evidence*, I thought

Carson went up to Koenig's front door and pounded on it, shouting something. He and the state patrolman conferred for a moment and then Carson kicked the door, hard. His leg went right through the thin wood and he had trouble getting it out of the door. He kicked again, this time up by the lock, and the door flew open.

The sheriff rushed through the door and then came right out again. He shouted something to his deputies and one of them opened up the trunk of his car. He brought out two long flashlights and gave them to the Sheriff and the state patrolman. They switched them on and went back in to the dark. *I wish I'd had one of those when I was in there*, I thought.

I watched the moving lights through the side windows as they slowly made their way back into that filthy cluttered house. A few minutes later, I saw the lights coming back towards the front. When the two men came out of the door, they had Koenig between them, half carrying, half dragging him. He was shouting something but they ignored him. They looked like they wished they had gloves on.

Somehow, Koenig managed to wriggle free of them. Then, Carson grabbed him. But instead of restraining him, he shoved him out into the yard into the midst of the deputies who had formed two lines on either side of the walkway. Koenig stumbled, but managed to keep his feet. He looked at the lines of men and started back towards the house. But Carson met him with the rolled up magazine in his hand and began hitting him with it the way you would a naughty dog. He drove Koenig back into the gauntlet, and then the men began kicking him and hitting him with the butts of their rifles

They're killing him! I thought.

Suddenly, the state patrolman ran forward into the frenzy, shouting and holding up his hand. When he saw this, Carson also held up his hand and the kicking and hitting stopped. The patrolman stood Koenig up against the porch rail. His face was streaked with blood and there was fear in his eyes.

The sheriff showed him pictures from the magazine and screamed questions at him. Koenig looked at him out of the corners of his eyes and said nothing. He looked like a frightened animal. I started to feel a little sorry for him until I remembered why they were questioning him. Then I thought, *Make him talk before it is too late!*

Suddenly someone shouted from the back of the house. One of the deputies was running through the vegetable garden carrying something above his head. I couldn't see it clearly, but it looked long and thin, like a bat. The deputy handed it to Carson. The sheriff looked at it carefully and then shook it in Koenig's face. Koenig cowered back, shaking his head and shouting something I couldn't make out. One of the deputies stepped forward and put handcuffs on the little man. He dragged him, still shouting, towards the sheriff's car and threw him roughly into the back seat.

Carson looked up at that moment and saw me looking out the window. He averted his eyes. Then he saw my father on the front steps and walked towards him still holding the mysterious object. He showed it to Father. I couldn't stand not knowing any longer. I opened the door.

The sheriff held the thing in his hands. It was an axe. Something dark had stained the handle and part of the blade.

"We found it lying right by his rocker on the back porch!" the sheriff was saying. He lowered his voice, sensing my presence. "We'll have to wait for the lab report, but that stain sure looks like blood to me!"

he sheriff drove off towards town with Koenig huddled in his back seat. The patrolman followed in his prowler. Most of the deputies began searching the house, their flashlight beams cautiously moving back towards the kitchen. I wondered if they would find the kind of things they'd found in Ed Gein's house. I especially wondered if Ellen—or parts of her—were in there. I watched them bring out boxes, but most were filled with the kind of magazines I had brought out of there. Nothing that looked like it could be made out of human body parts. Thank God!

The rest of the deputies milled around in the back and side yards. Some of them poked long poles with sharp metal prongs into the ground, apparently looking for soft spots indicating they had been recently dug up. When they found one, other deputies excavated it with shovels. They dug mostly in the vegetable patch, finding nothing but roots. I was a little sad to see Koenig's gardens being laid to waste. But I was mostly relieved they hadn't found her. Yet. My father also looked on at the search, pacing back and forth from window to window.

As soon as it began getting dark, the deputies packed up and left but not before sealing off the house and the front yard with strips of yellow tape. I let out a long sigh of relief when I saw them leave. They hadn't found her; there was still hope she might be alive.

About an hour later, the phone rang. My father hurried into the kitchen to get it. He listened quietly for several minutes, and then slammed the phone down.

"What is it, Father?" I asked.

"The axe tested positive for human blood," he said in a dead tone. "They'll have to send it to another lab to determine the type." I couldn't say anything. After a while, he added:,"Tomorrow morning, they're going to search the entire area from the bridge out to Lepke's woods for...Ellen. They'll use dogs. All the surrounding police jurisdictions will be there, along with the State Patrol. They're even going to use your old Boy Scout troupe in the search for whatever good that will do!"

I thought about Bobby and his friends scouring the countryside for Ellen's body, maybe even finding her. How obscene!

"Do you think that they'd let me search along with the Boy Scouts?" I asked

"Why would you want to join that bunch of thugs and hooligans?" he asked me.

"I can't just sit around here waiting! I have to be in on the search! I have to know what happened to her! Please, father, let me be part of it! They wouldn't even be looking for her if it weren't for me. Please! I couldn't stand for someone like Bobby Niebauer to find her!"

My father stared at me dubiously.

"Those people are not your friends. I've always suspected they had something to do with the attack in the alley! Are you sure you'd be all right?"

"Father, hundreds of cops will be there! I'll be fine!"

My father looked out the window as if staring at something a great distance away. Finally he spoke, "All right, if you're sure. I'll call Carson and find out if it's all right."

I went back up to my room sensing an awkwardness between us. An hour later, he shouted up to me that Carson had okayed it. We said nothing further that night, even when I came down for dinner. It struck me that this was how it would be in that house from now on. Dead silence.

That night I lay awake for a long time thinking about Koenig, and that filthy house, and the bloodstained axe, and that vision I had of Ellen's panicked face. After a while, I saw a familiar white flash in the corner of the room, over by the closet. Elena!

"Nooo!" I breathed. "No, Elena, not tonight!"

"What's the matter, little Teddy? Don't you want to play the Game?"

"No, I can't. Don't you know what's happened? Ellen's gone!"

"Oh, yes. I know. I am sorry, really. But why should that affect us?"

"I can't! I won't! Now get out of here!" I shouted.

"Well, if you can't, you can't! I won't force you!"

"Please understand, Elena. Let's do it another time. Can't we?"

She gave her sexy little laugh. "All right, little Teddy."

I jumped when I felt her cold fingers touch my arm. She laughed again.

"I will be with you tomorrow night instead. We'll have a good time then!"

In the morning I woke up shuddering, instantly aware that Ellen was missing. The sun was just starting to light the edges of the sky. I lay there for an hour thinking about Ellen and where she might be before the alarm went off.

I got up instantly and went down to breakfast. My father was cooking eggs. He said nothing, but the way he looked at me, and the way he'd gone out of his way to serve me an early breakfast, told me he was not angry at me. He just seemed overwhelmed. I thought I understood; as badly as he had treated Ellen, she was still his daughter. Maybe he even felt a little guilty.

He made me a bag lunch to take with me on the search. Just as I went out the door, he called my name.

"Yes, Father?"

He hesitated. His eyes were troubled and he struggled to say something. Finally, he spoke, "Good luck, Teddy!"

I nodded and went out. I was relieved to be out of that house. It was a lovely day for late fall. The sun was just above the trees and it was cool, with a wind coming off the river. Ordinarily I'd have enjoyed riding my bike on a day like that, but I felt tense and a little nauseous. I shouldn't have eaten, I thought.

I passed a lot of people, mostly on foot, heading towards the center of town. I was glad there were so many; they lessened the probability of an attack by Bobby and his friends. The staging area for the search was in the town square. When I got there, a big crowd had already gathered around the bandstand. Police from as far away as LaCrosse were there and I saw several state patrolmen in their broad hats. I parked my bike up by the library and walked down towards the bandstand. On my way, I saw several Boy Scouts clustered around a State Patrol van. Three big Dobermans were leaping at the bars of their cages at the back of the van trying to get at Bobby Niebauer who was teasing them with a stick. I was wishing the screen would tear so the dogs could eat Bobby, but no such luck. Finally, one of the patrolmen shooed Bobby off.

I noticed a car from the Lacrosse Tribune, the only daily newspaper in these parts. I saw a truck with the call letters of a Milwaukee TV station on it. I also noticed a man with what looked like a big movie camera on his shoulder, though I guessed it was for TV. He was following another man, in a suit and tie who kept shoving a microphone in the faces of some of the higher ranking cops. Most of the cops just shooed the man off, but I noticed Carson was giving the TV reporter a statement. This was probably the biggest story this town had ever produced and the media types were making the most of it. I guess I should have been angry that my sister's disappearance was being made into a circus. Instead, I was curious and a little excited.

The sheriff had a big grin on his face as he talked to

the reporter. But, the smile soon turned into an angry frown and he walked away. The reporter must have asked him about something he didn't want to talk about. I wondered if it was about the labor organizer. That had gotten a little play in the papers before Carson and the others hushed it up. It would be natural for the media to bring it up now that they were searching for another missing person.

I went up to the Sheriff. His smile reappeared, only to be replaced by another frown as if he remembered just then who I was.

"Hello, there, Teddy," he said, slurring his words slightly, "Listen, I'm sorry about your sister..." He stopped, obviously embarrassed. "What I mean is, I'm sorry she is missing. I'm sure we'll find her... That is, I'm sure she's okay!"

"Th-th-thank you," I said, quickly, more embarrassed than he was. But I was glad he was drunk. It meant he should be in a good mood. "My father said it was okay for me to tag along with your Boy Scout troop today."

"Why, sure it is," he said expansively. "You're always welcome in my troop. Matter of fact, I was never sure why you left!"

"I-I-I had a conflict in schedules," I said, and quickly walked away.

A crowd had gathered around the TV reporter, who was talking into the camera in front of the bandstand. I walked towards them.

"...only a year and a half after the same sheriff refused to order a manhunt for the missing labor organizer.

Authorities say this is the biggest manhunt in this town in just over twenty years. And in a strange coincidence, the last big search for a missing person in this town was for a girl from the very same..."

A sharp pain in my back distracted my attention from the reporter's words. I looked around and saw Bobby. He had his switchblade in my back, but the blade was not out.

"Nice to see you, faggot. We got you where we want you now. You can't run away this time."

"I-I d-d-don't know if you noticed but there are four hundred cops a-around here. I-I-I'm not worried."

"You should be worried, T-T-Teddy. The cops can't look everywhere at once. They'll be too busy looking for your sister!"

"Y-y-you shut up about my sister!"

"Why should I? Ellen and I had something really special. Maybe I know where she is. Maybe I put her someplace where they aren't going to find her. What do you think, Te-Te-Teddy?"

I wanted to kill him, but I couldn't. He had the strength; he had the weapon; he had the friends. Someday, perhaps, I'd be able to take revenge. For now, I wouldn't give him the satisfaction of seeing me cry. I turned and walked away. He didn't follow. Instead, he gathered the boys in the troop together. He soon had them in a semicircle around the bandstand. *He really can lead*, I thought grudgingly. But he won't lead me.

The sheriff was up on the bandstand, holding a bull horn and giving orders. He had a grim, businesslike expression, but you could tell he was enjoying himself

"Listen up, men!" he shouted. The horn gave out a shrill, feedback screech. He lowered the volume and began again. "In about five minutes, we will begin our search. As you know, a local girl, about fourteen years old, is missing, and we suspect foul play. We'll be looking for her corp...We'll be looking for her dead or alive!"

"We're going to go down to the river. Half of us will cross the bridge to search the other bank; the rest will remain on this side. Then, we're all going to turn east and search both sides of the river down to the girl's house which is about a mile and a half from here.

"Now the suspect lives next door to the girl's house. We've already searched the area around those houses. If we don't find anything by the time we get to his house, we'll go over into Lepke's Woods, over on Nuthouse... Seminary Road. Any questions so far?"

Some of the men shook their heads.

"Good! Now, as you know, our brother officers from all the neighboring communities have come here to help us. Of course, we want to thank them very much. The search and rescue team from the State Patrol is also here, with their canine unit. Also, our local Boy Scout troop is helping in the search.

"Now, I want to talk to you boys especially. We appreciate your help, but I want to impress on you...this isn't a game. Something terrible may have happened to a young girl all of you know. So this isn't a picnic and I don't want you to treat it as such. We're going to be looking for any clues as to what might have happened to her. So if you see anything suspicious, like a girl's clothing or blood stains, I want you to call me or one of my deputies.

"As for you law officers, I'm sure you've been briefed as to your responsibilities. But I'll go over the search plan again briefly to make sure everyone is on the same page. The state troopers will go first with their dogs, working both sides of the river. The rest of you men will cross the river and follow Seminary Road. Did I say that already? The Boy Scouts will be on that side, on your right flank... Is everyone clear on who will be doing what?"

There were a few yells of assent. The lawmen seemed tired of Carson's speech and anxious to begin the search. Someone yelled a question at him.

"No, there's no need to drag the river at this point."

I'll bet I know why you don't want to drag the river, I thought. *What if they found that union man?*

"Oh, one more thing," the sheriff said. A few groans rose from the assembled men. "Pipe down out there. This is important! If any one of you men finds her body... finds her, you're to fire one round into the air. If you find anything else significant, notify me or one of the state patrolmen. All right, let's get started. Everyone in their places."

We all formed a line along the south side of the square. The TV camera was down at one end of the line pointed in our direction. Most of the Boy Scouts leaned out of line to get in the picture. The sheriff immediately shouted, "Back in line!" The boys retreated.

I was excited in spite of myself. It was as if we were marching off to war; all the guns and uniforms, the dogs, the curious onlookers, even the TV cameras. I had to remind myself our objective was to find my sister's body.

I was at the very end of the line. I kept a few feet behind Bobbie's scouts. I didn't want to get too close to these people, but if I got too far behind, they might find her before I did.

"Okay, move out!" shouted the sheriff, and the line began to move down towards the river. When we reached the river, the troopers and their canine teams—who were in the lead—split up, each taking a side of the river. The other law officers crossed over the bridge as did the Scouts. Then we wheeled left, parallel to Seminary Road. I admired the military precision of the maneuver; it reminded me of diagrams I'd seen in books about the Civil War. The sight of the dogs sniffing the bushes by the river brought me back to reality. The patrolmen had asked Father for an item of Ellen's clothing to give the dogs her scent. Here we were looking for her body, and I was playing war games in my mind!

As we boys marched over the uneven ground sloping down from the road to the river, our line became ragged. We began to fall behind the men. We were scanning the bushes and weeds for "clues" but were not sure what a clue would look like. I became more and more bored and frustrated. Surely if she were this close to the road, she would already have been found. The important search was taking place in the thickets along the banks of the river and everyone probably knew it. So we walked along, picking through dirty rags, newspapers, and other trash, and wishing we could be with the patrolmen. We were constantly being stung by horseflies and picking nettles out of our pants. The day was unusually hot for late fall. The excitement we had felt at first was soon gone

To pass the time, some of the Scouts began telling "Geiners."

"What did Ed Gein say to the cops when they came to arrest him?"

"Aw, come on, fellas! Have a heart!"

"Why doesn't anyone want to play poker with Ed Gein?"

"Because he always comes up with a hand!"

One of the kids said he'd heard Ed Gein had escaped from Waupun.

"Bullshit!" said Bobby. "That would have been all over the papers and TV!"

"You don't know. They might not be telling us 'cause they don't want us to panic!" said the other kid

"You're so full of shit your eyes are brown!" Bobby said. The kid shut up and no one said anything for a while

Another boy said he had heard Old Man Koenig had already been arrested.

"Aw, they just got him for having some dirty pictures," said Billy Carson, the Sheriff's son.

"I heard those magazines showed kids having sex with grownups!" a boy said.

"That's right!" said Billy. "I saw the magazines!"

This was greeted with snickers.

"I bet you jacked off all over them!" a boy called out.

Billy flushed red.

"I didn't!" he cried, but the laughter increased.

"I know why they haven't arrested him for murder yet," said Bobby, and the laughter ceased. "Because they haven't found her body! They have to have a corpse to make an arrest."

An embarrassed silence followed. I had turned away when Billy started talking, but I felt their eyes on me. I slowed my steps hoping to get out of earshot. When I looked up again, I was twenty feet behind them. I speeded up again; I didn't want to lose contact in case they found anything

The sun was rising and I was feeling hotter and hotter. It looked like another Indian Summer day. I wished I'd brought a canteen like most of the other boys. My legs were getting tired from walking over uneven ground and my throat was bone dry. I considered asking one of the nicer kids, like Billy Carson, for a drink but then I thought, *The hell with them. I'll tough it out.*

I drew some comfort from the fact we hadn't found anything yet. We were already parallel with the school which towered over us on the right. I saw the chimneys of the asylum not far ahead. We were almost halfway to my house.

The boys were talking about Ellen's disappearance, and in spite of myself, I listened in.

"You know," said Billy Carson, "maybe she isn't dead. A lot of times these sex fiends don't kill their victims. She could just be hurt somewhere and unconscious."

Yes! I thought. That's possible. I felt grateful to Billy for giving me hope. Maybe she is out here somewhere, hurt, unable to walk or even cry out. Unconscious, maybe, but alive! Maybe we will find her in time! *Please, God*, I thought, *let it be like that!* Then I remembered I didn't believe in God. And I remembered the stain on the axe.

A boy said, "I heard that down in Mexico they still sacrifice virgins just like the Aztecs did!"

"How can they tell if they're virgins?" another boy said. Everyone laughed at his naïveté

"I bet you're a virgin!" someone called out, to general laughter

"Am not!" the boy said

"Sure you are!" said Bobby. "Otherwise you would know that virgins have a hymen in their pussy. Like a strip of flesh. And when that gets broken, they're not a virgin anymore! But I'll tell you what. I'm not so sure Ellen was a virgin!"

There was embarrassed laughter again. I could feel their eyes on me. *I'll kill him*, I thought. *I have to kill him.* I felt a pressure in back of my eyes. *I won't cry*, I thought. *He won't make me cry.*

"How would you know?" said Billy Carson

"Never mind. I just know. You really think a girl with tits like that could stay a virgin?"

Some kids laughed but most didn't. I felt a tremendous pressure building up behind my eyes and in my throat. Suddenly, I wheeled on them and screamed as loudly as I could, "Shut up! Shut up! For God's sake, just shut up!"

I turned and walked away from them. There were a few snickers, but amazingly they shut up for a long time—even Bobby. Then I heard someone walking up behind me. I clenched my fists, ready to try to kill him if he said one wrong word.

"I'm sorry!" the voice said. I recognized the voice as Billy Carson's. I mumbled something, and he walked back to the others. I felt tears running down my cheeks. All their cruelty hadn't been enough to make me cry, but one word of kindness had opened the floodgates. I wiped my eyes, hoping none of them had seen

After a while, the tears stopped. When I looked up, the boys were almost out of sight up ahead and I had to hurry to catch up to them. The sun was almost overhead. Looking down the road, I made out the roof of my house. We were more than halfway now. I heard the sheriff over his bull horn telling everyone it was time to break for lunch. He was over in his prowl car, resting while the rest of us were sweating! But I was glad it was lunch time. I was tired

I took my bag lunch out of my knapsack and went off under a tree away from the others. I'd thought I might not be able to eat but I found that all the walking had made me really hungry. I devoured the baloney sandwich and the apple with enjoyment. I was beginning to feel optimistic. Probably, this was a wild goose chase and we would find nothing. I had been developing my own theory about Ellen's disappearance, and the longer we went without finding anything, the more probable the theory seemed.

Suppose Ellen had intended to say something like this in her letter:

"Dear Edward. I'm afraid of Father and I can't live

like this any more. I have gone to live with Grandfather for a while."

The more I thought about this scenario, the more likely it seemed. She'd always loved Grandpa Waller, and he loved her back. On this last trip to Milwaukee, she must have come within a few miles of his house. It was natural that she would think of his house as a safe haven from our father. She might even have asked Grandpa not to tell my father, at least for a while, which would explain why we hadn't heard from him.

But the theory had its flaws. How could a girl her age get to Milwaukee from here? She had no money of her own. Perhaps she could have taken some money from Father without his knowing it? But he surely would have discovered the theft by now. And would Grandpa really have kept her whereabouts a secret, when he must have known we would all fear the worst? But maybe she hadn't reached Grandpa's yet. Maybe she was out on the road, hitchhiking. Yes! She had once talked about how much fun that might be! I told her only bums hitchhiked and a girl like her could get hurt if she tried something like that. But she just laughed at me

That was it! She was off hitchhiking somewhere! I should tell the sheriff right now so he could stop all this foolishness and start looking for her on the roads! But it wasn't likely he'd stop this major operation on my word alone. If the search turned up nothing, then he might be willing to listen. It made me nervous to wait: knowing all the time she might be getting picked up by one of Ed Gein's cousins or something. But I really had no choice.

When we got to my house, I would tell Father what I suspected. Carson might listen to him.

I heard the sheriff on the bullhorn again, telling everyone to move out. I saw my house clearly now, maybe a block ahead; it wouldn't be long until we got there. The Scouts desultorily drifted into line and the law officers were not much faster. Everyone seemed tired of the search and skeptical about finding anything. *Good*, I thought, *the sooner this is over, the sooner the real search can begin.*

Then, just a few minutes later, I heard a shot.

As if in slow motion, the birds lifted out of the trees by the river. The echoes of the shot were soon drowned out by the roaring in my ears. A darkness came over the sun, my own darkness. Out of the corner of my eye I saw Bobby and his friends running towards the river bank. I shook my head, fighting off the dark fit. *I can't let those bastards get to her first!* I thought, and began running towards the river. But the boys had too much of a head start. I'd never catch them before they got to the bank. I felt a terrible pounding in my head.

Another shot! It came from further down the river, towards my house. I felt a wild moment of hope. Two shots! That must mean something else! She can't be in two places at once!

At last, I reached the spot on the river bank where the first shot had come from. Bobby and two friends were looking on in silence while two state patrolmen tried to get something away from one of their dogs. They screamed angrily at the dog to drop it. The dog finally did so, wagging his tail. One of the patrolmen patted the dog on the head. Good boy.

The trooper reached down and gingerly picked up the object. As soon as I saw it, I began retching my lunch into the bushes, as if I could vomit out the sight. But I knew I would never be rid of those haunted eyes and those slobber-stained cheeks. Somewhere, at a great distance, I heard Bobby's quavering, horror-filled voice.

"My God, that's her head!"

13

I was at the bottom of a deep river. Far above me, light shone through the surface of the water. Had I fallen in? But this river was far deeper than the one which flowed past our town. Where was I? It didn't matter. I had to get to the top before my air ran out! I tried to swim, but my body was encased in something thick and viscous, like wet concrete. I ascended but with agonizing slowness. I told myself, *Just hold on a little longer!* At last I was close to the shining surface. I reached my left hand up towards it. Something grabbed the arm. It was biting me, hurting me!

I came awake screaming, trying to free my arm. A man in a doctor's white coat was struggling to hold it down. Someone else in a blue uniform grabbed me by the right arm.

"Hold him down!" said the doctor.

I recognized my father's voice.

"Ellen!" I screamed. It all came back to me—the axe, the search, the slimed head—all frozen together in a tableau.

"Hush, Teddy!" Father said. "It's going to be all right!"

"That's a lie!" I said. "It will never be all right again."

My father sighed and said, "I'm going to give you something to make you feel better."

Suddenly exhausted, I relaxed and stopped fighting.

"All right!" I said quietly. I hoped what he gave me would make me die.

I felt a pin prick in my left arm. It did not even distract me from the rush of horrible images which overwhelmed my mind. But gradually, wonderfully, I began to drift above all the images, and the boy who was seeing them. I saw him twisting and writhing as they put him on a stretcher and loaded him into an ambulance. I watched the expressions on his tortured face with great interest. *He seems to be undergoing a psychotic break*, I observed with clinical detachment. I observed the boy's father get into the ambulance which then drove towards the center of the town, leaving me behind. I noticed that there were still lots of police and troopers gathered around where the body had been discovered. I noted a man taking pictures of the site. I saw what looked like a body under a tarpaulin. When I saw the body, I began to slip downward. *No*, I thought. *I don't want to go there!* I could feel the detachment slipping away to be replaced by panic. I heard myself scream and then the darkness closed over me.

When I woke up again, I was in a hospital bed. I tried to get up, but soon realized I was in restraints. A call button lay within reach of my hand and I pressed it. A few minutes later, a nurse appeared. I saw pity and curiosity on her face. *I guess I'll be getting a lot of that*, I thought.

"Hello, Teddy. How are you?" the nurse said with a professional smile.

I couldn't tell which irritated me more, the stupid question or her calling me Teddy. I'd never seen her before and never wanted to see her again. I just wanted to be home, in my room, away from everyone.

"Puh-puh-please can I s-s-s-see my father?"

"Your father isn't here right now, but I'll let him know you asked for him when he comes back here in the morning. He'll be so happy to see you're all better!"

"I-I want him now. P-please! I cuh-can't spend a whole night like this!" I shook my restraints for emphasis.

"We just don't want you to hurt yourself, Teddy."

The syrupy sweetness in her voice made me want to vomit. I'd rather have had Bobby there sneering at me. At least he wasn't a hypocrite!

"Puh-puh-please!" I screamed, shaking the restraints so hard it seemed they'd have to give way

"All right!" she said, her smile giving way to a frown. "I'll call him!" She strode away, obviously irritated. I liked her better already.

About half an hour later my father walked into the room. His face was grim and he would not meet my eyes.

"What is this all about?" he asked.

"What's it about? They've got me trussed up like a turkey here! Please, Father, tell them to let me go!"

"Teddy, I gave the order for the restraints!"

"Why, Father?"

"Because I was afraid you would hurt yourself. You were hysterical in the ambulance."

I remembered seeing myself being put in the ambulance. *Yes*, I thought, *I did look pretty bad*.

"I know, Father, but I wasn't myself then. I'm better now, really."

He looked into my eyes.

"Really?"

"Please, Father!"

"If I let you go, will you promise not to hurt yourself?"

"Of course! But please, can't we go home? I can't stand being here! Not tonight! I feel so sad, so lonely here!"

"Well, I suppose so. But you have to promise to take some medicine I'm going to give you. It will calm you down."

"Of course."

He leaned down and loosened my restraints. I let out a deep breath I hadn't known I was holding. I was free!

In a few minutes he had my release papers signed and we left the hospital. I saw several of the staff watching me with the same expression the nurse had: the one you see on onlookers at a bloody traffic accident. I was glad I was leaving them behind. If my plans worked out, I wouldn't be seeing them ever again.

We drove in dead silence. When we got home, my father gave me two white pills and had me swallow them with a glass of milk. In a few minutes, I began to feel some of that blissful detachment the shot had given me. *Good*, I thought. *It will make what I have to do that much easier.*

I said goodbye to my father at the foot of the stairs. I could feel his eyes on me all the way into my room. I listened until I heard him walk into his room. Then, I locked my front door and the one to Ellen's room.

I wasn't floating above myself as I had when I got the shot, but I observed my activities with the same clinical interest. Now he glances at the huge holes dug in Koenig's yard, apparently with a back hoe which was now parked in the rear of the house. Now he pulls down the shades. Now he lifts up his mattress looking for something. Yes, he has it. Something sharp and gleaming—the scalpel he'd stolen from his father's medical bag when he last considered suicide. He tests the edge by rubbing his finger along the edge. He draws blood. He sucks his finger. He takes the scalpel into the bathroom. Now he is running cold water on his finger. He looks at the finger and shakes his head. Now he turns on the warm water. He rolls up his left sleeve and folds it back. He takes the scalpel in his right hand and takes one last look in the mirror and sees Ellen's face!

I was jerked back into myself. I dropped the scalpel and stared at her. Her eyes were wide with horror. And then the lips moved.

"Help us, Teddy!" the lips said. "I'm afraid!" I recognized Ellen's voice, though it seemed to come from a long way off.

I felt my eyes bulging. My throat was constricted and I couldn't talk.

"Only you can help us!" she said, in a distant but urgent tone. "If you don't, we will belong to him forever!"

"I don't understand!" I said in a strangled voice.

"You're dead! You don't need to be afraid of anything ever again."

"You're the one who doesn't understand. You think when you're dead, the fear ends. But that's when it really begins!"

I looked down at the scalpel lying on the floor. I felt ashamed. She still needed me! I'd let her down once by failing to protect her. Now, I'd been about to betray her again

"What can I do? I want to help you. I will help you! Tell me how!"

"Find him. Stop him. If you don't, he'll come for us when he dies and we will be his, forever."

Her image began to fade to be replaced, point by point, with my own features

"Wait!" I screamed. "Don't go! Who is he? And who is 'we'? I don't understand!" But she was gone from the mirror, from the world. I couldn't feel her presence anywhere.

I put my hand down on the sink to steady myself. I was dizzy and nauseous. After a moment, the wave of sickness passed and I felt better. I reached down and picked up the scalpel. I felt again that sense of shame. *Don't worry, Ellen*, I said into the void, *I won't let you down again.*

I walked down the hallway and into my room. I put the scalpel under my mattress again until I had a chance to put it back in my father's bag. I sat down on the bed and put my head in my hands. I'd promised to help her but I had no idea how. But it wasn't my fault! Why couldn't she tell me straight out who her killer was? Why did she have to talk like the Oracle at Delphi? Or was that one of the rules for communicating with those on the Other Side; that they could only talk in riddles and couldn't say what was on their minds? If so, it was a stupid rule no matter who made it!

"On the other hand," Sherlock Holmes said, "you always wanted a murder mystery and now you've got one! You've even got a few statements from the murder victim herself which is more than I ever had. Now let's see what we can make of them.

"'Help us!' That implies more than one victim. That would make sense if Koenig was a mass murderer, like Ed Gein. On the other hand, if Koenig was the killer, why would she need your help? The authorities already have him. So that implies that Koenig is not the killer. Which does not surprise me in the least.

"For one thing, Keonig never used violence before against his sexual victims. He always attempted to lure them into his web. We'll leave aside his more or less justified attempt to kill you for the moment."

This cavalier treatment of my near demise irritated me, but I said nothing.

"Also, the case file showed that his previous victims had been much younger than Ellen. Your sister was very well developed for her age. He could never have mistaken her for a child. I also doubt that what he yelled at you after you escaped from his house proves anything at all. Would he really have referred to Ellen as a little girl? More likely, his alcohol-soaked mind had regressed to the time when he'd been arrested for molesting a little girl. I believe that it had nothing to do with Ellen!

"Finally, where did that axe come from? You came within three feet of Koenig on his back porch and you didn't see it. And you were on the lookout for a weapon. Also, if the axe had been right by him, why did he not just come at you with that? Instead, he had to search through that dark, cluttered kitchen for a knife."

"So the axe was planted?"

"I have no doubt of it. This throws suspicion on Sheriff Carson since it was one of his men who 'found' it."

"He is a logical suspect anyway. He hates me, and my father, and he's had his eyes on Ellen for a while. He's certainly capable of violence and deceit. I strongly suspect he had a hand in the "disappearance" of the labor organizer. I doubted his men would risk something like that without a nod from him," I said.

"Yes, but you have not provided a strong personal motive for his killing of Ellen. And wasn't Ellen afraid of him? Would she really follow him into the night?"

"No, I don't think so. But there is one person she might have gone to meet. Bobby Niebauer! Her troubles with Father might have driven her to him. He is crazy and evil enough to commit this crime…and he hated me and my family."

"Once again you are letting your personal animus towards this young man cloud your reasoning powers. What was his motivation for killing her? I find a general dislike for you and your family a poor motive for murder. Also, how could he have planted the axe? How did he gain entrance to your house or, how did your sister leave the house to meet him? Finally, his surprise when you told him Ellen was gone and his horror when he saw her head seemed genuine."

"But aren't some psychopathic killers natural born actors?"

"You are on the wrong trail. We must follow the evidence wherever it leads us, not distort it to cover your personal enemies."

"What do you mean?"

"Well, for example, what about your father? They had argued violently recently and he had in fact struck her. She might well have left her room at his command. And the letter you found might well have been addressed to him. His name is Edward as much as yours is."

"But how could he have planted the axe? I was watching the front of Koenig's house during the only period when he could have planted it and I would have heard him if he'd used a ladder or vaulted over Koenig's fence."

"Yes, that is a valid point" Holmes admitted. "However, you are missing the point. You are making the worst mistake of the amateur detective: theorizing without data. The fact is, you don't have enough evidence to include or eliminate anyone as a suspect."

Holmes was right. Not only did I not have any evidence, I had no idea where to look for evidence. The more questions I asked, the more arose and I couldn't answer even one. But there was one person who seemed to know everything. She had said that it would all start on the night Ellen was killed. She had known beforehand! And she had to know who the murderer was and how he had done it.

She must know also what Ellen was talking about when she said that, unless I caught the killer, she and the other victims would be under his power when he died. The whole idea was insane! Except...

I had read that some psychotic killers who had killed women, believed that, after their own deaths, their victims would be their slaves forever. And now Ellen was telling me this psychotic delusion was the literal truth! This seemed bizarre, even a little blasphemous. Why would God allow innocent victims to be trapped and tormented eternally by their killers? But it was hypocritical to invoke God I'd never believed in. Perhaps the world of the spirits was as insane and chaotic as ours, and the weak souls were at the mercy of the strong. It was that way in this world: why not in the next?

I thought of Old Man Washburn looming over his victims in the window of his farmhouse. He'd said after he'd killed them, "They'll mind me now!" I remembered his hand, beckoning to me. Why? Was I to be one of his victims, or was he inviting me to see his slaves? And why had Elena's voice led me to Washburn's farm? Did she wish to show me something about the spirit world? Was there some connection between Ellen and Elena? My mind was going round and round, hitting the same points over and over.

A sudden thought hit me. Old Man Washburn had not only been arrested for his family's murder: he'd been hanged. Why would bringing Ellen's killer to justice release her spirit any more than it had released Washburn's victims? I shrugged off my doubts. Ellen had told me it would save her, and Ellen had never lied to me! But the point was that Elena knew about Old Man Washburn and she must know about Ellen's killer too... No longer would I be satisfied with Delphic statements. I would get the truth from her. Once I knew what had happened, I could figure out how to prove it.

I lay in my bed all the rest of that day, thinking about how I could force Elena to tell me the truth. I was distracted only by the sounds of digging from next door. They were excavating the back and side yards, including all the vegetables. That seemed a shame after the work Koenig had put in on his garden. *But what if his land was so fertile because there were dead bodies buried there?* I quickly dismissed the thought. Koenig was not the killer. Ellen had all but told me so. But how could I convince the police of that?

There were dozens of uniformed cops, state patrolmen, and men in civilian clothes swarming around the house. Men were still probing the yard with long metal rods and calling in the backhoe when they found a soft spot. I could see bright lights shining through the dirty windows of the house. Periodically, they brought out more boxes of material from inside. Probably, they were looking for corpses or body parts in there too. In Keonig's front yard stood the same TV camera I saw at the start of the search. The same TV reporter was there, talking into the microphone. I could imagine what he was saying: Could this man be another Ed Gein? *You're famous, Ellen*, I thought. *Soon they'll know about you and our peaceful little town even in places like New York or Chicago where murders are commonplace.*

I felt like running down there and screaming into the microphone: They have the wrong man! They're looking in the wrong place! But they'd ask for evidence, and what could I give them? A cryptic letter? A vision from the dead? A ragbag of deductions and suppositions? They'd laugh at me. They had their killer: a certifiable madman and pervert, and they had the murder weapon found at his house. Why should they look any further?

Now the TV camera had moved in front of our house! Yes, we were famous too. I felt like going down to my father's workshop, grabbing one of his axes, and driving them away. Leave us alone! But I knew I could never do it. The phone rang every few minutes and I listened in on my father's side of the conversation. Several times, I heard him say, "No, I have no statement to make. Please don't bother us in this time of grief!"

That felt good. He could always say the things I couldn't. He also had several calls about funeral arrangements: from the funeral home, from the florist, from relatives who would be coming in. I heard him talking to my grandfather. I almost ran downstairs and asked to talk to him, but I heard Father say, "No, he is under sedation now. You can talk to him when you come to the funeral!"

It hurt not to be able to speak to Grandpa and to be treated like an invalid. It was also hard to hear him talk so matter-of-factly about the funeral arrangements for someone who meant almost everything to me. I felt like the whole world had died and he was calmly arranging for its disposal.

As the day drew on, the pace of the digging next door slowed, and finally stopped. The backhoe drove off, and soon, so did the rest of the searchers. They left only the yellow evidence tape, strung across the front door and between the edge of his porch and our fence. The TV people had gone long ago. I supposed I could see them on the six o'clock news from LaCrosse, but I had no desire to do so. Nor would I read any of the newspapers. They didn't know her like I did. No one did, not even my father. Only I really loved her, and I'd let her down.

But still, I was curious about what the cops had found at Koenig's. I asked my father about it when we sat down to dinner.

"Yes, Teddy. They found your sister's locket. He had hidden it under the stairs," he said.

I gave a little laugh. *What an obvious plant!* I thought. Who would hide anything in a place so easily accessible? My father looked at me curiously but said nothing. We were both silent after that until I got up from the table.

"Teddy," Father said, "how are you feeling?"

"I'm okay." I said. "As well as can be expected."

"Do you want another sedative to help you sleep?"

I shook my head

"To tell you the truth, Father, the last one made me a little sick."

"All right," he said. "Good night, Teddy."

"Good night, Father."

He looked at me as if to ask what he should say or do. But there was nothing more to say, and he'd never been one to hug or kiss his children, so there was nothing more to do, either.

I went upstairs. I was glad he was letting me alone. I didn't want to talk to anyone or to think about anything except catching the killer. I had figured out how I might get the information I needed from Elena. Force wouldn't work, but pleading just might.

I lay in bed and clasped my hands together as if in prayer. *Please, Elena*, I thought, *please show me his face. Help me to catch him!* But there was no reply. *Perhaps, this isn't the kind of prayer she wants*, I thought. I cupped my hand around my organ as I had done before she first appeared and again invoked her name. Again I asked her to show me his face, or at least how it was done. Again, there was no reply.

But something about the room had changed. Bright moonlight illuminated the room. I'd have sworn just a minute ago that the sky had been dark. The night before last had been like this; moonlight bright enough to read by. I got up and looked out. Koenig's yard was lit up as if by a spotlight. But there were no holes in the yard, no dug up vegetables, no yellow tape! What was going on?

A sound rose from somewhere downstairs. It was somehow familiar—a metallic whir and whine. Yes! I'd heard it the night Ellen was murdered! The sound slowed and stopped. Somewhere below a door creaked open. A few moments later, I heard a low soft step on the stairs.

He was coming up! It was the killer. I knew it was. And tonight was, somehow, that night! I had been transported backwards in time and I could stop him! I could keep the murder from happening!

I rushed towards Ellen's door and put my hand on the knob. That was when I realized I had no hands. I was invisible and couldn't affect anything in this world. I tried to scream, to warn Ellen. But I had no voice either. I was only a pair of floating eyes, doomed to watch what was about to happen without being able to stop it or even close my eyes.

There was a soft, scraping knock on Ellen's door. I heard the door open. There was a whispered exchange and then I heard her door close. I heard them both going down the stairs. I stared helplessly at the closed door to my room. I couldn't even follow them.

Suddenly, I was moving towards the window. It was open as it never was at night except on the hottest summer nights. I was sure it hadn't been open that night. No matter, I was moving out through the window. I tried to grab the sill, but of course I couldn't. I had a moment of vertigo looking down ten feet at the fence below. I glanced over at Koenig's house. It was dark and silent.

I was moving towards our back yard. I was just above the kitchen door when they came out. She was dressed in the white cotton nightgown they found her in. He had on some kind of dark robe with a hood on it. I could not see the man's face. He seemed a little taller than Ellen, about my size in fact. He walked in front of her carrying a large metal flashlight which he shone ahead as he walked. She moved like a sleepwalker, slowly, occasionally stumbling.

Go back, Ellen! Run! Scream. Don't go like a stupid cow to the slaughter! I tried to shout these things, but no sound came out. Still she followed him, out into the yard and towards the back fence. *Where are they going?* I thought. *There's no gate back there!* But he continued until he came to the part of the fence between two thick shrubs. He reached over it and did something with his hand, and part of the fence swung out into the open field beyond.

That's impossible, I thought. *I have lived here fifteen years and have never seen a gate there!* But they walked out into the field. The grass and weeds were as high as her head in places, but someone had hacked out a kind of trail there, and they followed it towards the creek. I was still floating above them. I tried to speed up so I could see the killer's face, but I had no control over my motion.

Ellen stopped to pick a burr out of her nightgown. He reached back and grabbed her arm, then pushed her in front of him. She stumbled again and began to half-run towards the river. She looked back at him and I saw the fear in her eyes.

Dear Edward, I'm afraid.

Now they were moving down the hill towards the river. Looking back, I could see our house and the asylum looming above it. *Surely someone up there can see*, I thought. But the building was as dark as the rest of the neighborhood.

Now they'd moved out of the grass and into the

woods by the river. The country was beginning to look all too familiar; I'd seen it on the search.

Run, Ellen, you're not there yet! It isn't too late! I thought these things, but had no mouth to say them. She moved on, slowly now, occasionally looking back at him. She said something I couldn't hear. His face was still hidden so I couldn't see if he'd replied. They were in the woods now, close to the river bank. She paused for a moment and he shoved her roughly. Then she was running, but in the wrong direction, down towards the river.

No! Go towards the house! He was close behind her, running hard, his robe flapping open. I could see her screaming now, but I heard nothing.

She was down! I could see the root she had tripped over. She tried to get up, but he pushed her down. Now she was moving crabwise on her back; one hand raised as if to avoid a blow. Something dark and heavy came down on her head. The flashlight! Pieces of the lens flew off on impact and landed on the ground. Now she was pleading, but I still heard nothing. I was glad; it would break my heart. How could he hear her and not be moved?

He stood there as if listening. Then, he reached inside his robe. He brought something out, something long and thin that glinted in the moonlight.

Get up, Ellen. He has the axe!

And she was getting up, slowly, as if she'd heard me. Groping her way in the moonlight, the wrong way, towards the river! He walked slowly towards her, holding the flashlight in his left hand. He had the axe in his other hand, but behind his back so she couldn't see it. She hesitated and then moved towards the light. The broken lens made jagged patterns on her face. Her eyes shone the way a deer's eyes shine when it's caught in the headlights. She probably didn't see when he raised the axe above his head.

Then, down! The black and white of the dream was lit up by a brilliant gout of red. Again! The blood burst out, smoking in the cool night air. Smoking! And absurdly, I thought, *Shakespeare was right; blood does smoke when it comes out!* The blood-colored the leaves, the ground, the front of his robe. Again! Again! And suddenly her head was rolling free, the face appearing and disappearing like a Jack in the Box. Her body collapsed back on the ground, twitching like a live wire.

Now the killer picked the head up by the hair and hurled it down towards the river bank. And then, he leaned over the body, which was still twitching slightly, the blood spurting from the severed neck. What was he doing? *Oh, no, you can't. You must not!*

He kneeled down over her, covering her. Then he unfastened the front of his robe. I could not turn away. Wake up! But I couldn't. I had to watch as he tore open her nightgown. No! Now he took something off her neck. Her locket, the one her grandmother gave her. He thrust it into the pocket of his robe. Now he began to move, up and down, spasmodically, as if his head had been cut off too. Faster and faster and faster he moved over her, more and more rhythmically until–

"No!"

And I was awake again, my hands still wrapped

around my organ, and something viscous and hot, like blood, was running down my thighs

"No!" I screamed again, and the room rang with the echo. "No, no," I said to myself, this time quietly, hopelessly. And still the foul thing between my legs leaped and spurted like a headless corpse. No.

It was then I really wept for the first time since they found Ellen. I wept and wept, the clean tears mingling with the foul stuff running down my legs. "I'm so sorry, Ellen," I said, over and over. So sorry.

There was a knock on the door.

"Teddy, are you all right?" my father asked.

"Sure. I...I'm okay," I said, but the quaver in my voice said something else. After a minute, my father moved away. I heard him walking down the stairs. In a few minutes, I got up and walked quietly down to the bathroom. I washed my stomach and thighs and genitals for at least half an hour. Every time I felt as if I were clean, I'd feel the gelid substance somewhere else. *Yet here's a spot*

I noticed some kind of hard lump in my bathrobe pressing against my leg. I reached in and pulled out a locket. The same locket I had just seen the killer rip off Ellen's neck. I dropped it in horror. At that moment, I was sure of the meaning of the dream. I was the one I was seeking. I had killed Ellen!

14

I awoke to bright sunlight. It was morning and a long day lay before us. Perhaps Ellen and I would go to our secret spot in the woods or down by the river if it was not too cold. It was nice down there especially in the morning when you could watch the mist rise up from the water... The river! I saw her head in the patrolman's hand. She was dead, and I had killed her!

The dream and its aftermath came back in a rush of shame and horror. How could I have felt such things, desired such things? I was a monster, a murderer! I'd be better off dead! I reached in under my mattress and brought out the scalpel. I had to do it, now! I couldn't bear this shame! I was a freak, a cosmic mistake, and the sooner I corrected that error, the better. Before I killed someone else!

I stared at the knife. It glinted in the sunlight and I flinched and almost dropped it. I hated sharp objects and I had good reason; I had been cut three times recently. I thought how the axe made me shudder when I first saw it in the deputy's hand. How could I have used it when I could barely stand to look at it? I hesitated. Maybe I was not guilty after all.

But the locket! I must be the killer, because he was the one who took it off her. I reached in the pocket of my robe. Nothing. Then I remembered my father telling me that the locket had been found under Keonig's back stairs. I *could not* have had it last night. So maybe I wasn't the killer after all.

This led me back to the dream. I didn't want to think about it, but I had to, because the key to Ellen's murder might lie there. Either the dream came from Elena or from my own subconscious. If from my subconscious, then I was probably the murderer. If it came from Elena, then she may have given me clues to the killer's identity, as well as to how the murder happened. But why these constant games? Why didn't she show me the face of the killer? Was she forbidden, by someone or something, to speak directly? Or maybe, she just liked playing games— the nastier the better.

I had no answers. But, if the dream was from Elena, and if she'd shown me the truth, I did have some clues. I knew the killer had knocked on Ellen's door, and she'd gone with him immediately as if by some plan. They'd gone out a gate in the back fence, which I had never found in fifteen years of living there. He was about my size and carried a metal flashlight. He had hit her with the flashlight and shattered the lens close to the murder site. And he had raped her after he had cut off her head. Some of these things could be verified. I could find the gate if it was there. I could probably find the shards from the broken lens. And the police must know if she'd been sexually violated. I could at least verify if the dream were true, or a lie.

And that was even more important if the dream came from my subconscious. If it had been just a sick fantasy, then I was just a pervert, not a killer! But if the dream was a true one, then it was based on my memory. I'd been the one who led her down there, killed her, and then raped her. I had to know the truth. If I was the killer, I would take the scalpel and correct the cosmic error that was me. That way, I'd spare the state the expense of a trial.

But how I could have killed her and not known it? I could have done it in a trance. I had been in a trance that lasted almost all that night. She'd have responded to my knock and might well have followed me down to the river. The figure in the dream had been my size.

But there were problems with myself as a suspect. For one thing, when I awakened that night, I heard the sound of whirring downstairs, and in the dream, the man had come up the stairs, shortly thereafter. Unlike Ellen's body, I couldn't have been in two places at once. Also, I didn't have a robe like the one in the dream, or a flashlight like that either. I'd not consciously known about any gate in the fence. And that was not all. When would I have had time or opportunity to plant the axe or the necklace? I had been in Koenig's house, true, but I was quite sure I had no axe when I went over that fence. And I was sure I never went near the steps.

But then the shame of the dream came back and with

it, the certainty I was the killer. Only a monster could have a dream like that!

"Teddy, it's time to get up."

It was my father's voice, unexpectedly gentle and with a tinge of sadness. His tone made me all the more reluctant to face him. If only he knew what a psychotic he had for a son! And he would find out. I could never hide anything from him. Never! I was suddenly tired of this whole melodrama. If only I had the courage to use the scalpel and put an end to it. If only I hadn't made that stupid promise to my dead sister! "I'll find the murderer!" I told her. That's easy enough. I'll just look in a mirror!

"Teddy?"

"All right, Father, I'm coming down."

He was waiting for me at the bottom of the stairs, his gray eyes scanning me carefully. I avoided his eyes. I walked over to the breakfast table and poured my cereal.

"I already cooked some sausages and eggs," my father said. "Don't you want any?"

"I'm not hungry," I said. I had my head down to avoid his gaze

"Teddy, look at me!" he said, with a familiar voice of command.

I looked up and directly into his eyes. They seemed to see into my heart.

"Did you sleep well?" he asked.

I nodded, but he shook his head.

"I heard you screaming last night. Your eyes have black rings around them and you can barely keep them open. Did you have bad dreams?

I hesitated for a moment and then nodded. I'd given up any hope of completely fooling him. I only hoped he wouldn't make me relive that nightmare.

"About her? About Ellen?"

Again I nodded. My father got up and walked to the window. I could see a row of stained glass red crosses on the top of the window glowing over his head. I was thankful he'd turned his back on me and couldn't see my face.

"When someone we love dies," he said, "we have many painful feelings. The things we're supposed to feel, sorrow, pity, a sense of loss, are difficult enough to deal with but other darker feelings, which we can't acknowledge, freeze this process of mourning, so it can last a lifetime. These feelings come out in our dreams"

He turned to look at me again.

"One of these feelings is betrayal. How dare she die and leave me alone! Of course, this feeling isn't rational, but whoever said feelings should be rational? When my sister died, I felt a tremendous sense of betrayal. I knew she didn't want to die. But we have inside us a totally selfish, irrational beast who knows only what it wants. It doesn't really believe anyone else exists. Don't be ashamed of this beast, Teddy. Deep down inside, that is who we all are.

I was silent. He hadn't yet put his finger on my guilt but I could feel, almost see this beast inside me. This thing had lusted after my sister, even as she was dying, even after she was dead. Could my father, too, have such a beast inside him?

"Teddy, even darker thoughts, even more hidden longings lie inside every one who mourns. Negative thoughts towards the dead person, anger, even hatred. Hatred is the shadow of love and it always lies behind love, as the Devil lies behind God. And because we had these feelings towards the lost one, we imagine we somehow brought about her death. We may even identify with the murderer. We think: After all, didn't I want her dead? Perhaps my wish killed her!"

He sighed deeply.

"But we're not magicians, Teddy, and our wishes create nothing—positive or negative. We're not even responsible for our wishes, they rise out of the depths of our souls without being called. We're only responsible for the things we do! Do you understand me, Teddy?"

It was my turn to sigh, a long slow outrush of breath. I felt as if I'd been holding my breath ever since I saw Ellen's head. Now, I could breathe again. Of course, I was not responsible, not for my dreams, not for my hidden desires. Only for my actions! The next minute, I was weeping again, half from relief, half from pent up sadness. Oh, Ellen!

I felt the light touch of my father's hand on my shoulder. It was quickly withdrawn, but it left a warmth there. When I looked up, my father was smiling

"Remember, Teddy, there is a murderer inside each of us. The trick is never to let him out!"

I said nothing to this. The thought made me uneasy. I could still feel that beast inside me. How could I subdue him so that he never came to the surface?

After breakfast, I asked permission to go out for a walk. My father agreed. I went across the street into Lepke's woods, to the special spot where Ellen and I lived out our most wonderful fantasies. I sat down inside the circle of trees and tried to conjure up the days when she and I would lie there and pretend to be in an underwater kingdom. But all I could see was her severed head.

I cried some more. It was good to cry. But I was not out of the woods yet. It was still possible I was the killer. Even if I was not, I needed to find out if that dream was a true one or not, and was not sure how to go about it. But at least I felt like a member of the human race again. Somehow, my father had the ability to look into the foulest caverns of my soul without disgust or judgment. I wished I had the same ability; I had no harsher judge than myself. In any event, I was profoundly grateful to him.

But one thing puzzled me about my father's little lecture. He'd told me how angry he felt when his sister died. My father was always secretive about his early life. But I'd always thought that he was an only child!

I only felt better for a few hours after my father and I talked. The talk had somehow opened me up, made me feel more vulnerable. Later, I lay in my bed for a long while racked by deep sobs that tore up my insides. Afterwards I felt still and empty. Whenever I saw the images from the dream, I'd put my hands over my eyes as if to blind my mind's eye. Or I'd dig my nails into my forehead just above the eyes until the imprints burned. But nothing could erase the dreadful movie which continued to play in my mind.

I'm so sorry, Ellen! I prayed again and again. But there was no absolution. I might not be a murderer, but I *was* the pervert who'd had that horrible wet dream. How could someone like me help her? How could I catch the killer and bring him to justice when I was no better than he was?

At last, I got up and went down to the bathroom. I drew myself a bath, as hot as I could stand it, then a little hotter. I undressed and looked at the steam rising from the water. Finally, I put my foot in. The heat seared my skin, but I forced my body down into it, even my genitals. I gasped with the pain, but somehow it took away the terrible images...the terrible guilt. I knew then how the medieval monks must have felt while scourging themselves to remove their sin

Afterwards, I felt clean, inside and out, and much calmer. I went back to my room and lay down. Downstairs, my father was answering one of a seemingly endless series of phone calls. I'd always thought death was an ending. But for those left behind, it was just a beginning, of arrangements, and explanations, and regrets. Fortunately, my father was taking care of all the details, leaving me with the regrets.

"You really feel sorry for yourself, don't you, kid?" Sam Spade said. "Your regrets, your guilt... Ellen is the one who died! But you want center stage. Maybe you would have been happier if you had died!"

"Yes," I answered him. I'd have been much happier.

Suddenly, I heard my father calling me from downstairs.

"Teddy, come down. It's your grandfather!" My grandfather! I had forgotten all about him and everything else except my pain. Once again, I felt ashamed of my self-pity. I rushed down stairs and grabbed the phone out of my father's hand. The sound of Grandpa's voice, gentle and yet strong, made me want to cry again.

"Teddy?"

"Yes, Grandpa?"

"How are you feeling?"

Oh, Grandpa! How could I even begin to answer that question?

"I'm okay," I said, realizing as I said it how stupid it sounded.

"I'm sorry, Teddy. I can't tell you how sorry I am."

I believed him. I could hear the tears in his voice. I wanted to hold him and be held by him. I knew my father loved me and wanted to comfort me, but only Grandpa could hold me like I wanted and needed to be held

"Grandpa?"

"Yes, Teddy."

"Are you coming?"

"Yes, Teddy. I'll be coming on Sunday for the...for the funeral."

"Grandpa, I don't think they'll let me go to the funeral."

My father stared at me a moment and frowned.

"No," Grandpa said. "You will be there. I've already discussed this with your father."

My father was still frowning as if he could hear or guess the subject of our conversation. I gathered that they'd had another fight about this. It made me feel guilty all over again.

"Grandpa, I really loved her!"

"Of course you did, Teddy. Of course you did!"

There was a long silence as if neither of us could think of anything to say. I wanted to say, *I have a demon lover in my closet and I think, maybe, I raped and killed Ellen! Grandpa, I just had a wet dream about her murder!* But of course, I couldn't say any of that.

"Teddy, try not to worry! I'm going to be there in two days and then we can sit down and talk about anything you want!"

"I'd like that," I said. But I knew I could never talk about the things preying on my mind.

"Teddy, just remember one thing. Ellen isn't really gone."

I was startled. Did he know something?

She is in Heaven now, Teddy. I'm sure of it."

"Okay, Grandpa," I said. But I didn't believe it, although I appreciated his trying to make me feel better. Wherever Ellen was, it was not Heaven. Heaven wouldn't send her back with such fear and horror on her face!

"And remember I love you very much."

"I know, Grandpa. I love you very much, too."

"Now, please hand the phone to your father. We have to discuss some arrangements."

I did as I was told and sat back to listen to my father's side of the conversation. He was telling Grandpa he and I would drive to Milwaukee to pick him up. Father told him he'd put him up in the hotel in town. That seemed very cold to me

"Father," I broke in, "can't he stay with us?"

My father stared at me, his eyebrows raised.

"Certainly not!" he snapped. Then, more softly, he said; "For one thing, the only place we could put him is in Ellen's bedroom and I don't think that would be appropriate. Now please let me get on with my conversation."

I sat listening as they finalized the details. I looked forward to seeing Grandpa, but the long, silent drive to Milwaukee would be terrible. And then an idea hit me: why not stay here? It would give me almost a day to check out the details of the dream. I had to find out if it was a true dream or not. If it was, perhaps I could find some proof I could show someone: to the State Patrolmen, even to Grandpa.

"Dad," I said, after he'd hung up the phone. "Can I ask you a favor?"

"Of course, Teddy. What is it?"

"I really don't want to go to Milwaukee with you. I'm feeling too tired and upset to make a trip like that right now."

"What? You don't want to go to Milwaukee? Don't you want to see your grandfather?"

"Of course I do. But he's going to be here for at least a couple of days isn't he? I'm sure I'll get to see him then."

"Well, yes, of course that is true. But I can't think of anyone we could have you stay with while I'm gone."

"I don't need to stay with anyone. I'll be fine here alone."

"No, no, that's not possible. You're too upset to stay here alone!"

"I'm too upset not to! Please, Father, I just want to be alone to think about things. All these arrangements just depress me. Please, Father, let me mourn her in my own way!"

He stared at me hard, the way he did when he thought I was holding something back from him.

"Don't you trust me?" I asked.

He lowered his eyes.

"No, it's not that. It's just...you're all the family I have left. I couldn't bear it if something happened to you because I left you alone."

"What could happen to me, Father? In a quiet little town like this?"

"I thought the same thing about your sister."

"But they've caught the killer. Haven't they?"

He stared at me again, with suspicion in his eyes

"You wouldn't do anything foolish, would you?"

"Like commit suicide? No, Father, I have a lot to live for."

Like finding out who killed my sister, I thought. *Finding him and making sure he pays!*

"I didn't mean that. You will stay around this house, won't you?"

"Of course, Father. Where else would I go?"

He sat down and put his head between his hands. For a moment, he looked like an old man with too much on his shoulders, and I felt sorry for him. The next minute, he was the same calm, controlled man he usually was.

"Very well, Teddy. I'll let you stay here, on two conditions. First, you're not to leave this house. Second, if you need any kind of help, or even if you're just lonely and need someone to talk to, you're to call your grandfather. I should be there tomorrow afternoon by four. He and I will leave the next day about one in the afternoon and get here about five. Do you understand?"

"Yes, Father, you don't need to worry about me."

"Very well. Oh, and if anyone calls me, simply take a message."

"Of course."

I hadn't expected it to be so easy. He suspected nothing. I was better at lying than I'd thought. I felt excited. Now I had a real murder mystery to work on! I remembered one of my favorite lines from Sherlock Holmes.

"Come, Watson, the hunt is up!"

My father seemed very uncomfortable with the decision to leave me alone. All that day, I felt his eyes on me, pondering, judging. I finally asked permission to go back upstairs, which he granted. Once up in my room, I felt free. I began making preparations for the next evening's adventures. I got out my old biology kit. I had used it for collecting specimens for my Science class but the plastic envelopes in it would serve very nicely for preserving small pieces of evidence. I took the permanent black marker from the kit and labeled the envelopes exhibits A through E. The kit also contained tweezers which I could use for picking up evidence, and a small microscope for examining it. I decided not to think about who, if anyone, would look at my evidence once I'd gathered it. First, I had to convince myself I had found the killer before I tried to convince anyone else.

"Quite right," said Sherlock. "If I'd waited to convince Scotland Yard before I began my investigations, I would never have started."

I heard footsteps outside my door. I quickly stowed the items in the kit and closed it up. But the steps continued on past my room down the hall. A few minutes later, I heard footsteps in the attic. Then, only silence. I opened my kit back up again but I couldn't help listening for sounds from upstairs. But I heard nothing.

The nearness of my father made me nervous all day. I couldn't concentrate on my plans. I felt that somehow he could hear me or see me, and this made me feel guilty. I put away the kit and opened up my Shakespeare. I tried to read *Timon of Athens,* but the words were just a collection of letters. I put the book down and lay down on my bed to take an afternoon nap. I fell into a troubled half-sleep. I saw Father peering down into my dream from above, a scowl of disapproval crossing his face.

About an hour and a half later, I woke up to hear him padding quietly down the hall. He hesitated for a moment outside my door, and I was afraid he would come in. But then I heard him walking down the stairs. I got up and went back to my preparations, keeping an ear out for my father. I heard him sawing something down in his work shop. I relaxed; he seldom spent less than an hour at a time down there.

I was able to complete what I'd started. I began to wonder if I really could see blood well enough under the microscope to distinguish it from animal blood. I decide to do an experiment. I reached under the bed for my father's scalpel. I ran my finger over the sharp edge. It cut deeper than I had expected and blood gushed out. I got a wash cloth and applied direct pressure over the wound. Soon, the bleeding stopped. I wiped some of the drying blood on a slide. That would show me what dried blood looked like if I should happen to find some. There! I could actually see the red and white cells. Of course I had no animal blood to compare it to, but the police would know the difference if I could get them to look at what I'd found. I could hardly wait for Father to be gone so that I could begin my detective work.

My father spent hours down in his workshop, and so we had a late dinner. He looked at me carefully as we ate. I saw him examining the band aid on my finger.

"You've cut your finger," he said.

"Oh, yes. I was doing a biology experiment and I needed some blood."

"Why did you need blood?" he asked.

"I wanted to see the difference between white and red blood corpuscles."

I saw suspicion in his eyes.

"Teddy, I don't like this. I think you should go with me."

"No, please, Father! I'm much too sad and nervous to

go out now. I don't want anyone to see me like this, even Grandpa. I'll be all right. I...I just need some time alone!"

His eyes softened a little.

"All right. But this is against my better judgment!"

"Thank you, Father. You won't regret it."

I ran quickly up to my room. That had been too close. I was excited and uneasy. I was glad Elena hadn't shown up this night. I felt myself drifting off to sleep, floating up off the bed. No! Not that dream again. But there was no moonlight. In fact there seemed to be some sort of storm outside. The whole house was creaking and groaning as if it were being buffeted by strong winds. It sounded as like it could collapse any minute.

"Help me, Father! The house is falling down!" I was shouting.

Somehow, my father was in my room sitting at my desk. He smiled and looked up at me. He seemed to be writing in a diary. I recognized it as Ellen's, and I thought, *He shouldn't be writing in that. That is private!* He closed the diary and locked it. He slipped it into the pocket of the dark robe he had on, then he said, "Don't worry, Teddy. There is just something rotten in the walls. But the house itself is strong, it won't fall."

And then I heard another voice, muffled as if it was speaking through some kind of heavy material. It might have been a woman's voice but I wasn't sure. "Not in the walls!" the voice said. "In the basement."

My father's smile vanished.

"Don't listen to her!" he snapped. "She is a lying little bitch! There is nothing in the basement!"

The creaking and groaning grew in intensity until it became a shriek. I woke up with a start, sitting bolt upright. Someone or something was moving around downstairs! I put my ear to the keyhole of the door. I heard the refrigerator open. I smiled and relaxed. Perhaps Father was having bad dreams too.

I woke up again in bright daylight. I must have slept a long time but I didn't feel rested. I felt I'd been wrestling with something all night long. Something about the dream. What had so disturbed me about it? The storm? My father being in my room? The voice from the basement? No, these had been disturbing all right, but they were not what was bothering me. What else?

The diary! When I had gone into Ellen's desk, I hadn't seen the diary. And the diary was not on her when she was found. The dream showed my father with the diary. That would place a lot of suspicion on him if he really had it.

Perhaps I was wrong. Maybe I just failed to see the diary last time. Well, it's easy enough to check on that. I went over to the door to Ellen's room and opened it. Her room seemed terribly cold and deserted, as if no one had ever lived there. I went directly to her desk and opened the drawer. I was right! The diary was gone!

Just then, I heard a knock on my bedroom door. A moment later, I heard my door opening

"Teddy? Where are you?"

My father's voice

"In here, Father!" I said, hurriedly closing the desk drawer.

My father poked his head into Ellen's room.

"What are you doing in here?"

I thought about telling him the truth and then decided against it. What if the dream was right and he had the diary?

"I'm just sitting in here...remembering things."

My father sighed.

"I hope you're not going to do this morbid kind of thing when I'm gone. It doesn't help the mourning process to think about how she was when she was alive. You have to understand, really understand, that she is gone and won't be coming back! Now come on down to breakfast!"

I nodded. But the fact was...she had come back. I had seen her twice since she'd died! The only way to "complete the mourning process" was to find her killer so she didn't have to come back again.

My father seemed both tired and distracted during breakfast. There were black circles under his eyes. I wondered if he'd slept last night. He seemed to be taking Ellen's death harder than I'd have imagined, considering how he'd treated her. But maybe that was why he was taking it so hard; maybe he was feeling guilty.

My father seemed to take forever to get going and his slowness was agony to me. I had so much to do, and the longer he delayed, the less time I had to do it. He'd told me he'd leave just after noon, but noon came and went and he was still making phone calls, writing letters, editing the obituary for the local paper. He seemed very reluctant to leave me. I appreciated his concern for me...if that was the reason for the delays. But what other reason could there be? Could he be afraid I'd find out something? It was hard to take him seriously as a suspect in Ellen's murder. But, on the other hand, I couldn't think of anyone else who could have taken Ellen's diary. Except me, of course. The thought made me uneasy, and for a moment I was glad my father was dawdling. I was suddenly not so anxious to go poking around. I might find something I wished I hadn't.

Finally, though, my father had finished all his arrangements. By that time, it was almost dark. He asked my help moving one of his suitcases out to the car. As he opened the trunk, he looked at me and said, "It's not too late for you to change your mind."

I looked up at him and said nothing. His words seemed to swell and echo in my mind until they became huge and portentous. Not too late. But it *was* too late. I had to know who killed Ellen. Even if it turned out to be me.

"No, Dad. I have to stay here."

He nodded and closed the trunk. The heavy sound had a terrible finality to it. I seemed to hear my father's voice again, only this time inside my head, *"You should have gone. Something horrible is going to happen, and you're not ready!"*

I again had that terrible feeling of wrongness which always came with that inner voice.

My father shook hands with me. Then he got in the car and drove out towards the town. I felt a chill going down my back, like a wave. Something horrible is going to happen. I stared at the car until it was out of sight. I looked back at the house and for a moment, I saw thick black smoke pouring out of it. *It's on fire!* I thought. But when I looked again, there was no smoke.

This is stupid! I thought. You're wasting your precious time on silly fantasies. You have only a few hours and very little daylight. I ran back up to my room. I set up the microscope. Then I put all the little plastic envelopes in a paper bag, along with a set of tweezers. What else would I need? Oh, yes, a flashlight. By the time I got started, it would be nearly dark. Besides, I wanted to duplicate the dream as nearly as possible. He'd used a flashlight and walked by night: so would I. I wanted to put my self in his place; to think what he thought and feel what he felt on that night

Now where did Father keep the good flashlights? The basement. I'd seen my father using one of those big cop flashlights down there once. That was the kind I needed! I took the bag and went down to the basement. As I had feared, the door was locked. I almost decided to use my own little flashlight. But then I remembered last night's dream. Something rotten in the basement. I remembered the sound I had heard the night she was killed, that seemed to come from down there. No, I had to get in.

I went up to the kitchen and got a hammer out of the tool drawer. I went back down and started pulling on the pins that held the door hinges in place. In a few minutes, I had the hinges off, and the door swung out freely. I hoped I'd have time to put the door back on before my father came back. He'd be very angry if he knew that I had invaded this place I was rarely allowed even to visit. I fumbled for the light switch and turned it on.

I was again struck by how small the room was compared to the house itself. There must be some kind of crawlway in back. If so, there had to be a doorway to it; I had never seen any evidence of it, but that didn't mean it didn't exist. If I had time, I would check on that.

The room was, like most of my father's things, neat and a little sterile. All the tools which wouldn't fit in the drawers or the big tool box on the work bench were hung on racks over the bench: axes, hammers, saws, wrenches. Only something seemed a little wrong compared to the last time I'd seen it. It looked like the room had gotten bigger somehow. There seemed to be more room between the row of axes and the walls. A pile of sawdust lay under the lathe at the end of the bench. I was not surprised. I'd heard him sawing. What else was different? The tool sharpener was in its place, at the opposite end of the bench from the lathe. Everything else seemed to be in place.

Well, no matter. I had to find that flashlight. I opened up the drawer in the bench. There it was: almost a foot long: it looked like it could double as a weapon. I pushed the button. Yes, it still worked. But there was something odd about the light it cast: it seemed ragged. I turned the lens towards me.

The lens was broken and a piece was missing. I instantly thought of the dream, of the killer raising the flashlight and bringing it down on Ellen's head, shattering the lens. This was exhibit A! I examined it carefully. I found no blood on it, nor were there any dents. My exhibit proved nothing by itself. But if I could find that missing piece...

My search was off to a good start. I had found evidence the dream was a true one. I looked around the room. What had the woman's voice said in last night's dream? *Something rotten in the basement.* I tapped the floor with my foot—nothing but solid concrete. Well, one dream at a time. I was anxious to get out of the place. I again had the crazy impression that the room itself had grown.

15

I turned off the basement light and hurried up the stairs. Looking down at the awkwardly hanging door, I shook my head. My father would kill me if he ever saw that. The heft of the flashlight in my hand seemed familiar. That was strange; to my knowledge I'd never held it before. Unless I held it that night, which would mean I was the killer! I wished I could get fingerprints. Which reminded me, I was getting my own fingerprints all over it? Some detective! I went back up to the kitchen and wiped the handle where I had touched it. Of course I might also be wiping off the killer's fingerprints, but that couldn't be helped now. I got a pair of kitchen gloves out of a drawer and put them on. At least, I wouldn't screw up any other evidence I found.

Now I was ready. I walked slowly towards the fence, imitating the slow cadence of the walkers in the dream. They'd found the gate between two large shrubs in the center of the back fence. As I walked towards the bushes, I still couldn't see any hinge to indicate a gate was there. If there was no gate, then the dream was phony. That would also mean that the visions of Ellen had been phony. What a weight that would be off my shoulders! I could go back to mourning my sister, instead of trying to avenge her. It was too much to expect of me! I was just a kid! By this time I was hoping and praying there would be no gate.

When I got to the fence, I still couldn't see any join or hardware indicating the existence of a gate. I got up on the wooden rim on the bottom of the fence so I could look over. More heavy bushes grew against the fence on the other side, but I couldn't see any latch. Thank God! I let out a deep breath I felt I'd been holding in since Ellen died. It was all a bad dream!

I jumped down off the rim and, as I did so, I felt the fence move outwards and heard a metallic clank. I knew at once what that sound meant. There was a gate there! Damn!

I'm just a kid! I thought. *Just a kid.*

"Maybe so," Sam Spade said, "but you've got a man's job to do! Now, get to it!"

I sighed. Then I got back up on the rim and ran my hand along the other side until I found the metal latch. I lifted the latch and pushed out. The gate swung open into the field beyond. I noticed that my hand was wet and sticky. I put it to my nose and sniffed. Oil! Someone had recently oiled the gate. I also noticed someone had made a path through the bushes and high grass down towards the river, just like in the dream... Now that I had started, I had no choice but to follow that path to its end. I walked slowly along the path, hoping I was not destroying or covering up evidence as I had done with the flashlight.

I thought of the dream, trying to recreate it with my steps. The killer had walked as I walked, carrying this flashlight. But Ellen had been walking in front for most of the time. How could I recreate that?

"Remember how you first saw me? Do the same thing now!"

I couldn't mistake that voice. Elena! She was here with me! I was half frightened and half relieved. At least, I wasn't totally alone. I did as she told me, turning my head so I could see the tunnel through the tall grass ahead with the corner of my eye.

There! A seductive white figure, like the one in the dream. Walking in front of me, stumbling in the darkness, shivering in the cold. Ellen! Or was it Elena? No matter, I had to follow her. I focused on her and instantly, she disappeared. I turned my head to the side and she was there again, just in front of me. I could almost reach out and touch her. She looked back over her shoulder at me and I saw the fear in her eyes. I moved on, feeling the excitement of the hunt rising in me mingled with a sense of unreality.

We reached the crest of the hill and headed down towards the river, through the weeds which were chest high on me, head high on her. I saw the soft curves of her body as she walked, which added to my excitement. She stopped for a moment, her nightgown caught on a nettle. Yes, I remembered that from the dream. There! Something white was caught on the nettle. I shone the flashlight on it. It was real! A fragment of white cloth which looked like it could have come from Ellen's nightgown. I reached out and plucked it off the nettle and put it in one of my evidence envelopes. Exhibit B!

"Leave a little of the fabric on the nettle for anyone who might come later to find in situ," said Sherlock

I did as he suggested, but I had an uneasy feeling of being watched. In the dream, I had been floating above the killer. I looked quickly up. Nothing. What had I expected: a disembodied eye? I looked for the girl and saw her moving well ahead of me. I half-ran after her. We were nearing the river now. The line of trees where they'd found her, loomed starkly black against what remained of the twilight.

I was almost on her when she lurched forward as if she'd been pushed. Yes, this is where he pushed her in the dream. And in that clearing up ahead is where she began running. She ran now and I started running, too, the burrs catching at my clothes as they must have caught at hers. Suddenly, she was down, just in front of me, staring up at me with fear and shock in her eyes. Yes, this is where he hit her! Right here by this tree.

I shone the light at where she lay. Of course, I couldn't see her. But I did see something else, shining in the grass. I leaned down to examine it. A thin shard of glass. Its shape was somehow familiar. Of course! I leaned down to pick it up, and then held it up against the broken lens of the flashlight. A perfect match for part of the missing lens at least! Furthermore, the shard seemed to be stained. I knew the stain would turn out to be blood when I looked at it with the microscope. I reached in the bag and pulled out another envelope. With satisfaction, I put the shard inside.

Exhibit C! I saw a couple of smaller shards and left them "in situ" I was getting pretty good at this detective stuff.

Out of the corner of my eye, I saw the white form crawling along the ground just as Ellen had crawled in the dream. The unreality of the situation hit me suddenly, making me shiver. Was this just another dream? But the cold night air and the weight of the flashlight in my hand told me it was real. I saw the pinkish white of her woman's legs underneath the white clothing and began getting excited again. The line from Sherlock Holmes came back to me.

The hunt is up! I was gaining on the crawling form, watching her scramble to her feet, trying to run. *You can't get away now!* I thought and quickened my pace. I seemed to smell her panic and it excited me.

Suddenly, I ran into an obstacle strung across the path. It was like a rope, only soft and yielding. I turned my light on the thing. It was a yellow strip of tape with writing on it: "Crime Scene: do not enter!"

Of course. This was the kind of tape they strung around Koenig's house. I hesitated. If I entered the crime scene, I would be violating the law and could wind up in jail myself. On the other hand, I'd gone too far to turn back now. I looked through the corner of my eye but I couldn't see the white figure. I'd lost her! I lifted the tape over my head and went under it. I heard a metallic click and whirled around. I was blinded by a bright light, but not before I saw the glint of a long gun barrel pointed right at me!

"Stop! Who goes there?"

It was a harsh, familiar voice. The sheriff!

I froze in place. My hands jerked into the air as if by themselves. I was at his mercy now. He could do what he wanted, including shoot me...

"It...It's m-m-me, Sheriff. T-T-T—"

"Is that the Schoendienst boy? What are you doing out here so late at night?"

My brain went blank thinking about that shotgun and the police car waiting close by. I couldn't think of any lies to tell so I told the truth.

"I-I-I'm looking for evidence, sir."

The Sheriff exploded in spluttering laughter.

"Well if that don't beat all! Looking for evidence, just like Sherlock Holmes. Tell me, did you find anything?"

I looked back up and saw he'd lowered the shotgun and the flashlight. He had that superior smirk on his face. Well, I would show him.

"Y-y-yes. I did. I have the exhibits here in my bag."

I reached into my bag, but the sheriff waved his hand dismissively.

"Don't bother bringing it out. We got our man and all the evidence we need."

"B-b-but this is new. Pl—"

"You don't understand, son. It really doesn't matter. There's not going to be any trial, so why do we need more evidence?"

"N-n-no trial?"

"Son, you must be the only person in the whole town who hasn't heard. That old pervert Koenig hanged himself with his belt. We found him this morning in his cell!"

I was too stunned to say a word, but the sheriff was too drunk or self-absorbed to notice.

"So you don't need to worry about evidence, son. Your sister's death has been avenged and we got one less pervert to keep track of. Course, it's too bad about him committing suicide and all." He chuckled. "Yes, sir, too bad. He should have had his day in court. On the other hand, he sure saved us a lot of trouble! Reporters prying around here, looking into things that don't need looking into! And the taxpayers paying for a trial! What a waste! The way I figure it, he felt too guilty to go on. And who am I to say he was wrong? We probably would have hanged him anyway!"

He shook his head as if to clear it.

"Anyway, you go on home now. I'm just wrapping things up around here. Go on now!"

It appeared from the raw smell of his breath that wrapping things up included generous helpings of alcohol. I didn't feel like arguing, particularly since he still cradled his shotgun loosely in the crook of his right arm. I left quickly, feeling sick and scared. Suicide! With his belt? I'd read that the belt was the first thing cops took from their prisoners. Unless the sheriff was too drunk or too stupid to bother.

Then I remembered how the sheriff had hit Koenig with the rolled up newspapers and how his deputies went after him with the butts of their guns. I'd thought then, *They're going to kill him!* And now, maybe they had.

The only question was whether he'd died through negligence or by malice aforethought. I saw again the despair and fear on Koenig's bloody face when they dragged him into the prowl car. Yes, he could have killed himself. But how, in such a small jail? The sheriff lived just above the holding cells. Wouldn't he have heard something? But if he was drunk enough to forget about the belt, he might have been drunk enough to sleep through Koenig's death agonies.

"You're not seeing the big picture, kid. Your sheriff is real happy that there won't be a trial. That reporter had asked about the labor organizer even before they found Ellen's body. The longer the trial, the longer the press would have to "poke around" your little town and the more they might find. Sheriff Carson isn't the only one who might want to avoid that. What about Old Man Lepke and his semi-feudal hold over this town? Would he want that looked into? Or what about the Town Hall Boys? A lot of people will be happier that Koenig was dead, and most especially the man who killed your sister. You can bet on it: Keonig was murdered. And you're the only one who can bring him and your sister justice." It was Sam Spade

"You've got to be kidding! How can I possibly solve not one, but two murders, when a whole town doesn't want them solved? The last thing they'll want to see is proof that one or more of their numbers are murderers."

"But you've got to try, kid. I know you don't care that much about Keonig, But what about Ellen? You loved her! You know you did. And if somebody kills your sister, you're supposed to do something. Don't tell me that you're going to walk away from this as if nothing has happened."

"That's exactly what I'm going to do. And you can't stop me, because you are only a part of me, remember?"

"Okay, maybe I am a part of you. But I'm a part that will make you miserable if you don't do something now. You will regret it, maybe not now, but soon and for the rest of your life!"

"That isn't even Sam Spade's line. That's Rick from "Casablanca!"

He fell silent and I was glad. As I walked slowly back up towards the house, part of me felt relieved. Well, that was it! No one could expect me to fight the sheriff and the whole town! My detective days were over. Maybe, after all, Koenig had killed Ellen. And maybe, just maybe, he had killed himself. If he hadn't, I'd never be able to prove it.

"But what about justice?" Sherlock said

"What about it! "I said. "Is it just that Negroes are lynched down South? Was it just that six million Jews died in the gas chambers? Is it just that the whole world could blow up in half an hour if someone presses the wrong button? Life is unjust! Live with it!"

The voice said nothing. I felt a sense of triumph. Well, I had told him. Probably all my worrying about catching the killer was a way to postpone my sadness and depression. Maybe my father was right. What I needed to do now was to mourn Ellen. Nothing more.

And all these visions, of Elena and of Ellen. Weren't they just bad dreams, after all, creations of my subconscious, just like the voices?

I'd won for now. But I felt uneasy. As I approached the house, I had a mental picture of black smoke billowing out from it, everywhere. And the strangest thing was the smoke was cold, icy cold! I felt the cold as I approached, even though the smoke had gone. I shivered as I let myself in through the gate I had first seen in my dream. Enough of that, I thought. A dream is a dream and a vision is only a delusion. I was through with them both!

I walked up towards the kitchen, glancing briefly at the cellar door hanging off its hinges. I'd have to fix that in the morning. I was tired now, desperately tired. The feeling of cold grew as I entered the house. It was not just a physical cold. It was like I was an interloper in the house now, even an enemy. I ran up to my room and put on a sweater. I put the evidence bag in the closet. Later on, I'd figure out what to do with it. The sweater didn't make me feel any warmer. Perhaps I needed to turn up the heat.

As I walked past my sister's room, a great blast of cold came through her door. I felt gooseflesh rise on my arms. Ellen! As if in answer, I saw an image form against her door. It was at first just a whirl of darkness, which coalesced into a round shape.

No! Ellen, please, not again!

But the image continued to take on form. That pleading, fear-stricken face.

"No!" I screamed aloud.

The lips of the figure moved.

"Help me! Help us! Save us from Hell!"

The darkness and the roaring rose protectively around me as I sank to the floor unconscious.

When I came to, the figure was gone, but the brutal cold remained. I could barely get up. Nothing. All my imagination! But in my mind's eye, I still saw it; and in my mind's ear, I heard her voice. "Save me from Hell!"

Save her from Hell? How? I couldn't even imagine. I had to get out of here! I ran downstairs, and opened the door. I stared into the darkness outside. All right, genius, where to now? You should have gone with your father! Then all this could have been avoided. Where in this town will you be welcomed? And I had to admit, there was no place. I closed the door and went back into the cold, hostile house.

So how was I supposed to get through the night now, alone with the fear of what else I might see or hear? What I needed was a drink! Only liquor, a lot of liquor could blot out all this horror. Either that or one of my father's pills. But I had foolishly refused to take any kind of sedative, and I had no idea where he kept his drugs. Well, it would have to be alcohol then.

"Your father's cognac!" said a familiar seductive female voice.

I looked around. Was that my own voice, or Elena's? Either way, an excellent idea! I remembered the smooth taste of the liquid and the warmth which rose to my brain when my father poured me that toast to McCarthy's death. Yes, a great idea.

I walked into the dining room and over to my father's liquor cabinet. There it was, the clear brown liquid tempting me in its shining crystal bottle. But the cabinet was locked and I had no idea where the key was. I jiggled the crystal door knob in frustration.

"Your father's room!"

That voice again! How could I trust it? It had led me to Old Man Washburn's house of horrors, and, tonight it had put me in Sheriff Carson's sights. But on the other hand, what it said made sense. My father's room was the only place I could possibly find his keys. And I really needed to get drunk tonight.

"Just so you know I'm not going to be your stooge any more!" I said into the stillness. "My detective days are over."

There was only silence. *Good*, I thought, and walked over to my father's room and unlocked it. Nothing had changed, and I could see no keys on his desk or his nightstand. Probably he took his keys with him, I thought, or else locked any spare keys in the desk, or the file cabinets. In any case, this was a wild goose chase.

"The books."

Now the voice was getting annoying. My father was much too neat to leave his keys lying around on the book case.

"The books!"

All right, I thought, *I'll look there. But I won't find anything.* A cursory examination of the shelves revealed nothing out of place. But the voice hadn't said the book shelf. It had said: the books. Could the keys be hidden in one of the books? I'd heard of such hollowed out books, mostly in detective novels, but I'd never seen one. My father was not whimsical enough to buy something so crass. Something like that could have been given to him as a joke. But would he have kept it?

There were hundreds of books here. How could I find

such a book even if it did exist? I sat on the bed to think. A gag gift would have a gag title. Fortunately, most of my father's books were carefully arranged by subject matter. The book I was looking for would be out of place.

I went back to the book case. Nothing changed. Mostly Psychology books...some books on sociology and politics. One book on music.

Music? My father hated music. I took a closer look *The Well Tempered Clavier* by J. S. Bach.

Very odd. Shouldn't that be clavichord? Besides, I never knew Bach wrote books.

Then I had it. Clavier was another name for key. That was just the sort of weird intellectual joke that might appeal to my father's friends. I picked up the book and was rewarded with a metallic rattle. I opened it and found several key rings mounted on small pegs. *Which one,* I wondered. I focused on a large ornate ring I had seen my father use for the attic door. The keys hung from a blue and white ceramic rectangle. It had a lovely, but faded floral pattern and the initials E.B.S. on it. Edward Schoendienst, my father.

"No," said the voice, "but those are the right keys."

I was puzzled. Not his initials? Oh, wait; my grandfather had the same initials. That's probably what she meant. No matter. After carefully replacing the book, I took the key ring and went into the dining room. I quickly found a small brass key which matched the lock on the liquor cabinet, and opened it up. I brought the ornate decanter out and removed the stopper. The pungent odor of the cognac made me a little dizzy. I noticed that my hands were trembling. *Don't worry*, I told myself, *your medicine is coming soon.* I took out a small brandy snifter, filled it from the decanter, and then quickly gulped it down.

Ah! That was better. The liquor had a little afterbite, but was very smooth going down. A rush of warmth came up from my stomach and into my chest. *Thank you, mysterious voice*, I thought. I poured another snifter and raised it to Elena.

"To ghosts!" I toasted.

"To you," came the voice.

I laughed out loud. This was all getting very cozy and friendly. And indeed, she and I had done many cozy and friendly things together, in my bedroom. Why should I be afraid of her? I took another big gulp; the glow in my chest rose into my face. I felt my lips relax into a smile. My muscles, which had been so tense, were relaxing too. Soon, they'd melt, and then my bones would too. Good, I thought, and took another drink.

I felt the tension explode out of my body. I'd been so tense, for so long. I felt tears on my cheeks. I observed their course down my face with some interest and even tasted some when they ran into my mouth. I felt no sadness, though, nor much of any other emotion. I seemed to be looking down on my self from some distance. Good! Three cheers for dissociation!

I laughed again. But this was a harsh, bitter laugh that seemed to tear something as it came up. I thought of all my weird dreams, of the look on Bobby's face when he saw Ellen's head, of Koenig's doomed, calf-like expression as he went to the slaughter. It was all so grotesque, like one of those freak shows that came into town with the carnival: See the bearded lady! See the boy with two heads! Or, like the kids telling Geiners as they searched for my sister's body.

"Aw, come on, fellas, have a heart!

They were pretty funny at that! I laughed again. I could feel the house, listening.

"I don't care what you think!" I told the silence. "I'm out of it! Dammit, I've done enough! I can't do any more! I'm just a kid!"

The only reply was emptiness.

"I'm sorry Ellen is dead, but it isn't my fault. I didn't kill her!"

Was there laughter, somewhere deep in the house? I didn't care. I took another drink. My eyes and body were becoming very heavy. Everything was slowing down. If everything slows down enough, does time stop? Perhaps I'd find out tonight. They say Heaven and Hell are both out of time. But who says that? The thought disturbed me, so I took another drink. The thought floated away like all the others.

Suddenly, the warmth I had felt vanished, replaced by intense cold. The cold seemed to start in my heart and spread outwards towards my limbs. Is this what death is like? I thought. If so it doesn't seem so bad. I watched the goose flesh move down my arms like ripples on a pond. It seemed strange but I felt no particular emotion about it

After a while, I said, "Well, it's time for bed!" The

words echoed off the high ceiling. It made me aware of how big the house was and how small I was.

The thought brought fear to the edge of my consciousness. I was afraid someone or something would answer me. I decided to leave the lights on. It was a terrible waste of electricity, but the lights kept the fear at the edge of my thoughts. I dreaded having to go into my room and turn out the lights. But I couldn't stay here all night. I took another drink, but it seemed only to increase the cold, inside and out. Time to go to bed.

I put the decanter back in the cabinet and locked it up again. Then I went slowly up the stairs. The darkness at the top was like a living thing, receding from the edges of my sight the way Elena always moved.

I don't want you, I thought into the darkness. *Just leave me alone! I want to sleep and never wake up again!*

16

The noise awakened me. It sounded like the groaning of bed springs and came from Ellen's room. I was angry at Ellen for being so noisy and inconsiderate. If she couldn't get to sleep, she should just get up quietly and read, like I did when I had insomnia.

I sat bolt upright, remembering. Instantly, my whole body erupted in goose bumps, as if I had fallen into icy water. This had to be a dream! But the feel of cold sweat on my skin told me it was not. *Well then*, I thought, *I was wrong about the noise*. It may be just the house settling. But as my ears strained toward the source of the sound, I heard someone moving around on her bed. And I felt a presence in that room which had been without a presence since that night.

Anger rose in me, contending with terrible fear. I'm tired of this! Whoever or whatever was in that room was dead! It had no right to break into reality, or to try to terrify me into doing its will. I was going to confront it, here and now. It would have no choice but to fly away as Elena did whenever I looked at her straight on. *This is my world, not yours!* I would say. *You're not real! You can't stand the light!*

"Good boy, Teddy!"

It was my father's voice in my mind. I knew it must be part of me, but its approbation warmed me. Still, I couldn't force my body to obey my will. I lay there as if paralyzed. The squeaking noises from the bed grew louder and louder. Then the giggling began, high-pitched and girlish.

It is Ellen, I thought. *She has come for me from Hell and she wants to take me with her! She is angry because I won't find her killer for her!* And if I open that door, I'll see her bloody head or her decapitated body, and she'll open her arms to me...

"Stop it!" I screamed. "Go away! I can't stand any more!"

There was silence. I've done it, I thought. I've made her go away! But then the squeaking of the bed began again. And I was up, moving unsteadily towards Ellen's door, the wooden floor cold and rough under my feet. I saw a light under the door. Whoever or whatever is in there isn't afraid of the light, I thought. Well, I've got to see her, or it, face to face. I just hope it has a face.

I was standing at the door, my father's old key ring in my hand. That was strange...I didn't remember picking it up, and anyway, I didn't need a key to open this door! Maybe this is a dream. But then I heard the giggling and felt the cold glass of the handle under my hand. I opened the door, my mind gathering for a scream.

The girl was lying on the bed, dressed in something

filmy and white. I was relieved to see she had a head! She also had a red scarf around her neck. But when she turned towards me, I staggered back. It was not Ellen! There was a resemblance; she was about Ellen's age and had her cool gray eyes, and prematurely seductive body. But her face was much fuller than Ellen's and the frank, teasing sexuality of her gaze and posture was nothing like Ellen. My anger and fear turned to confusion.

"You're not my sister!" I said, stupidly. She laughed a low throaty laugh that was somehow familiar.

"All right, Edward!" she said. "I'll play along with your little fantasy if it makes it easier for you to play the game. I'm not your sister!"

Her words were so bizarre that I couldn't say anything in reply. I could do nothing but stare at her filmy nightgown, which clung to her full, womanly curves. I realized to my embarrassment that I was becoming aroused.

"But who are you?" I asked, again feeling stupid. I ought to know, but I didn't.

"Who do you want me to be, Edward? You know I'm game for any fantasy."

"Why do you keep calling me Edward? Edward is my father's name!"

"And your name, too, whether you like it or not! But tell me who you want me to be and I'll play along!"

"Teddy! Teddy is my name!"

"Teddy! I like it. It's a cute name. But this name game is really boring. I know a game lots more fun than this!"

"You don't understand. This is my sister's room. You don't belong here!"

She hitched her nightgown up, revealing most of one splendid thigh.

"Are you sure you want me to leave, Teddy?" She pointed a finger at me, then turned it over and crooked it invitingly. "If you do, you'll have to come and get me!"

A big part of me didn't want her to leave and it was getting bigger all the time. But the more I looked at this room the less I wanted to go any further into it. The dimensions were all wrong for Ellen's room. It was much bigger and the ceilings were high and peaked, not flat like Ellen's. It had two dormer windows and Ellen's room had none. If I didn't know better, I'd think this was the attic. I'd never been there but the dimensions and the location of the dormer windows looked right. The furnishings were nothing like the ones in my sister's room. The old fashioned four-poster bed had a lacy canopy over it, and there were frilly coverings on the bed which my sister would have hated. Their blue and white floral pattern looked familiar, though. An old-fashioned Currier and Ives calendar hung on the wall open to June and showing a young girl, dressed in a frilly white gown on a swing. Several pretty oil paintings hung on the wall. They looked like originals. Most were of flowers, and several continued the blue and white pattern of the bed clothes. I realized where I'd seen that pattern: on the key ring in my hand!

That was not all I recognized. That full throaty voice, that seductive laugh!

"You're Elena!" I said softly in wonder. I could finally see here face to face!

"Yes, Edward, your own beloved sister. I'm so glad you finally recognized me! Now we can drop these tiresome fantasies and get down to business! Don't you want to play?"

I stared at her. Part of me wanted to take her then and there, but with me on top this time, me calling the shots! But another part wanted to get as far away from her as possible. Everything was wrong here: the room, the furnishings, the antique calendar, the bright red scarf around her neck, the way she called me by my father's name. I felt I could lose my soul inside her and never get it back. But I'd never seen anyone so desirable, even in my wildest fantasies. And she wanted me. Me!

"What's the matter, Edward? Don't you want to play the Game?"

Yes, yes, I wanted to say. I had to have her now! But I could feel danger here. I began to move towards her without thinking. This is so right! It has to happen! I felt the same kind of inevitability as when I was about to come.

"That's it, Edward. You know you want to. You can't help yourself, can you?"

She hitched her nightgown higher on her smooth white thigh. I put out my hand towards her. Then, she laughed and moved to the other side of the bed.

"Now, now, Edward, don't be so hasty. Why just last night, you told me you would rather die than play the Game with your own sister!"

"You're not my sister!" I said angrily. "You're not even real. You're just part of my dream!"

"That's not what the bird said!"

I stared at her stupidly.

"The bird? What bird?"

"The bird that said my name. The bird that's dead. The bird that had its head cut off!"

I backed up, beginning to panic.

"I don't understand what bird you mean!"

"The bird that looks like this!"

Suddenly, she stood up on the bed, towering over me, and tore off her scarf. With a jolt of horror, I saw she had a deep red scar—no, a deep red wound all the way through her neck. How could she be alive?

Her voice rose to a deafening screech, like an immense bird.

"Elena, why did you come back?"

I screamed and ran towards the door, but somehow she got between me and the door. Her hand shot out and gripped my right shoulder like a huge talon. I felt icy cold nails sinking into my flesh, sending a wave of shock towards my heart.

"What's the matter, little boy! Don't you want to play the Game any more, now that you see me as I am? Are you too chicken?"

With strength born of panic, I managed to pull away from her and run towards the door. But somehow, she had got in front of me! Her arm came up and hit me, hard, across the face. I felt as if I'd been hit with an immense icicle. I saw blue stars, then nothing.

When I woke up, I lay on the floor of my own room. The top of my head felt as if someone had dug into it with his fingernails. My mouth was so dry I could hardly swallow and my belly churned. So this is how a hangover feels! So much for getting drunk! My face and my arm also hurt. I guessed I'd fallen on them when I passed out. Well, the booze got me through the night. Just that one scary dream and now I was alive and safe! The daylight shone through the curtains, and I was no longer afraid.

That certainly was a strange dream though. So vivid! It started out like the best wet dream ever but it turned ugly fast! I guess you can't expect pleasant dreams when you're mourning someone you love. But the more I thought about the dream, the more depressed I became. If Elena was only a figure in my dream last night, then probably that was all she ever was. I had loved her so much, longed for her so hard, and in the end, she was only another wet dream. Now, I had to live without both Ellen and Elena! One more cause to mourn.

I wondered if I looked as bad as I felt. I had heard from the bad kids that getting drunk was supposed to be a manhood ritual. I decided to see if I looked any manlier after last night.

I walked over to the mirror and took a look. My heart leapt once and seemed to stop. All across my face was an angry red welt in the shape of a woman's hand! Slowly and dreamily, I put my hand up to the mark on my face, using the mirror for guidance. The skin at the red part was raised and felt ice cold. Beads of some kind of clear liquid oozed out of it. I looked at my right shoulder. The same raised marks, the same inhuman cold, the same clear ooze. But here, her talons had dug in and there was blood mixed with the liquid. I sat down suddenly on the bed. I felt sick, scared, violated. She'd insinuated herself into my dreams and now left her coldness in my flesh.

Leave me alone! I screamed in my mind. I thought I heard her low harsh laughter. It was all too clear now: she, and Ellen, were not going to leave me alone. They were working together! But why did they wish to torment me? Ellen at least had told me what she wanted, even if I couldn't do it. But what did Elena want? I saw again the horrible, impossible wound on her neck. It looked like the head was balanced on the neck, with nothing to connect it. Just like Ellen. And hadn't Ellen asked me to save "us?" Maybe Elena had been killed by the same person. Maybe she too wanted justice...or revenge. But why not just say so?

Clearly Ellen's death and Elena's arrival were related. Elena had shown up only a few weeks before that night of the murder, and had actually shown herself to Ellen and me. And perhaps not only to us. I began to doubt that the person who screamed "Elena, why did you come back?" was Ellen. If Elena and Ellen were killed by the same person, that person must have been the one who screamed Elena's name that night

This brought me back to the bird. It had screamed Elena's name as part of a phrase, and last night Elena had repeated the same phrase. She said something else about the bird; something I needed to verify. I suddenly knew where I had to go. And I had a hunch I could find a much easier way into Koenig's back yard than I'd used the last time.

I dressed quickly and went down to the back yard. Now that I was on the hunt again, I didn't feel so sick and weak. I felt now that I had the house and its spirits on my side. I opened the hidden gate and walked over to the fence in back of Koenig's place. As I'd suspected, a gate opened out onto the field in back, with the latch on this side. As I lifted the latch, I noticed someone had oiled this gate recently as well. Undoubtedly the same person, and probably the killer. I wished I had a real finger print kit—his prints might be there.

Koenig's back yard was still ripped up; no one had bothered to fill in the holes they'd dug and it looked like no one ever would. I picked my way through what looked like a battlefield and onto the back porch. The yellow tape was still up but nobody was around. I thought I had better hurry before the sheriff decided to do more housecleaning. I lifted up the tape and went under it.

The back door and all the windows were wide open, probably to air the place out. Lord knows it needed it, but I felt sad. Koenig had always been such a private person, and now his inner sanctum was open to the world. Of course he didn't know about it, so I guessed it didn't matter

The place was still filthy and cluttered, though almost all of the dirty magazines were gone. With all the windows open, I easily found my way to the bird's room. The door was closed; I wondered if the cops had even gone in there.

I listened for a moment but heard no sound from within. I pushed the door open.

The bird lay on the floor of its cage. I felt a flash of anger. Wasn't it enough they'd killed Koenig and ransacked his house? Did his pet have to die of starvation, too? But, maybe the bird could be revived. I ran over to the cage. As I leaned down to pick up the bird, I realized that it was smaller than I remembered. When I picked it up, the problem was obvious.

Someone had cut off his head! Poor thing! His brilliant colors were fading quickly into a dull orange. I stood there holding the headless bird and my mind went back to the dream. Elena had said the bird was just like her; her with the horrible wound all the way through her neck. Of course! He'd cut off all their heads—the bird, Ellen, and Elena. The pattern was complete and I knew who the murderer had to be. Elena had hinted at it last night when she called me by my father's name and said that she was my sister. Only one man could have had a connection to all these decapitations and it was not me!

You bastard! You killed my sister! Why did you do it?

And the answer came back, in Father's own voice, "Because I wanted you for myself!"

I felt as if the bottom had fallen out of my world. I could see the darkness rising and hear the roaring

"No!" I said to the darkness. "Go away! I won't be punished for what my father did!" And as if in reply, the darkness receded.

"Good," said my father in my mind. "You are right.

Never accept the blame for what someone else did. You have learned something important."

"Why should I listen to you any more! You're a murderer!"

There was a pause. "Yes, but I'm also your father. And you must listen to me or you will never be free!"

"Free of what? I don't understand!"

"You will understand and you will remember. You must remember. There is very little time left!"

The truth of this knocked everything else out of my mind. I had to act fast. The sun was rising higher in the sky. Our basement door hung off its hinges. It was all so clear now. Father was the only one who could have persuaded Ellen to go out with him. He was the only one who could have known about the back gate. It was his flashlight which was used to club her. And he'd used the back gate to plant the evidence on Koenig's back porch

What remained was to prove it. The problem was that most of the evidence I'd developed could be turned around to point at me. I too could have persuaded Ellen to go out that night. My fingerprints would be on the flashlight. And most of all, I was an unstable teenager while he was a prominent psychiatrist with important friends. I couldn't prove his guilt without establishing a motive. Why? Why, why would an intelligent man like my father commit such a hideous crime against his own daughter? The answer, I believed, had to lie in the past. The secret of Elena lay somewhere in the past too. I thought of her room in the dream, the old fashioned furniture and bedclothes, the Currier and Ives calendar.

The way she called me Edward, my father's name, and said she was my sister. Then there was my father's strange statement about his sister's death. I could guess her secret now, but I needed proof.

Within a few minutes I had locked up the house and was pedaling my bike toward the library. I was risking an attack but the risk was not a big one, I thought. The boys in the Scout troop had mocked me on the search but hadn't attacked me. It was as if my family tragedy had given me a temporary immunity. Unfortunately, I didn't know when that immunity might run out

But my ride went smoothly, and within minutes, I was locking my bike on the rack outside the Library. I went in and asked the treacherous blonde for microfilm copies of the local paper from 1934 through 1936. She looked at me strangely. I put my hand to my face and realized the red marks were still oozing. Without a word, the woman gave me the reels I wanted, and then looked away quickly. I must look a sight! Well, I didn't care what she thought of me as long as she gave me what I wanted. The radio reporter had said the search for Ellen was the biggest search in this town in just over twenty years. I believed I knew who they'd been searching for last time but I needed proof. I also needed to know if they'd found her.

I took the reels up to the Time Machine and inserted the first reel beginning with June 1934. The calendar in Elena's room had read June. But June 1934 was uneventful. FDR's new agencies were hiring some local people. Germany, Italy, and Japan were beginning to cause trouble internationally. There were weddings, anniversaries, and county fairs but no disappearances. I sped quickly through the rest of 1934 and the beginning of 1935. At June 10, 1935, I found what I was looking for:

"HUGE MANHUNT BEGINS FOR LOCAL MINISTER'S DAUGHTER!"

And there in front of me was Elena's face! She was about the same age as when I'd seen her last night, but her neck was intact. She had the same gamesome eyes and cynical smile. I could almost hear her laughter, as if she were reading over my shoulder. I pushed the button to copy the whole page. My hands trembled as I picked up her picture. Elena was my aunt! My face flushed red when I thought about what she and I had done all those nights. She was my aunt for God's sake! Of course, I didn't know that at the time, but she did! How could she have done it?

I felt sick at my stomach. How I had loved her! Writing her name over and over, thinking of her constantly! And what a little fool she'd made of me! Necrophilia and incest—not too bad for a first romance! I seemed to hear her hoarse laughter once again. I felt as if everyone, including the librarian, could see my shame!

I shook my head. I didn't have the time to feel ashamed. I had to find out more. I looked again at the page in front of me:

Elena Beatrice Schoendienst (EBS, the initials on the keys!), *fourteen-year-old daughter of prominent Methodist minister Edward Schoendienst, had disappeared two nights ago. A search by Sheriff Carson* (the father again) *and his deputies had turned up a red scarf—apparently belonging to Miss Schoendienst—by the river, behind her home. The scarf was stained with human blood. As a result, Sheriff Carson had asked for the cooperation of police from several surrounding jurisdictions, as well as the Wisconsin State Patrol, in searching for her. Even the local Boy Scout troupe joined the search, which concentrated on the banks of the river from the bridge down to the girl's house and the adjoining Seminary. Unfortunately, no further evidence was found...*

I rolled down to the following day's headlines: "MINISTER'S DAUGHTER STILL MISSING". A picture of the sheriff made me do a quick double-take. The father looked almost exactly like the son. The story told about a scaled-back search in the woods around the Schoendienst residence. Lepke's woods? Nothing further had been found, but Sheriff Carson said the case was still open and volunteers, including the family of the victim, would continue the search along with members of his department.

So my father was out there searching for his sister. And all along...he knew exactly where she was! But where was that?

"There is something rotten in the basement!"

The words echoed in my mind. Where had I heard them before? Oh, yes, the dream about the storm. But how could my father have dug through the concrete floor? When would he have had time to bury her anywhere around our house, with my grandfather there?

"The basement."

It was her voice again. All right then, I'd look in the basement. But it seemed useless. I had very little time as it was. I brought the reels back to the blonde behind the counter and paid for the photocopy. At least I had confirmed my hypothesis that Elena was my father's sister. I also had a motive for her murder. In last night's dream, Elena had pretended to be my sister, and asked me to play the Game! I knew very well what that meant! So, Elena had tempted her brother too. Elena's taste for incest was nothing new. Perhaps this terrible temptation had driven my father over the edge.

I thought about what he'd said about my dream: There is a murderer inside each one of us—the trick is not to let him out!

I hopped on my bike and pedaled as hard as I could towards home. The sun was almost overhead which meant I had very little time. If Bobby or any of the others showed up, I'd just have to outrun them. But no one bothered me, and within a few minutes, I was home. I dropped the bike in front of the house and ran towards the basement. The door was still hanging off its hinges: I would have to reattach it before Father got home. I turned on the light and began to examine the concrete. My father would have been about my age in 1936 and I couldn't imagine him being able to dig through that concrete and then somehow repair the damage he'd done.

"No! Look up on the wall."

Obediently, I looked up. I noticed again the dimensions of the wall seemed wrong in relationship to the row of axes hanging on the wall. The axes! Of course. There were six axes hanging up—lined up left to right according to size. The biggest axe on the far right was about twice as long as the smallest on the far left. But there was a jump in comparative size between the third and fourth axe from the left. There should be one more axe, midway in size between the two, to make the series look even. And the missing axe was about the size of the one the deputy found on Koenig's back porch!

I went up closer to the wooden rack on which the axes hung. There it was! You could just see where Father had sawed through the rack in two places and then glued it back together. Some glue had oozed out of the join and had hardened, turning dark against the lighter wood. Some sawdust had fallen down on the bench. I leaned over the bench and saw that some of the sawdust had got in behind it. This surprised me. I'd always thought that the bench was joined to the wall. I leaned over and saw something in back of the bench.

Something like a door.

So there was a basement behind this one. I had always believed there must be but this proved it. I tried to pull the bench away from the wall. The bench was quite heavy, so I was only able to move it an inch at a time. At last, I had swung the bench out enough so I could get in back. But then I saw the door was padlocked. Stymied! I knew that her body was back there somewhere, but I had no way of getting in! I looked around for a tool to break the lock.

"The keys."

Once again I'd forgotten my lines and had to be prompted! I was sick of all these voices in my head. I wanted to tell them all to shut up. But they'd been proven right too often. I fished in my pocket for Elena's old key ring. The lock was an old Schlage, so I looked for and found a matching key. I turned it in the lock. To my surprise, it opened right away.

A gust of cold musty air billowed out. There was another smell—something like rotten meat. But the smell was faint, I could have imagined it. The crawl space was very dark: the lights from the basement seemed to be swallowed up by the thick darkness.

Are you in here, Elena? I thought into the darkness.

"Not any more," came the answer.

"Then where are you?"

"Up in my room."

Her room. I thought again of the dream, the huge, cold room, and the dormer windows. The attic!

"You're such a smart boy."

Yes, I'll come up there, but first I must do something here. I went around to the front of the bench and took another flashlight out of the drawer. I shone it into the close darkness. The light picked out a wooden beam at least forty feet away, on the other side of the room. This place was huge. It would take ten men a whole day to dig this place up; even if I could convince them there might be a body here. And what were my chances of doing that?

"Come up to my room," said the voice.

What an invitation! But I had to decline! I had only a couple of hours left and I still had to put the door on the hinges.

"Come up now!!"

All right! I thought. *But this is hopeless. Hopeless.*

I ran out of the basement, leaving the back basement door open and the basement door hanging on its hinges.

All right, let him find it. Let him know that I know! But what will he do when he finds out?

"Come."

"All right. I'll leave it in your hands then. You make the plans!"

"I will."

I walked up the steps, taking a last look at the tell-tale door as I did so. *I hope I can trust you!* I thought. There was no reply, not even laughter.

I went up the stairs slowly. I was remembering a strange dream I had once, in which I saw a dark, cold fog pouring out of the attic. Somehow, it hadn't felt like a dream. I also remembered all the times I'd listened, straining to hear the sound of the Monster moving up there. I remembered last night and the marks she'd left on my flesh. I remembered the scream which must have come from there: *Elena, why did you come back?* I now thought I knew why she had come and the discovery didn't make me anxious to go up there. But I had no choice. I needed her help and I had to ask for it face to face.

I reached the stairway to the attic. I felt her presence in there; it flowed and oozed towards me like a freezing mist. My hands were shaking as I put the key in the lock. I braced myself to see something horrible when the door opened. I saw only darkness. I fumbled for a switch, half expecting a cold hand to reach out and pull me in. There! The room sprang into light.

Yes. This was the room I'd been in last night. Across the room were the dormer windows, covered with thick blinds to keep out the light. Closer to me, I saw the poster bed and the roll top desk. Even the calendar was hanging on the wall, open to June. There were the paintings and the lamp. Everything had the same floral motif and colors as the ornate key-ring in my hand.

I looked around the vast room. It was totally clean, not a cobweb anywhere. My father had kept it like a shrine to Elena. He'd come up here every Sunday for years to worship her. And yet it must have been my father here in this room who had screamed: "Elena, why did you come back!"

Maybe it is better to worship our gods at a distance, I thought. What must my father have thought when his "beloved" sister, the one he had murdered, returned to him?

I looked more carefully at the paintings. All of them were signed EBS. They were quite good, especially for a fourteen-year-old girl. The flowers had a sensuous exuberance most such studies didn't have. You could almost smell them.

You were quite an artist, Elena, I thought into the darkness.

"My best work is yet to come."

"What does that mean?"

"Open up the desk."

I searched through the keys until I found one which was made of the same brass as the lock on the desk. I put it in the lock and turned. To my surprise, the lock turned easily. I pulled up the roll top. There were about a dozen cubby holes of different sizes.

"Upper right-hand cubby."

All right, all right! I thought. I put my hand in the top right hand cubby and brought out an old fashioned book with gilt on the edges and a leather cover. It had a golden lock and the initials EBS on the front cover.

"Check the cubby again."

Obediently I put my hand in again and dragged out another book. It was Ellen's diary!

The hunt is up! I thought. And this time the prey is in sight!

17

ow at last I had a chance to get behind Elena's mask. This was her own diary. She had granted me this for her own reasons. Perhaps the time for revealing herself, the time she had promised me would come, was at hand.

"Yes!" came out of the darkness. She was following my thoughts, commenting on them. It was an intimate moment in spite of the anger and fear I felt towards her. I felt that she too was excited by this intimacy. It had been a long time since she had been able to share her heart with anyone. I quickly found the ornate gold key that matched the lock. The diary slid open easily. My hands trembled as I leafed through the pages. I wasn't even sure what I was looking for. There must have been two hundred pages of her florid but neat handwriting, and I certainly didn't have time to read it all.

Then I began to see the drawings. Delicate and lovely drawings of flowers, of trees, of the river in the distance. There were also portraits. One was clearly my grandfather: her father. He had that same Old Testament sternness as in the photograph downstairs but with no trace of the same fierce love, only disapproval and judgment. I guessed he hadn't loved her any more than my father loved Ellen.

"Yes!" she said again. I heard anger and pain in the voice this time.

I saw several portraits of a boy I recognized as my father. He was about my age, a little older than in the photo downstairs. In most of the drawings, he had the same uncertain, haunted expression as in that picture. But in the last drawing, near the end of the diary, his face showed something else: a strange mixture of hatred and intense desire. And he was looking right at the artist, at Elena. I'd seen that expression on his face only once before: when he had caught Ellen naked in the shower. And not long after, Ellen had been raped and murdered. I decided to start reading a few pages ahead of this drawing, to see what lead up to it.

"April 10, 1935: Billy was looking at me at school. I could tell he was interested. I saw the outline of it jutting out of his pants!"

I felt warmth in my cheeks. I had no idea girls thought like that, especially back in 1935! But it did sound like the same young woman who had played so freely with her nephew on so many fevered nights.

"Admit it! You liked it!"

"Of course I liked it. But it was wrong! I'm your nephew!"

I heard again her coarse laughter. *Damn you, get out of my mind!* This was too intimate. But I couldn't get rid of her, so I just kept reading. I saw some very explicit drawings. I wondered how she was able to draw a man's penis so accurately and in such detail. In spite of myself, I was becoming aroused. I read on.

"May 14, 1935. Edward is hopeless. What an iceberg! I can't believe he doesn't feel what I feel. Am I the only person in the world who has this desperate hunger?"

I felt my heart rise into my throat in sympathy. *I understand, Elena. I feel the same way. You're not alone!*

In the silence, I heard her harsh, sardonic laughter. Apparently she didn't like pity any more than I did. I read on.

"May 8, 1935: This evening, I persuaded Edward to begin the Game. We didn't go too far: just a kiss, a little more affectionate than usual; a hug that was a little closer than most brothers and sisters give each other. But I felt him respond! The icicle is beginning to melt! And I have all summer to finish thawing him. I can't wait!"

And below was the last drawing of Father, looking at her with the same mad eyes I had seen watching Ellen after the shower incident. I felt a chill. Apparently Father couldn't wait either. And no, she didn't have all summer. She disappeared just about a month after that entry. In fact, there were only two more entries in the diary.

"June 7, 1935: Two more days and Father will leave for his conference. Then, Edward and I will play the Game again. But this time, I don't think either of us will stop! I can't wait!"

You were a little too impatient, Elena.

There was no reply.

"June 9, 1935: Tonight, it will really happen! Now

that the time is here, I feel guilty. Frightened, too, as if he and I were going to some place no one has ever gone to before. But no one can stop what's going to happen tonight."

I felt the chill again. *No, Elena, no one could stop it.* You melted the icicle and found a murderer and rapist underneath. But he didn't rape you first. First, he cut off your head, so you couldn't see what he was going to do to you. Just as he did with Ellen his own daughter. You gave him that taste for incest. But you didn't teach him how to kill. That came from inside: you only helped free it. And he was your older brother! He was supposed to look out for you! But then I thought of how poorly I had looked out for Ellen.

I had it all now: the motive, the method, even the place of burial. But how could I prove it? I decided to look through Ellen's diary to see if she could give me an answer. Unfortunately, I didn't have the key. My father must have hidden it elsewhere.

"Break it open!" came from the darkness.

I can't! I thought. This diary was so important to her. It's bad enough for me to read it. To break it open feels like killing her all over again.

"You have no time! Break it."

I looked outside and saw the sun declining towards the hills in the West. She was right! I smashed the lock down against the edge of the desk again and again until the diary flew open.

I'm sorry, Ellen, I thought into the darkness. There was

no reply, but then I'd expected none. I skipped towards the end of the diary and began reading.

"October 4, 1957: I'm feeling so bad about poor Teddy. He is totally alone now except for me and Father. I love him so much, but I can't help him. It's so unfair! Why should I have all these friends and he have none?"

I blinked back tears and skipped to the next entry. Like Elena, I hated pity, even self-pity.

"October 12, 1957: I had the dream again last night. Elena is so frightening. She overpowers me, and I have to do what she wants. She says she only wants to teach me, but the things she makes me do are so disgusting and frightening! I don't want to learn them! I hate her! Something dark hangs around her!"

Yes, Ellen, you were right. She lives in darkness and brings it with her wherever she goes.

"October 13, 1957: Last night, in the dream, she led me down to the basement. I heard a scraping sound behind the wall, as if someone were digging in the darkness. I told her it scared me and I wanted to leave.

She said: 'Don't be afraid. I'm not. This is my home!'"

You tried to tell her and me where you were buried, but we didn't understand. Now I know, but I can't do anything about it

"November 5, 1957: Today, Father saw me naked in the shower! He got so angry and I was so scared. He hit me, hard! He looked so crazy; I had no idea what else he might do! Then he accused me of leaving the door open deliberately. I told him I'd never do such a thing. But would I? Sometimes, lately, I don't know why I do certain things, like flirt with boys. It's as if someone else is doing it, not me! I usually am careful to lock the door, particularly when Teddy is around, but today I didn't. Why? Why?"

I think know why, Ellen. You have given me a missing piece of the puzzle. I almost have it all now.

"November 13, 1957: Teddy was such a dear today. He comforted me and told me he'd never let anyone hurt me. If only I could believe him. But his arm felt so good around me."

At least I'd given her that!

"November 15, 1957: It is a miracle. Not only is Father talking to me, but he acts so sweet and kind. It is hard to trust his kindness because I don't know why it began or when it will stop. Still, it feels really good right now."

"November 16, 1957: The way Edward has been towards me lately is like a dream. He has been so kind, so attentive! He even wants me to go to Milwaukee with him to shop for clothes. I have prayed for something like this all my life. Why then am I so afraid?"

She called him Edward! The letter she left was written to him. I knew it!

"November 17, 1957 (The night of the murder!): I'm still shaking! I can't bear to think of what almost happened. And the worst of it is, part of me, the stranger in me, wanted it to happen: I was some other girl, having a nice romantic date with a man, shopping for dresses, eating in nice restaurants, and the kinds of things that had never happened to me. And all I had to do was give him sly glances, brush by him in a certain way: the things

Elena taught me. And it was okay because I was Elena, just like in the dream. But then it started to get serious; he kissed me; he touched me in places he shouldn't and then I was Ellen again. I screamed and ran away. And he was so angry! I thought he'd kill me right there in the hotel room."

No, Ellen, that wouldn't have suited his cautious nature. The bastard, the cowardly, murdering bastard!

I closed the diary and collapsed on the bed. My hands were clenched in helpless rage. I should just kill him like he killed her. Just wait for him, with one of the remaining axes! But I couldn't even picture myself using it on him; bringing the blade down on his head. Whenever he turned those piercing eyes on me, I became a coward, just like him!

No, I had to force him to admit what he had done. But first, I had to put it all together so there was no weak link he could exploit. I had most of it. But something about the letter I'd found in Ellen's room still confused me. She must have written the diary entry just after she got home that day. I had seen her putting away the diary. So then, after I had gone to bed, he must have approached her and asked her to go with him that night, just a little walk, to talk things over. But why would she have gone? Maybe he made her weak, just like he made me. Perhaps she couldn't say no to him face to face. So she started to write it down in a letter: that might have been easier for her. *Dear Edward, I'm afraid of you!* Then she was interrupted by his knock... No, that was wrong. He must have told her when he was coming up for their little walk.

But he came up before she expected him. That was it! Hearing him, she lost her courage and threw the crumpled up note in wastebasket. But he didn't stop at her room. He went up here to the attic. And then he screamed out the words I and the parrot had heard. And she must have heard it, must have! And she must have known that he was insane and dangerous. So why didn't she run—to Bobby, or the sheriff, or anyone? Or to me! Or at least why didn't she lock the door to keep him out? Perhaps she knew she couldn't keep him out for long. She must have been hypnotized by him just like I was; him and his eyes reflecting fire and ice! But he was not the only one hypnotizing her! Was it she that answered my father's soft knock that night or the stranger who had planted herself inside her? Was it she or Elena who followed my father so willingly to the slaughter?

If it was Elena, why had she done it? That was the one remaining mystery: Why had she tempted me and my sister and finally my father? Was it just a love of the Game? But no, she must have had a deeper motive. She had ignited a fuse inside us all that had blown our little family to bits and led directly to my sister's murder. Why?

Was it because she was his slave? Was it true that murder victims became the slaves of their killers after death? But my father was not dead and she hadn't acted like a slave towards him. Instead, she had driven him to madness. He had screamed her name like an animal that night

But what had he meant? Had he opened Elena's diary that night? No, he must have done that a thousand times:

the pages were worn and smudged with use. There must have been something else that reminded him of Elena.

Of course. It was Ellen herself. She herself had said in the diary she felt like she was Elena when she flirted with my father. He must have recognized her; something about the movements, or the eyes, or the attitude! When he killed Ellen, he must have thought he was killing Elena again! And then suddenly, it all fitted together in my mind. I knew why she'd come back!

So now, what to do? From the angle of the sun in the sky, I had at most an hour to expose my father as a murderer. If I left now, I could repair the basement door in time and act as if nothing had happened. And live the rest of my life in this house knowing my beloved father had raped and murdered my sister! But I knew that, based on what I had now, I'd never be able to convince anyone in authority to even look into this matter, much less indict Father. I had no choice but to ask Elena for help, though I knew her to be a vicious and manipulative liar, and very possibly a murderer! I couldn't live with myself if I didn't try to avenge my sister. The trouble was, she seemed to have vanished while I was reading the two diaries. Had my thoughts driven her away?

"Elena," I said into the stillness. "I need your help."

There was no reply.

"Elena, I don't have enough to go to them with. Please help me!"

"A fine Sherlock Holmes you turned out to be!" said a familiar, scornful voice. "I gave you all these clues and what did you do with them? Nothing!"

"So why couldn't you just tell me what I needed to know."

She laughed. "What fun would that have been?"

The voice was coming from the bed. She wore the same flimsy nightgown she had on in the dream. She had on the bright red scarf which almost hid the horrible scar all around her neck. In her hands, she held a familiar looking dark robe.

"Yes, that's right; this is the same robe you saw in the dream. The same robe he wore when he killed Ellen... and me!" She threw it in my direction. It landed in front of me. I stared at it in wonder. She could move physical things with her hands!

"There! Show that to the cops! It has Ellen's bloodstains on it, and maybe even mine. He wore it to kill me, too!"

"I can't! Don't you understand?"

"Understand what? That you're a fool and a coward? I understand that all too well."

"You don't understand. If I accuse him, who will listen to me? I'll be standing there stuttering, barely able to get a word out, and he'll be the great doctor explaining to them how crazy I am. "He ought to know," they'll say. He's the headshrinker."

"How could I have expected anything else of you? Poor little Teddy! You couldn't have figured out any of it without my help!"

I was getting angry now.

"I did figure one thing out without my help!" I told her.

"What was that, little Teddy."

261

"I know why you came back!"

"Explain it to me, Mr. Detective!"

"After he killed you, you couldn't rest until you got your revenge. But you couldn't kill him yourself, could you?"

"No, I don't have that kind of power. Not yet."

"So you had to get at him indirectly. Your chance came when Ellen and I came along. You were the monster who came to us in our dreams when we were children. Right?"

She laughed.

"Wrong again, Sherlock. That was not me!"

"Really? Well, no matter. A few months ago, you started coming to me, hoping to get me under your control. Then you invaded Ellen's dreams."

"And why did I do all this?"

"You knew you couldn't get either one of us to kill him. But you could get him to kill Ellen! All you needed was to arouse her sexual desires. You made her into a temptress...into another you! Then you got her to tempt him. You knew what he'd do after that. After all, he'd done it to you!

"Then, after he committed the crime, it was my turn. I was supposed to gather the clues and put him on Death Row. Am I right so far?"

"So what if you are?"

"Well, if I'm right, then you're just as much of a murderer as he is. You killed her!"

Elena glared at me. I could swear that her eyes flared red, like an animal's in the headlights.

"Congratulations! You did figure something out! Now see how much good it will do you! Goodbye!"

I saw her beginning to fade into the sunlight.

"No, wait!" I screamed at her. "Don't go. I still need you! And you still need me!"

The fading reversed itself and she was soon as real and solid as she'd ever been. But she was not smiling.

"So what do you want?"

"We have to figure a way to even the odds between my father and me."

She stood quiet for a few moments, as if thinking. Then, she smiled. "There is one way. As long as he is the eminent doctor, so calm and collected, no one will listen when you tell them he is a killer. We have to make him lose his cool demeanor for good."

"How can we do that?"

"You need to draw him a picture. Of me."

"I can't draw, Elena."

"But I can. All I need to do is borrow your body for a while."

"I can't do that. I don't know how. No!"

She stretched out her arms, longer and longer, impossibly long, until they reached inside my chest! I felt my self being pulled out of my body. I struggled to remain inside, but the force pulling me was too strong. Then, I was floating free, just above my head and then higher, up to the ceiling. I tried to tell her I was afraid, but once again I had no mouth and no hands. I saw something huge and white looming over my body and then slipping my body on like a piece of clothing. I wanted to look away, but I couldn't. Then it was inside and my body was sitting at the desk with a pad and a pencil, drawing. Elena was still lying on the bed, her legs curled up, showing almost all of her lovely thigh. I couldn't understand how she could be in two bodies at the same time. But then, it was becoming clear she could do almost anything she put her mind to.

I stayed up there, floating near the ceiling, for what seemed like an eternity. I could see the drawing take shape. It was amazing to see my own hands skillfully creating her image. I felt clumsy and stupid, knowing I could never produce such beauty.

I watched as "I" finished the drawing, and then glanced over at Elena to compare the image to the reality. My face smiled as if in satisfaction and then looked upward at me.

"Come down, little Teddy," I heard my own voice say. Then I saw the huge white shape slip out of my body. The next thing I knew, I was sitting at the desk, staring over at Elena. I shuddered.

"That was horrible!" I said.

"Poor little Teddy. But the job is done…that is the important thing. Now all you have to do is show him the drawing."

"But what will he do when he sees it? Will he confess?"

"You'll see, Teddy. You'll be amazed at the change in him! You have to trust me, Teddy. I know what I'm doing."

Trust her! The person who planned and accomplished Ellen's death! But what choice did I have? The die was cast: my father would be home in a few minutes. The basement door was still off, and I had no time to put it back on. Evidence of my father's crime was spread all over the house, in the basement, in the paper sack in my room and here in the attic.

I took the drawing and went downstairs. I didn't say goodbye. I had no reason to be polite. As I waited in the living room, I began shaking. This was madness! My sister's funeral was tomorrow! How could I turn him in to the police now even if he did break down and confess everything?

But the more I thought about Elena's plan, the more sense it made. I'd once compared myself to Hamlet. Well, then, my father was Claudius. By showing him I knew he'd murdered Ellen, I would get a reaction from him, just as Hamlet did with his play within a play. That way, I, like Hamlet, could make sure that my suspicions were not just part of my madness. Most important, I would make him lose his cool superiority.

"The play...no...the drawing's the thing wherein I'll catch the conscience of the king!" I said aloud.

The bombastic paraphrase of Hamlet echoed in the empty house. It made me feel pretty silly. I sat down, quietly, to wait.

I didn't have to wait long. Within minutes, I heard my father's car pulling into the driveway. I looked out and saw him getting out of his car. He was alone. I was glad, because I didn't think I would get the desired effect if my grandfather were there. He got his suitcase out of the trunk, and walked towards the door. I noticed that my hands were trembling. I pressed them hard against the chair arm until they stopped.

The lock clicked, and the door opened. I looked at my father as if for the first time, now that I knew he was a murderer. Strangely, he didn't look any different than he ever had

"Hello, Teddy, sorry I'm a little late. I had to help your grandfather get set up in the hotel in town. He is getting more and more helpless! His hand shakes so much he could barely sign the register! How are you?"

"F-f-fine, Fa-Father!"

He stared at me in astonishment. I was no less surprised. As far as I knew, this was the only time I'd ever stuttered in his presence. Maybe his being a murderer did make a difference, to me at least.

His eyes grew sharp, and once again I felt he was peering into my soul. I felt like the hunted, rather than the hunter.

"What's the matter with you?"

"Nuh-nuh-nothing, Father.

"You're lying! Something has happened. What was it?"

"Nuh-nuh-nothing has happened!"

But my eyes involuntarily turned towards the upstairs, and his eyes followed mine.

"Something happened up there. What was it? And what do you have in your hand?"

I put the drawing behind my back.

"Ju-ju-just a drawing"

He snatched the drawing out of my hand.

"Just a drawing! You never drew anything in your life. Now, what's this?"

He stared at the drawing with that hard, all knowing stare. Then, he seemed to see it for the first time. He brought it up closer to his eyes, as if to convince himself it was real. Then, he let the drawing go. It fluttered to the floor. His eyes seemed to fuzz over as if he were looking at something a long way away. Or a long time ago.

It's working, Elena, I thought.

The veins on his neck began to stand out. He swallowed hard, once, twice. The fuzziness left his eyes to be replaced by a hard if unfocused stare. I thought I saw his eyes flare red as Elena's had done. Perhaps it was the blood that was flowing into his whole face, including the eyes. I'd seen him like this only once before: just after he hit Ellen. This was not a good sign. I began to back away.

"Where do you think you're going? You little bitch!" he said in a choked voice.

"No, father. Look at me! I-I-I-I'm your son!"

He lowered his head and charged me. His head rammed into my stomach. I doubled over in shock and pain. His head drove me backward until I hit the wall. I heard one of the photographs fall and shatter.

He had me pinned against the wall, and I was too weak to move I felt his hands close around my throat. I tried to push him away, but I had been lifted off my feet and was powerless. I couldn't breathe: It felt like he was crushing my windpipe

"You little bitch! Why did you come back? But you

won't get away this time! I'm going to finish you off for good!" he screamed.

It worked, Elena, I thought. *Just the way you knew it would! What a fool I am!* And then the blackness and the roaring closed over me.

18

I awoke to pain, fear, and darkness. The pain was centered in my chest and my throat. For a moment I thought I was back in the hospital after the attack by Bobby and his little pals. But then I remembered my father's hands around my throat. I was lying on a bed; it felt like my own. I was very cold. He'd apparently stripped me stark naked except for my undershorts. My hands seemed to be tied together and attached to the headboard over my head. I struggled to free them, but the more I squirmed, the tighter the knot got. *Must be a slip knot*, I thought, remembering my Boy Scout days. I stopped struggling. I turned my attention to my legs, which were spread-eagled, each one tied to a rail in the lower part of the bed stead. I felt angry and humiliated to be so exposed. But then, I had bigger problems than being nearly naked. If he thought I wouldn't run outside if I ever got these ropes off, out of false modesty, he was dead wrong!

I could hear him rummaging around in the attic, banging into things up there. He sounded enraged. All the evidence he'd so carefully hidden lying out in the open, everywhere! I smiled a little. It would be all right. Sooner or later, he'd come to his senses and realize that I hadn't shared this evidence with anyone. He could simply destroy it, and no one would ever be the wiser. And if I tried to say anything, he could simply have me committed.

Yes, that was what would surely happen. After all, tomorrow was Ellen's funeral. He could hardly report another one of his children missing without arousing a lot of suspicion. Even the sheriff might raise an eyebrow at that. And if they searched the house, they'd probably find Elena even if they didn't find me. No, my father would never get away with this. Surely, he must realize it.

But he didn't seem to be calming down. The noises grew louder, and I could hear choked screams coming from upstairs. They sounded like the scream I'd heard the night Ellen died.

I thought of what Elena had said. *"We have to make him lose his cool demeanor for good."* Elena had seen what would happen from the beginning. *"You'll be amazed at the change in him,"* she'd said. I was amazed, all right!

She knew the sight of her drawing would drive him into a murderous frenzy that wouldn't be appeased until I was dead! Then, and only then, would he regain his cool demeanor. Then he'd start thinking about how to hide his crime. But this time, it would be too late! They'd catch him all right, but it would be too late for me.

But maybe that was part of her plan. She must have hated both Ellen and I: Ellen, because she'd taken her place and even her name. That, I could understand.

270

But why did she hate me? Then I remembered the look of anger and contempt on her face when she threw my father's robe at me. She hated me for frustrating her plans to get my father arrested—and maybe just for being his son. And I think she hated me even more for figuring out she was responsible for Ellen's death.

Well now, unless I could figure out some way out of this trap, she'd have her revenge on us all. I tested all the ropes again. No luck. They might as well have been made of steel. So I couldn't break the ropes. What other chances did I have? I could scream. But there was no one within earshot. If anyone did happen to hear it, they'd probably think it was coming from the asylum. And my yelling would probably just madden him even more.

I could try reasoning with him. Fat chance! The last time I'd seen him, he'd looked like a wild animal, and from the sounds coming from upstairs, he had gone downhill from there.

I stared upward into the darkness. So there it was. Checkmate. I somehow was not as afraid as I had thought I would be. After all, my life hadn't exactly been a rose garden. And now, one of the two people I'd ever loved was dead, and the other one was just about to slaughter me like an animal. I couldn't see how I was going to lose anything very valuable. I should have ended it with Father's scalpel which was now under the mattress. I just hoped the end wouldn't be too painful. I wished he had finished me off in the hall. He'd been very close to it.

Why hadn't he done it? Why did he have me trussed up like a turkey, my legs spread wide open? Something about this line of thinking disturbed my fatalistic calm. I felt the beginnings of panic. For some reason, I remembered those nightmares I used to have of The Man in the Moon! The tremendous footfalls on the stairs, the dark monster with great moon eyes, the sensation of being crushed down against my bed. I'd accused Elena of being that monster.

That wasn't me, she said and laughed. And she was right. That was not her. That was him! It was his footfalls on the stairs, his glasses shining in the moonlight like full moons, his body pressing mine against the bed. It was him all the time. And now he had me here, half naked, spread-eagled on the bed! "You little bitch!" he'd said. And now he was going to give me what he'd given Ellen and Elena! What he'd given Ellen and me when we were small children. His own children!

No! I twisted and writhed, lifting myself up off the bed. It was no use. The bonds were so tight now I could hardly feel my hands or my feet. No. I thought. Please, no.

And then I heard the laughter coming from next door. I could hear the bed squeaking as if someone were on it. It must be Elena. She must be loving this: my panic, and the thought that what had happened to her would happen to me! Enjoy yourself! You murdering bitch!

I heard my father coming down the hall. Is this it? *Please,* I thought, *just kill me before you do it to me. You did that much for them!* Faint, long repressed body memories of pain and fear and deep shame rose in my mind. I couldn't bear the thought of experiencing that again! But he continued down the hall and then down the stairs. I let out a deep breath. Perhaps I was not so resigned as I thought I was. Maybe, deep down, I wanted to live.

And then the giggling started again next door. But this time there were two voices: one, Elena's throaty tenor and the other a high alto. I thought I recognized the new voice.

"Ellen!" I said. "Is that you?"

"Shh!" said two voices. "Not so loud."

"Ellen! You've got to help me! He's got me tied up and he's going to—"

"SHUT UP!" hissed Elena. "You're going to spoil everything!'

"She's right, Teddy," said Ellen's voice. "He has to hear our voices, not yours. Otherwise, it won't work!"

"Ellen! Oh, God, is that really you?"

"Yes, Teddy, it's me." The voice was sad, but somehow distant.

"Oh, Ellen, I'm so sorry!"

"You don't need to be sorry, Teddy. I know you did your best."

But her voice still had that strange coldness, that distance that I'd never heard before. But then, she'd never been dead before.

"Ellen, what's the plan? What do I do?"

"You don't do have to do anything, Teddy. Just leave everything to Elena and me."

Just then, I heard a strange sound coming from below. It was a whirring and the scraping of metal on metal. I recognized the sound; I'd heard it the night Ellen died. But this time, I knew what it was. I'd just been down in the basement and I had seen the sharpener on the work bench. My father was sharpening an axe, for me.

Suddenly, it seemed important not to rely completely on a plan hatched by two ghosts, one of whom was a murderess herself. A backup plan seemed like a good idea. But what could I do? Suddenly, I remembered the scalpel, lying just under the mattress. Fortunately, it was close enough to the edge so I wouldn't have to lift the mattress with me on it. If I could get hold of it, I could cut the rope and get free.

The metallic sounds from downstairs stopped. Apparently, Father was satisfied with the edge. I could see him running his finger over it. Yes, that will do. I heard the sound of the back door opening and closing. He was on his way.

"Ellen?" I called.

"Yes, Teddy?

"I love you!"

There was a pause, as if she were trying to remember something. Then, she said, "I love you, too, Teddy."

But there was something wrong with the voice. It was low and dull, dead somehow, in a way that Elena's wasn't.

"What's the matter, Teddy?" came Elena's sardonic voice. "Don't you love me? And after I've been so nice to you! Much nicer than she has!"

Somehow, her low scornful laugh didn't bother me as much as it might have. Ellen loved me, and forgave me. That was the important thing. And although I didn't know all the details of their plan, I did know one thing. A trap had been set in this house, and it was not set for me!

Whatever their plans were, though, I couldn't be sure they'd work. Since my life was at stake, I'd better do what I could for myself. My father had tied my hands together just above the wrists. If I could work the ropes down on my right arm and partially free the right hand, I might be able to reach the scalpel. I tried to twist each hand in a separate direction. I felt the ropes tighten, but I also felt a little more free play to the hands because the ropes had worked further down on my arms. I tried again. This made the ropes so tight I could hardly feel my hands. I worried that they might be too numb to grip the scalpel if I was able to get hold of it. I also worried I might lose the hands if the blood flow stopped for too long. But if I didn't get out of here, I'd lose my head

A noise downstairs. A creak in the linoleum in the kitchen as he walked across it. He was moving slowly, as he had in my dream about the murder. It was like he was performing a religious ritual. I somehow knew he was wearing the robe like in the dream, and was holding the axe under the robe as he had then. I tried once again to free my right hand... The knot tightened again shooting pain up through my arms. Let it. Let me develop gangrene and lose the arm as long as I can get out of here. A wolf will chew its leg off to escape a trap. I would do the same, if I could!

I could hear him now at the bottom of the stairs. I twisted the right hand again and I felt it working free of the left, while the rope rode further down on the right arm. Now all I had to do was somehow twist my body over so I could grasp the scalpel. I could hear him climbing the stairs, one at a time.

"Teddy."

It was my father's voice and it came from inside the room! I looked up and there he was, right over by the closet! I let out a little scream.

"Don't worry, Teddy" he said. "I won't hurt you. I can't hurt you. I just want to remind you of all the things I have told you."

I took a closer look at him. He was wearing his three-piece suit and he was glowing as if he was in a spotlight. What was he: a visual hallucination? Here was one more symptom of schizophrenia. Or could he be real? He was clearly not a ghost because his body was climbing the stairs!

"I'm sorry, Father, but I really can't talk right now, especially to an illusion. You see, the real you is coming up to kill me!"

He smiled sadly.

"I am the real me, Teddy. That thing down there is an angry and frightened animal."

I laughed.

"I'm glad to hear it, Father, but unless the real you can untie me, he's not much use to me!"

"I can't untie you, but I can tell you how you can free yourself. Remember what I told you? You can't live anyone's life for them. In the end, you can't save anyone… especially from themselves. Never identify with someone so much that you lose your own soul. Above all, remember this: the transference must end!"

The transference must end? I knew what Freudian transference was: the too-intimate bond between the psychiatrist and patient. And I knew that the patient must grow beyond it for healing to take place. But with a homicidal maniac coming after me with an axe, I didn't see the point in a review of Freudian theory!

"I don't understand."

"You will. Don't forget these things I have told you! This will be your last chance to break free!"

Then he was gone. The light he brought with him was gone, too. I stared into the black vacancy he left, disturbed and uncomprehending. I again had that feeling of wrongness. That's not the way it happened!

The footfalls were louder now. He was approaching the top of the stairs. I twisted my body as far as I could towards the right side of the bed. As I did, my head rested on my right arm, further cutting off the circulation. I could see that my hand was below the level of the mattress and in about the area where I remembered putting the scalpel but I could barely feel my fingers. I doubted if I would feel the scalpel even if I did put my hand on it. And what if I dropped it?

Checkmate.

Come on! Where is it? There. I felt my hand brush past something. Go back. There! I closed my hand on the sharp edge and felt a surge of pain in the almost numb hand. I've got the scalpel, all right, I thought. But he was at the top of the stairs and heading towards the door. I brought the scalpel up towards my face. God! My hand was covered with blood! I worked my hand down the scalpel until I was no longer gripping the blade. The blood spurted onto the handle, making it slippery. Don't drop it!

I twisted my right hand until the scalpel was almost touching the rope on the left wrist. No time for delicacy. I sliced through the rope and into my wrist. The pain was intense, but my left hand was free! He was just outside the door! I transferred the scalpel quickly to my left hand and hacked at the ropes on my right wrist. Ow! Now I cut my right hand. But it was free, though also covered with blood. The sheets were becoming soaked. I saw the door handle twisting. Too late!

And then I heard the giggling again, unnaturally loud and clear in the darkness. He must have heard it too because the door handle slipped back to its original position. There was a silence. He seemed to be listening, just as I was.

"Oh, Edward!" It was Elena's voice.

"Edward!" It was Ellen.

Then the giggling began again, along with soft whispering. Once again, I heard the choked, inhuman scream, this time right outside the door. "Why did you come back?"

More laughter.

"Edward?" they chanted in unison. "We're both waiting for you! Don't you want to play the Game?"

The question echoed in the darkness. Then I heard his footsteps going down the hall to Ellen's room. I heard the doorknob being tried tentatively. There was a low scornful laugh from inside, and then the door opened. The laughter grew louder.

What was I doing? They were buying me time, but I had to use it to get out of there! I quickly cut the ropes off my left foot and then my right. Free! I tried to stand but my legs were too numb and I fell to my knees. I heard movement in there. He seemed to be moving towards them, slowly, warily. I crawled towards the door to the hall. They seemed to have him occupied: now was the time to run for it. I pulled myself to my feet, using the doorknob for support. Pain flooded into both legs. But that was good: feeling was returning! I should be able to walk soon.

Suddenly, there was a high-pitched scream from Ellen's room. One of the girls? But, no, it was Father!

"No! Keep away from me!"

I pulled the door towards me. I almost fell but was able to use the door knob to remain standing I let it go and took a couple of hesitant steps towards the hall and freedom. There was nothing to keep me from getting away now! But I stopped, listening.

There was a swishing sound and then a 'thock'. I heard a thump as if something heavy had hit the door. Still, there was mocking, insinuating laughter. Then again, I heard swish, thock, bump! And then nothing. Still, I waited, my heart pounding. And then I heard the most horrifying scream I could ever imagine: there was in it fear, horror, loathing, and above all...evil. And it wasn't human. And still I didn't go!

I could have walked out. Gone down the stairs and outside. Got on my bike and pedaled to the sheriff's office and told him...Something. Anything. As long as I got out of there! I could have left the whole unearthly mess for the police or the coroner or the psychiatrists to handle. It was no longer my responsibility. And now, frozen in time as I am, I see myself doing that, just walking out and leaving it all behind. But no, I'm stopping, I'm turning back. And I hear a voice screaming, "Teddy, whatever you do, don't open that door!" It was Elena's voice

And yet, I'm opening the door. I have always opened it. I have no power to do anything else. But why, when I'd just been warned, when I knew nothing good could lie behind it? Was it curiosity? I had lived this story from the beginning; it was only natural I should want to see the end. Or perhaps it was stubbornness. Elena had been leading me by the nose for too long: perhaps I didn't want to follow her orders any more, even if they were for my own good.

In the end, though, I believe it was love. In spite of all my father had done and all that he was, I loved him and wanted to see what had happened to him. And so I opened the door and saw:

My father naked under the robe, cowering on the bed, his hand still limply grasping the axe. Its edge was slathered with a dark liquid. His eyes were blank and spittle oozed out of his mouth. And there were Ellen and Elena, naked, crawling all over him, pinching and caressing him, and everywhere they pinched, dark, oozing welts appeared like the ones Elena left on my shoulder and face. His body was now covered with the welts, but still they crawled and pinched.

The girls had no heads. Their severed heads were on the floor by the bed. Their mouths were still open and they were still laughing and giggling while from their necks burst forth dark upwellings of blood!

had always been here, and they had always been here too. Somebody once wrote that Hell is a small dirty room with a spider in it. My Hell had three spiders... no, make that five if you count the three bodies and the two severed heads. I watched my sister and my lover/aunt crawl obscenely over my father, covering his body with oozing sores. I heard the raucous laughter of their heads.

Emotions burned me inside: pity, horror, shame and hatred. This is my family! I heard the roaring and sensed the darkness gathering behind me. *Good! I can't bear this!* It was as if I were the one being tortured by those two headless corpses*! Come, darkness, and take me into oblivion!* But would it be oblivion? I remembered the dream in the library and the constant feeling of déjà vu that I had from then on. No wonder! I had lived through this nightmare period dozens, possibly hundreds of times, always beginning with that dream and ending in this horror. Maybe I was already dead like Ellen, and this was my endless, immutable Hell.

But wait. In this last repetition, something had

changed. Whenever I heard my father's voice in my head, and also when I saw his glowing figure in my room, I had had the feeling: It didn't happen this way. It was as if he had entered my endless nightmare and changed it ever so slightly. But how, and why? I could not figure out the how, but as to why, my father had told me in my room that if I could remember and understand his words, I might be able to escape. But how? My father's blankly staring eyes seemed to be looking at me. What can he want me to do or say?

Incredibly, my father's lips began to move.

"Remember all that I told you! You must speak now!" he says. The body which was Elena's began to tear gouts of flesh out of his body.

"I should have known you were trying to help him! Well, you won't get away with it! He is mine!" her head snarled.

"Remember!" my father groaned, until Elena's corpse clapped her hand over his mouth.

I did remember—too much in fact. The horror overwhelmed me and I could not remember anything clearly. What had he said? I must remember!

"Poor Teddy. I don't blame you! He is asking too much of you. Listen, the roaring is louder. It is coming for you, and you will never have to worry again," Elena's head whispered.

I could hear the roaring all right. She was in league with it; she always had been. And if I let it take me over, she says I'll never have to worry again! But she was lying!

The darkness would only bring me back to the dream

in the library, and to all the horror that followed. She loved to watch, because she thought that I would never escape. But my father had told me that I could escape. If only I could remember what he said!

I must remember!? Oh, yes, people have only the power over us that we give them. I looked at my father and Elena but nothing had changed. Obviously, I had to say something, not just think it, to escape from this Hell. But what could it be?

I open my mouth but all I could say was: "I-I-I..."

Elena laughed.

"Poor little Teddy!" her head cooed. "Stop trying to speak. It's much too hard for you."

"I-I'm only a kid!" I managed to get out. But I saw by the despairing look in Father's eyes and the gleam in Elena's, that it was exactly the wrong thing to say. Only a kid? Unless I grow up fast, I'd never be a man. What had he said? I have to remember

The roaring is becoming deafening now, and the room has become visibly darker. I have only minutes, no, seconds to find the right words. He had said: Never identify with someone else so much you lose your own soul. And something else. In the end you can't save anyone, especially from themselves. And more: the transference must end! That was it! I could tell by the gleam in my father's eye that he approved. But what do I need to say?

"I-I-I..."

"Too late, Teddy," hissed Elena's head. "You are mine for good now!"

And then I saw in my mind the illustration from

Dante's Inferno showing Dante in a boat. A sinner was stretching forth his hand and Dante was striking at the man with his paddle. And then I understood what was needed without further cues or prompting:

"I hate you, Father! You killed the only person I ever loved and you're getting what you deserve!"

And the scene suddenly began to fade, and I thought, *too late!* The darkness was on me and soon the endless nightmare will begin again. But no, the scene was getting lighter! Light flowed through it as if a movie screen had been cut to shreds, revealing a projector behind. I had time only to see the anger and loathing on Elena's face and the look of love and triumph on my father, and then they, and the rest of the scene, vanished.

And I awoke to find myself in my own room at the Waupun State Mental Hospital.

Epilogue

My awakening caused considerable excitement in the ward. Within minutes, a small, mousy man in a doctor's coat was asking me questions.

"I-I-I'm too confused now. I can't answer any questions," I said. "Puh-please, just let me go to sleep!"

"Son," he said in a gentle voice, "you've been asleep for two years! Maybe it's time you woke up!"

Two years! My God!

"Wh-where have I been, for two years?"

"Here, for most of it. But I'll tell you what's been going on on the outside if you'll tell me what has been going on inside your head."

"I-it's a deal. But please tell me, w-what is your name?"

"I am Dr. Harry Kunsler."

"Aren't you a f-friend of my father's?"

The doctor smiled.

"Yes," he said. "We've been friends since our University days."

"But where is my father? I n-need to see him!"

He shook his head. "I'm afraid that's not possible

right now. But you can be sure that he's getting the best treatment we can give him."

"So he's here at Waupun?"

"Yes, but it wouldn't do either one of you any good for you to see him now. Let's you and I tell our own stories, and in good time I'll let you see him. Who knows? Maybe you can give us information that will help us treat your father!"

So began a series of sessions in which he skillfully drew out of me my whole story. When the sessions began, he was calm and professional and I was still shell-shocked and trembling. But I found that telling my story was very therapeutic. At the end of the sessions, I was relaxed and hardly stuttered at all while Doctor Kunsler was the one who trembled and looked frightened. What I'd told him—particularly about the final scene with my father, Ellen, and Elena—had obviously badly shaken him.

"Are you all right, Doctor?" I asked.

He smiled, professionally.

"Of course I am. You don't need to worry about me. But that really is quite a story!"

"Do you believe me?"

"I believe you're telling me what you actually experienced."

In other words, no.

"Doctor, I n-need you to tell me what hu-happened to my father. You promised that you would tell me what has been going on. Please."

He made a little tent with his fingers. Obviously, he didn't want to tell me anything.

"Please, Doctor. I have to know. How can I ever get better if you don't tell me what happened to him?"

This argument finally swayed him. He began telling me a story which was, in its own way, as bizarre as mine.

When my father didn't show up to help prepare for Ellen's funeral the day after I went into my coma, several people called him without reply. Finally, Sheriff Carson and one of his deputies drove out to our house. The front door was unlocked, so they went in, calling for my father. When they got no response, they went upstairs and found my father and me in Ellen's room, both in catatonic states. No one else was there. My fingers and wrists were cut and there was evidence I'd been tied up in my own bed. There were also strange red bruises, in the shape of a hand and fingernails on my face and right shoulder which oozed a cool liquid.

My father was in far worse shape. His whole body was covered with the same red bruises, also leaking a cold clear liquid. Both of us were in comas, but his was far deeper. I would occasionally moan, but he made no sound at all and gave no sign of consciousness. Sheriff Carson immediately called an ambulance and had us both taken to the hospital.

Then he began investigating the scene. His curiosity had been piqued by his discovery of an axe near my father's body which was of the same type and almost the same size as the one used in Ellen's murder. Based on ligature mark on my arms and legs and the cut rope in my bedroom, it looked to Carson as if my father had tried to kill me, but that I'd somehow escaped. It was natural for the sheriff to wonder if he might have killed Ellen as well.

In my room, he found the exhibits which I'd so carefully collected. At first, he couldn't make much out of them. Then, he remembered meeting me near the murder scene that night. He compared the glass shard to the flashlight lens, which he also found in my room. (He later went back to the path near the murder scene and found the smaller shard which I'd left there. This matched the larger shard and the two shards also had blood on them. An analysis determined that the blood was the same type as Ellen's.)

Upstairs, he found Ellen's and Elena's diaries and my father's robe. (It was later discovered that the robe had blood stains of the same type as Ellen's.) When he went down to the basement, he found the join my father had made in the rack for the axe handles and was able to draw the correct conclusions, aided by the fact that one axe was missing. He also found the "crawlway", and since my father was now a suspect in Ellen's murder and my attempted murder, he decided to dig it up to see if he'd killed anyone else. They found Elena's body close to the doorway.

Carson had found my photocopy of the newspaper headlines about Elena's disappearance and he also had her diary, so he knew whose body he had. (This was later confirmed with dental records). He'd also heard of this girl's disappearance from his father, who had always been upset that the girl was never found. His father was now dead, and it must have given him considerable satisfaction to solve a case that his dad couldn't. As for me, I was astonished. I never would have believed Carson had the makings of a real detective. I was also amazed he could admit he was wrong about Koenig. But, he'd never liked my father, and I think he was glad to be able to destroy his reputation. As for me, I was glad my sleuthing hadn't been wasted.

Somehow, Ellen's funeral was completed. The question then became: what to do with my father and me? My father was now a suspect in two murders so it was decided to remand him to Waupun to determine if he was capable of standing trial. It was soon obvious he wasn't, so they left him there in Doctor Kunsler's care. No one had any idea what to do with me. The doctors were so unnerved by my father's condition and mine, especially the oozing sores which baffled even the medical journals, that no one could be found to treat us. Doctor Kunsler requested that I be moved to Waupun where he could treat us both. Since I was underage and not suspected of any crime, the judge was reluctant. So Doctor Kunsler promised I would have my own, secure room and that as soon as I was out of the coma, I'd be moved to a more appropriate site. He told the judge our two cases were absolutely unique and he needed to study them to make sure that whatever illness we had wasn't communicable. The judge finally agreed. Thus it was that my old premonition came true and I became a resident of Waupun.

Now that I am out of my coma, Dr. Kunsler says I'll be out of Waupun in a "short time." He isn't sure where I'll be placed: probably in some kind of "half-way facility" for emotionally disturbed youth. This doesn't sound promising to me. It sounds like I'll be put in with a bunch of Bobby Niebauers! But I'm trying to make the best of it. The doctor has said I'll only be there for a little while, for evaluation. I am grateful to him for being so straightforward and kind. But when I asked him if I could see my father, he just shook his head.

"That isn't really your father, Teddy. Not the way you or I remember him!"

He said my father hasn't uttered a sound in two years. The marks on my face and shoulder have long since healed, but his wounds are constantly being renewed. They have become more serious lately: it looks as if something is tearing great gouts of flesh out of his body. Dr. Kunsler says he can't last very long at this rate.

However, he has a theory about what happened to my father and me. He says that we were a victim of "*folie a deux*", a psychological condition in which two persons share the same delusion. In our case, the delusion was caused by my sister's death which caused the violent and unusual psychosomatic illness which struck my father and, to a lesser extent, myself.

It is a very neat theory—and total bullshit. For one thing, both Ellen and I were haunted by Elena which would make it a *folie a trois*. And obviously Ellen's condition could not be caused by her own death. Moreover, I made every effort to prevent my father from knowing about Elena and he certainly never told me about her...

Which raises the question of how we could have participated in the same delusion if neither one of us knew that the other one knew about Elena. The only person who knew that we both knew about Elena was Elena herself. So it would have to be a *folie a quatre* with one of the four victims being the delusion! But there is no argument so absurd that a scientist will not use it to explain away anything which he can't reduce to a scientific formula.

But Dr. Kunsler was right about one thing. That oozing vegetable they have attached to IVs in some private room here isn't my father. Nor was the psychotic who killed and raped his own sister and daughter. My real father is the man who found a way to break through the torment Elena was inflicting on him, and free me from my own prison. I don't know how he got into my mind or how he was able to lead me to health and sanity. But he did it. And now, he is paying the price for helping me, which may include death. At the very least, it included rejection by the one person he loved, and whom he risked everything to save.

The thing you were most wrong about, Father, was how you should never love anyone. Love is the only thing that gives life its value. If you hadn't loved me, you would never have risked so much to help me. I don't take back anything I said in that room. I do hate you, for killing Ellen! And yet, in spite of all you have done and been, Father, I will always love you as well.

But the thought of Ellen still in that place breaks my heart. The look in her eyes when last I saw her severed head wasn't even human. Total possession. I must have looked that way when Elena had hold of me. And I remember the deadness in Ellen's voice. Under it all, she must be suffering. Perhaps she is overwhelmed by the darkness and the roaring as I was when I was possessed. What kind of sick games is Elena making her suffer through, now? Perhaps something even worse than the games she made me play. But there is no hope for Ellen, as there was for me, because she doesn't even have a body to come back to! She did nothing to deserve this Hell, except to trust me! If, when she came to me about Elena, I'd told her all I knew or suspected about her, Ellen might be alive today! Someday, perhaps, I will find out how to save her. Until then, I will have her on my conscience. I have made a vow to Ellenand to my father that I will find a way to release them both from Elena's Hell, just as my father found a way to release me.

As for Elena, I won't waste any sorrow on her. Oh, I know, if anyone ever deserved revenge, she did. She'd been betrayed, raped and murdered by her older brother, who should have looked after her and helped her get through her sexual confusion, which was so much like mine. But she took her revenge at the expense of Ellen's innocent life. Now, she has what she wanted. She is the queen of her very own Hell, where she can torment her brother and my sister endlessly! May she have much joy of it! For she has to stay in Hell too! And someday I will find out how to send her down to the real one!

Incidentally, I now know why she led me to the old Washburn farm. Somehow, Old Man Washburn had somehow shown her how to execute the perfect revenge on my father and his children who had stolen her place in her house. She wanted me to go to his house to show me how her killer might trap her and Ellen. But all the while, that was the fate she had in mind for our whole family

My grandfather came on visiting hours today. He hugged me tight. It was wonderful! I'd forgotten how good human warmth and love can feel.

"Teddy," he said, "I'm so happy that you're awake again. (I could not say anything, so I just held on to him.) I know that you're having a lot of difficulty with…all the things that have happened. I just want you to know how terribly sorry I am about Ellen and your father. I need you to know that you will always have a home with me, if you want it. You know that I love you very much"

So I thanked him and hugged him again and told him how much I loved him. But I also saw how frail he was, and how his hands trembled. I don't want to be a burden to him. Doctor Kunsler agrees. After I get out of the half way house, he says I'll stay with a foster family until I complete my education. He has even suggested, shyly, half stammering, that I might come to live with him and his wife. I think I'd like that. He is intelligent, perceptive, kind. I can see why my father chose him as a friend. In fact, he reminds me a little of my father, or what my father might have been if he hadn't been a homicidal maniac.

Meanwhile, everyone here is nice to me, even the guards who are often brutal to the other inmates. I can't say that I blame them: the inmates sometimes attack them and are often hard to deal with. But I've made my first friend among the patients. While I was telling my story to the doctor, I was allowed to mingle with the other patients at mealtimes. My new friend, Eddie, is terribly shy; always walking around with a Bible in his hand, mumbling to himself. But he went out of his way to be nice to me when I was first allowed to eat with the others. He must have seen how scared I was and he introduced himself and offered to be friends. I was very touched and said Yes, I'd like that.

He and I don't seem like a good match at first sight. He's not terribly bright, and is always quoting from the Bible. But I have had enough of my father's demand that I only mingle with my intellectual equals. In practice, that means connecting with nobody. I don't really mind about the Bible either. At first, it did irritate me. But then he taught me the rest of the 23rd Psalm that I could not remember when I was in the Valley of Death, that "thy rod and thy staff will comfort me." And after all that I have been through, I now know that Mrs. Goethe was right: there are more things in Heaven, Earth, and Hell than were dreamt of in my father's philosophy. Maybe there's something to this religion stuff after all.

As for my new friend, I think he was surprised and touched that anyone would want to be friends with Eddie Gein. You may well wonder why I would want to be friends with Wisconsin's most famous ghoul. I'll tell you. He says he reads his Bible to keep away the "bad thoughts." I know those bad thoughts all too well, and I too need a refuge from them. Eddie's friendship helps. When I look into his eyes, I know that he too has seen Hell. That is something he and I will always share.

And somewhere, as if from a distance, I hear Sam Spade say: "Kid, you've got a long way to go."

Duncan Lloyd is a retired civil servant, whose avocation as a writer has lasted over 50 years, He was born in Illinois, but spent most of his childhood in the Wisconsin of the 1950's, the time and place in which this novel is sent. He swears, however, that this is not a memoir, and those who read the book will well believe it.

Nevertheless, two of the figures who appear here, and set part of the book's grim tone, were quite real: Senator Joe McCarthy and Ed Gein. The Senator gave us the word "McCarthyism", a synonym for fear-mongering and demagoguery. Gein was a ghoulish serial killer, who was the model for the novel "Psycho", and for Alfred Hitchcock's classic movie of the same name.

One of the grimmest chapters of this book, in which Teddy along with his old boy scout troupe, searches for his sister, Ellen, was also based on reality. The author joined his Boy Scout troupe in a similar search for a missing teenage girl about 55 years ago. The search was unsuccessful, but it has since been speculated that the girl might have been one of Gein's victims. However, since this was well before the discovery of DNA, the identity of many of Gein's butchered victims may never be known. However, Duncan Lloyd wrote his first short story about a more successful search for a girl. It could be said that he has been writing about some elements of this novel for 50 years, but the full version has only taken about 15 years. He has in the meantime sold several stories and non-fiction pieces but this is his first published novel. He lives in Oakland California with Diane, his beloved wife of 47 years, and has two grown daughters.

Printed in the United States
By Bookmasters